Nothing Happened in 1986

Steve Beed

DEDICATION

For Annie, this wouldn't have happened without you, and to Martin, Steve and Dave for your help and encouragement.

CONTENTS

CHAPTER 1   THE END OF SUMMER
CHAPTER 2   JOURNEY
CHAPTER 3   FRIENDS
CHAPTER 4   MAKING A START
CHAPTER 5   THE WALK
CHAPTER 6   ANOTHER PUB
CHAPTER 7   HOMEWARD BOUND
CHAPTER 8   THE MORNING AFTER THE NIGHT BEFORE
CHAPTER 9   TERM STARTS
CHAPTER 10   EVERYONE COMES BACK
CHAPTER 11   EVERYTHING GOES WRONG
CHAPTER 12   THINGS THAT GO BUMP IN THE NIGHT
CHAPTER 13   IN THE BELLY OF THE MACHINE
CHAPTER 14   NO PLACE LIKE HOME
CHAPTER 15   CHRISTMAS
CHAPTER 16   NEW YEAR REVOLUTION
CHAPTER 17   THE PLAN
CHAPTER 18   THE START OF SUMMER
CHAPTER 19   UNTITLED
CHAPTER 20   1990
CHAPTER 21   POSTSCRIPT

ACKNOWLEDGMENTS

Everything in this book is made up and all the people are pretend, except the bits that are true and the people that inspired me. Thanks for that!

Chapter 1
The end of summer

It was the end of summer, but it was not the end of summer.

See what I did there? I alluded to Dickens, paraphrasing the opening of Tale of Two Cities. So if you couldn't guess, I'm smart, or at least I think I am. Smart enough to get into college, and smart enough to survive two years of academic rigour - so far. Confession time though, maybe not quite smart enough to realise that some hard work on my part would make that work less rigorous and bump up my grades a bit.

Anyway, now is not the time for dwelling on college work. It's the end of my summer. I have spent the last eight weeks selling ice-creams for all I'm worth. Cornettos, MrWhippys, 99s, orange lollies, any lump of frozen sugar you care to mention. I have been at my station every day this week and now I'm almost done.

The beauty of having parents who live by the coast is that there are always summer jobs to come back to in July and August, a chance to save up some cash to help survive the following months of student grant. I haven't saved all of it though, some needed to be spent on refreshments when catching up with old school friends, who had also been forced to return to the loving embrace of their families for the summer. Nevertheless, I do have over £500 in my bank account, which will surely help me through until Christmas, if I am lucky. Then, hopefully, there may be a job in a hotel organising festive coach parties for people who want to spend Christmas being waited on. There was always good money in that.

Most days by now I would be looking across the road at the hot sand, covered in sunburnt families, shading my eyes to look at the inviting sea that is asking me to wander down and wade into its cold waiting arms and wash away the heat of the day.

Not today though. Today the clouds are a dusty grey colour, filtering the sun, daring it to break through and warm up the determined huddles of families milking the most from their annual week by the sea. Today I have things to do. I collect my final pay packet from Cliff, the owner, thanking him for letting me leave before the end of the season and wishing him the best for the next few weeks. Cliff smiles and thanks me back.

"Come down when you're home for Easter, we'll see what the weather's doing and hopefully get you some shifts."

"Thanks, I'll come down when I get back. Have a good Christmas and all that."

It may seem strange thinking of Christmas in late August. But like most seaside business owners, Cliff would gradually start running down his stock over the next month. Eventually he will put up the shutters, lock the doors and go away to do whatever it was he did for those months, when nobody wanted to sit on the windblown, rain-soaked beaches. This is the time of year when the town belongs to the people who live here, and the timeless skies and winter storms are only witnessed by a privileged few.

I like working for Cliff, he is in his 50's with appalling beige dress sense, and hair that perpetually needs a cut, but he never actually has time to go to the barber. Instead, he keeps it swept back over his left ear, constantly pushing it back in the hope that this time it would stay. He is almost always too busy or distracted for small talk. As long as you do what needs doing without complaining or waiting to be asked, he pretty much leaves you to get on with it. He's always around to do what he needs to do to keep the wheels turning, and he pays regularly. Not only that, he pays more than the next closest ice-cream shop. Not a great deal, but more is more.

Cliff turns, wipes his hands absently on his sun faded tee-shirt and brushes his hair back with an unconscious sweep of his hand, before picking up his cloth and carrying on wiping down the tables and adjusting the chairs. His hair immediately returns to its previous state. My departure is already forgotten as he resumes ticking things off his mental to-do list.

I stride off into the afternoon. I pass the trays of lurid pink sticks of rock with the name of the town running through them, ready to be presented to friends and relatives of people at home. I pass the piles of buckets, spades, flags and racks of postcards with pictures of donkeys, cliffs, boats and risqué jokes. I pass the empty tables outside the neighbouring pub, waiting for the afternoon drinkers to make their return at 5.30. Some are already staking a claim to an outside table in anticipation. I go on past the neatly tended flowerbeds and sand blown lawns that punctuate the sea front.

Even though the pavement is less crowded than it had been the previous week I still cut through the back lane and along the routes heading away from the town and beach. Heading away from the people and into the alleys and passages that formed the secret routes of my childhood – short cuts that had taken a lifetime to learn and formed the childhood map of my world. Over deserted back roads, up steep hills and through half-hidden lanes overgrown with summer brambles and nettles that need to be pushed aside to ensure safe passage.

These are the same trails that we followed on our bikes when we were out and exploring in the new-found freedom of 11 and 12-year-olds. They now provide me with safe passage to my parents' house. The house I have spent most of my life in which now serves as a place to sleep, eat and arrange meetings with friends when I'm not away at college.

I let myself in and look through the small pile of post by the front door. I'm not expecting anything, and I'm not disappointed. I go upstairs and pull out my duffel bag from under my bed, look around the room at the various piles of clean and almost-clean clothes, the books and tapes, then go into the back garden for a cigarette.

Suitably braced, I go back upstairs and put on a record. No selection required, I just settled for The Stranglers as that was the last thing I had listened to and was still sitting on the turntable, waiting to provide the soundtrack to my packing. This has just the right amount of energy and noise pumping from the tinny speakers to motivate me into getting started.

There is no system or thought involved: some clothes, some books, some folders of notes and coursework waiting to be revitalised. I also add a bundle of cassettes. The tapes were the items that required the most discretion. After what felt like an entire summer of listening to Chris De sodding Burgh's Lady in sodding Red on the radio at work I am in serious need of some musical rebooting. Hopefully I will go to see some bands in the autumn, maybe something half decent for Fresher's Ball, and a chance to make copies of friends new musical acquisitions from the summer.

Once my packing is complete and my bag is bulging with assorted strange lumps and bumps, looking like an overfed snake, I move to the kitchen to find out what food is available. Here I find my sister on the same mission as me, between us we make some fried egg sandwiches and park ourselves on the sofa to watch TV. We are still there when mum and dad get back from wherever they had been and the house descends into happily organised chaos as more food is cooked (of course me and sis have some, food is food!)

After eating, teasing my sister and arguing about who was washing and who was drying, we drift off to our own parts of the house.

"Are you still okay to bring my stuff up to college?" I ask dad as we pass on the landing.

"Yes, not for a couple of weeks though. Make sure you take everything you need until then, and make sure you pack up all the things you want me to bring up before you go so I can put them straight in the car."

"Sure thing, thanks."

"Why are you going back early anyway?"

"Duh, I already told you dad."

"Well refresh my memory then."

"We're painting the common room; it's all been arranged. It needs to be done before everyone else gets back."

At the end of last term, a group from the student union had approached the college premises manager Mr Dudman (Duddi) and asked if the common room could be redecorated over the summer. For years posters for everything - from the horrors of vivisection, to supporting the Greenham Common peace camp, to advertising upcoming events and happenings, had adorned the walls. Now the accumulated tape and adhesives had taken their toll on the paintwork. Combined with the everyday wear and tear of hundreds of students passing through, it looked pretty grim.

Of course, Duddi gave this the very briefest consideration he could without appearing not to have heard it, then said no.

After some negotiations about the necessity of the work, he eventually conceded that we could do it ourselves if we wanted. He made a great show of his beneficence in arranging for rooms to be available for us to stay in and some basic rations to keep us going for a day or two while we did the work. Then, as a final insult to injury, he told us that all the materials we needed would be left for us by the decorators, who would be refurbishing the staff common room and canteen – we could have their leftover paint.

Still, a group of us from the student council had volunteered - Me, Sarah, Lisa, Stewart and Jo. Despite none of us having any decorating experience whatsoever, we were going to transform the common room. The wonderful optimism of youth, and the freedom offered by ignorance, meant that we were all looking forward to getting back to college early and having a relaxing weekend while we quickly took care of the painting.

Here, on my last day at home, I briefly consider calling round for Dave to see if he wants to pop out for a quick half. Then, in a rare moment of mature self-reflection, I decide to stay in and get an early night, so I am rested and ready for tomorrow's journey. I consider a bath, but it seems such a rigmarole, and will undoubtedly lead to arguments about the remaining amount of hot water available for everyone else. A shower is out of the question as the rubber attachment that joins onto the taps had split several weeks ago, so I decide on not bothering with either option. I settle down on my bed with a dog-eared copy of Angela Carter's Bloody Chamber that I had borrowed, and listened to a side of Who Dares Wins before getting lost in the story and gradually dozing off with the book gently collapsing onto my chest.

Next to my bed there is my brother's old bed, heaped with a pile of my assorted bits and pieces (He is away in the navy, sailing the seven seas.) The pile is disorganised and not contained in any way. I am confident that my dad will find a way of transporting it of course, he's my dad!

*

I wake up with the sun streaming through the gaps in the curtains where I hadn't pulled them all the way across. I grab at my bedside clock to make sure I haven't overslept and am relieved to find it is still early. I quietly creep down to the kitchen in my boxer shorts and a faded-to-grey black tee-shirt, and make some tea. Then I go and sit in the garden with a cigarette.

Yesterday's greyness has blown away and the day is bright and warm. There are apples swelling on the branches of the tree at the end of the garden, weighing them down and creating a topiary shrug. The grass is damp and needs cutting, but that's not my job anymore. I go back inside, pour some Coco-Pops and sit back outside with my bare feet in the damp grass.

I always have mixed emotions when I leave to go back to college. It is too far to visit with any regularity (which is maybe part of the reason I chose that particular college) and I rarely had enough 10 pence pieces for a phone call of any length. Combined with my near legendary non-letter writing skills it means I am mostly out of touch with home while I'm away. Most times this doesn't bother me too much. Occasionally, like when my parents had to have the locks changed (which was a surprise when I arrived home one holiday.) I feel a bit out of the loop.

Still, the separation of my two lives was mostly ok by me. 'What happens in college stays in college' type of thing. I could lead the kind of late night, lazy days, drinking and womanising (if I got the chance) that my parents would definitely not approve of. Carousing or gallivanting my dad would call it, not that he's old fashioned, he just likes long words. Disgusting or shameful as my mum would say, she's a straight-talking Northerner.

Once I have finished breakfast, I dump my empty cup and bowl in the sink and beat the rush to the bathroom, splashing some water on myself, in lieu of washing, and spraying on some Turbo deodorant, whose advertising tagline should be 'Smells foul – but it's cheap!' I then spend as much time again making my hair look disheveled and unkempt.

I pull on my jeans, socks, DM boots and opt for the same shirt I slept in, no point getting a clean one all messed up. I'm ready to face the day. By now the house is alive with the stirring sounds of a family emerging, familiar and friendly and ready to start writing the story of a new day.

Back downstairs I make more tea, a pot this time, while mum fries up some bacon (of course I'm having some, food is food!) everyone descends and eats, then leave for work. I say goodbye to everyone, and suddenly the long hours have turned to short minutes and it's time for me to leave too.

Walking to the station I look like the bees knees: frayed jeans (hole in one knee), studded belt, leather jacket with a selection of badges. Over one shoulder is my roughly packed duffle bag. In the other hand a cassette player and a cigarette juggle for space as I leave a trail of smoke behind me in the summer sunshine.

Chapter 2
Journey

The day passes in a series of minor non-events: Ticket, wait, board, sit, look out of windows, station, change trains, wait - you get the idea. The view from the carriage window changes from familiar to unknown as the seats fill up a little more at each station and the carriage fills with a hazy layer of smoke held in place by the shafts of brilliant sunlight lancing through the windows.

Angela Carter sits largely ignored on the table in front of me as I work my way through the crisps, sandwiches and biscuits mum got ready for me. The journey is broken by a trip to the buffet car for a foul cup of tea, a lean out of the window, a toilet break and a nap. Eventually I start to recognise some landmarks and soon we head into a station that could have come directly from the set of The Railway Children. I heave my luggage and belongings off the train and onto the middle of the platform where I load myself up and transfer to the bus stop that will take me on the final leg of my journey and deliver me to my destination – well, most of the way anyway.

At the bus stop I check the timetable. It is afternoon now; the sun is cooling and I have the bench to myself and my luggage as I impatiently wait the 45 minutes for the bus to turn up. Lazily I trace patterns in the mud turned to dust with my toes, as I sit watching birds making their busy way in and out of the bushes. I'm looking forward to getting back, looking forward to being independent again, looking forward to catching up with friends. Also, although it's deeply uncool to admit it, I'm even looking forward to my final year of study, finishing my degree and moving on in the world.

Me and my luggage bump our way onto the bus. The driver watches me with a cocked eyebrow as I edge through the rows and claim a seat on the near-empty bus. The final part of my journey is brief, winding through some hedgerow-sided roads and into the village, depositing me outside St John's church, with another keenly observed manoeuvring of bags and belongings.

No metropolitan higher education experience for me. I chose this college more by accident than design, it is 'in the sticks' as I'm sure you guessed.

The village consists of a church, a pub, a single shop/Post Office and a cluster of red brick cottages and houses. It is pretty enough to be on a postcard – though I'm not sure why anybody would want to send a postcard of such a secluded place. You can actually buy postcards of the church - St John's in the Post Office, it is of great interest to people who are interested in old churches apparently.

From the village you have a long walk down 'The Drive' which leads through quarter of a mile of fields and into a cluster of buildings, from the same vintage as the village you just left. Alongside these are an angular assortment of more modern buildings that combine to make a working campus. Blunt and uninspiring residential blocks stand guard as you approach, then education buildings disguised as a 1960's secondary school and an old farm building housing the art studios.

At the centre of it all is the mansion. It stands majestically over the lesser buildings, its crenulated rooftop and two towers covering two sides of a courtyard that is completed by old service buildings. The Mansion is where the staff congregate, not for the likes of us students without an appointment. The few times I have been inside have revealed the spectacular view from the tall windows looking down the long lawn towards the river in the valley below.

I cross the road and start down The Drive, through fields of stubble where the oilseed rape had been waving its yellow heads when I was last here. I walk past a small copse of trees, my bag now feeling like it weighs half a ton, until finally emerging into the familiar territory of the campus.

I balance my bag precariously on my shoulder for one final time, jacket and radio in the other arm I walk through the lazy afternoon with the buzzing insects and the far-off drone of the motorway keeping me company. A mixture of anticipation, hunger and weariness drive me on, the bacon sandwich feels as long ago as it was and I'm keen to see who else has arrived.

The answer is - everyone. I am the last to arrive. To be fair the others all live closer and had gotten lifts. As I round the last corner I see my friends sitting on the grass outside the open doors of the common room. There is a small flat area of grass outside the wall of windows and French doors that line the side of the common room. On nice days, when everyone is here, this grass would be covered with people drinking, eating and talking. Alongside this strip of grass runs a path leading to the mansion. On the other side of the path is a large ornamental pond with an erratic fountain, not working now, and a good layer of bright green algae with insects and birds swooping and darting around it. In turn there is another, larger rectangle of grass in front of the entrance to the lecture theatre and flanked by an old stable block on one side and a two-storey science block on the other.

This is the place I have called home for the last two years, the place where I have formed bonds and found this surrogate family. I break into a trot as I approach them.

Chapter 3
Friends

Everyone gets up to greet me, I drop my bags onto the floor and I am immediately surrounded by welcoming arms, hugs, quick-fire questions about my journey (did I get the horse and cart to the station? Ha!), my health, my summer and my need for a cup of tea. I frantically try to keep up with answers and ask similar questions of my own.

I take the cigarettes from my pocket and offer them around; Sarah takes one and we share a light. I join the others on the grass as they resume their places with fresh cups of tea all round courtesy of Lisa. I inhale, exhale and ask a set of questions of my own, but at a more sedate pace, as the sun starts to dip behind the building dropping us into shade.

In summary, everyone's answers were as follows:

Stewart and Jo had been to Glastonbury together. The long weekend had been the highlight of their summer, everything else paling in comparison. Most of the rest of it was composed of being with their families and away from each other, which had been 'not good' and had necessitated numerous train journeys to and from each other's homes when money allowed.

Lisa had been volunteering, something to do with woodland conservation that sounded like harder work.

Sarah kind of shrugs and says she's spent most of the summer 'in the pub.' This is ambiguous as her parents own a pub and she doesn't make it clear which side of the bar she has been on, I suspect both.

I take my leave of the others and carry my luggage to the row of rooms that have been set aside for our stay in the old stable block, next to the mansion. Even though I'm last to arrive I still have a choice of rooms as Stewart and Jo have opted to squeeze into one room, to no one's surprise.

There is nothing to choose between the remaining two rooms, I throw my things on the bed of the nearest one, next to the pile of folded bed linen. Making the bed is a job that can wait till later, right now I'm hungry.

I re-join the others as they are rifling through the provisions that have been left for us in the kitchen. A selection of sandwiches is created and cold quiche (disgusting – but as I said, I am hungry and food is food.) A new pot of tea and a dig into a catering size box of crisps completes the meal, we sit and eat at one of the numerous tables, still catching up and sharing news, filling up the ash tray and looking over into the corner every so often.

The corner contains a pile of dust sheets and a large collection of paint tins sitting on a low flat trolley with a low wire mesh siding to stop everything falling off. There are various colours, hints and hues, none of which appears to have been selected to go with any other tin in the selection. God knows what the staff rooms in the mansion must look like. There are also rollers, brushes and trays all waiting for us to pick them up. Now I look at it in the fading light of day there did seem to be quite a lot more to do than I had imagined, with a lot of very grubby walls to cover.

I'm pretty sure it's Sarah who suggests that we go to the pub for a drink, but we were all thinking it. As we have a consensus, we up sticks and make plans to head off back up the drive to visit the pub.

I go to my room and put on my jacket, in spite of the warmth of the day. It may be warm now, but it will quickly start to cool down by the time we are walking back through the fields. I glance at the payphone as I pass and briefly considered phoning home to let everyone know I arrived safely. I rummage in my pocket to see how much change I have left, only a couple of 10 pence pieces amongst the handful of coins. Deciding I might need them for the cigarette machine later I pass by the phone and meet up with the others.

As I arrive, they start walking, letting me catch up. I look at Stewart and Jo, from behind they look like they have just dropped by from the 60s. Their clothes are flamboyant and multi-coloured. Stewart is wearing his ubiquitous trilby hat and an embroidered waistcoat over a collarless shirt, Jo a long flowery skirt and a flouncy white blouse with her red hair tumbling down the back.

Lisa has had a recent haircut. It is short. Her dungarees and stripy t-shirt are pretty funky. They are also quite grubby, worked in. Lisa is studied and studious, I can't imagine her engaging in hard physical labour. More likely that Lisa will be the one out of all of us who will end up getting the sort of job where she can make an actual difference.

That leaves Sarah. Sarah is…well she's Sarah. She always looks like she's just come out of the pottery studio, today is no exception. Wild hair and a loose-fitting sweatshirt over baggy track suit trousers. Sarah didn't need to dress to impress, she was a force of nature. She was always ready to volunteer (which is why she was here) always ready to lend a hand, and always ready to have a drink and a laugh. True I hadn't asked everybody, but I didn't know anybody who didn't like Sarah.

I catch up and we walk together retracing my steps from earlier. We walk back to the church and then around the bend in the road to the pub, the Round Tree. As we approach we can see an empty table at the front, the table is duly claimed and me and Sarah go in to order 5 pints of lager. No discussion is needed, that's what everyone drinks. Inside is dim, only lit by the sun filtering dustily through the leaded windows and some wall lamps. It is maybe a quarter full of couples sipping beer and talking quietly while the fruit machine flashes in the corner. Chris De Sodding Burgh is playing on the juke box, what else would it be? I look around trying to guess who would have put that on, Dan the landlord seems the most likely culprit. He looks up from his paper as we approach, "Didn't think you lot were back yet."

Sarah replies, "Yeah, we're back early, 5 pints please."

"We're here to do some work in the common room" I tell him with a hint of pride that belies the fact that I'm not actually used to doing anything like proper work, unless you count selling ice-creams.

"Well, it's good to see you, welcome back" he says. He is already putting the second pint on the counter for Sarah to ferry out to the thirsty people waiting outside.

"Are you here all weekend?"

"Yeah, there's loads to do."

"Well, if you were planning on coming in tomorrow, we're closed to the public – private do going on. Sorry"

"That's fine," I tell him, "we'll figure something out."

It wasn't unusual for someone from the village or surrounding houses to book the pub for a wedding or a party, we had a contingency plan for when that happened, although usually it didn't worry us too much in term time as we had the student union bar. I pay, thank Dan and take the remaining drinks outside.

The evening starts to fade and the temperature begins to dip slightly. Sarah gets a second round of drinks in, just as Dan is ringing the bell for last orders, and we sit and enjoy them as Stewart and Jo regale us with tales of drunkenness and loud music from Glastonbury. I had to grudgingly admit that I would have quite liked to see The Cure and The Pogues. There were a lot of the other bands I couldn't say I was that bothered about. A weekend in a field with a lot of hippies though, definitely not something I would pay £17 of my hard-earned cash for! We argue the toss over my cynical attitude for a bit, until Lisa, the peacemaker, moves the conversation onto what we are planning to do to welcome the new intake for Fresher's Week. I sense that the semblance of a plan has been made before we finish up our drinks and take the long walk back towards our beds for the night. I am tired but don't mind the walk, I am with friends and I am where I want to be right now.

As I shout goodnight to everyone and go into my room I look down at the bed – my bag sitting next to a pile of neatly folded bed linen – and remember my earlier decision to 'do it later'. This seems to be a defining characteristic of my short adult life so far, carried over from adolescence. Although it has served me well until now, I sense that it might be time for a change. It might be time to start being more proactive and making decisions, hopefully good decisions.

"My beds not made!" I shout loudly enough for Lisa to hear from her room, which is next to mine.

"Make it then you lazy bastard!" she shouts back. I am making a mental note to revise my opinion of Lisa, maybe she could be a protester yet.

Right now I'm tired, it's been a long day, it's getting late and I've had a couple of pints of beer. I roughly spread the sheets and blankets over the bed, kick off my boots and jeans and climb into the middle of the pile of bedclothes. I am asleep soon after my head hits the pillow.

Chapter 4
Making a start

I wake the next morning to the sound of running water in the next room, Lisa's morning ablutions. I decide not to bother as I'm going to be decorating today, so who cares. I put on my jeans, rummage in my bag for my trainers and leave the room, lighting my first cigarette of the day on my way down to the common room.

Sarah is already sitting on the steps outside finishing her cigarette when I arrive. We greet and sit together in the sunshine; it's going to be another beautiful day.

"Sleep good?" she enquires.

"Like a log. And you?"

"Yeah, right up until the bastard birds woke me up at stupid 'o' clock."

"What were they shouting about?"

"Fuck knows, but I wish they wouldn't."

I've spent the last 2 months being woken up by seagulls squawking and shouting at full volume, so this seems quiet by comparison. I don't say this, I look up and see Lisa walking towards us,

"I'm going to put the kettle on" I announce, and go into the kitchen to locate mugs, milk and teabags. I briefly consider collecting some of yesterday's plates from the table as I pass, but decide it can wait till later – as I said prevarication should be my middle name.

While I'm waiting for the kettle to boil, I find some cornflakes. I pour some into a bowl, add some milk and a liberal heaping of sugar then eat them while simultaneously making three cups of tea.

As I am fishing out the tea bags and dumping them on the draining board, Lisa and Sarah come in, Lisa rummages in the fridge and pulls out a large pack of bacon which she opens and starts spreading out under the grill. Sarah slurps her tea and starts buttering some bread while I find the packets of ketchup that will add the finishing touches.

Stewart and Jo arrive, all smiles and holding hands, as we are finishing our bacon butties in the sunshine. Lisa moved out some chairs from the common room to avoid sitting on the wet grass. Stewart collects two more chairs and joins us as Jo goes in to make tea and cook bacon for them. I follow her to make another one for myself, fuel for the day ahead.

"All good?" I ask.

"All good," Jo replies "so nice to be back, I miss you guys when I'm at home."

She gives me a hug, which feels nice. Having her body pressed briefly against mine reminds me of how long it has been since I had a girlfriend. My last relationship, with Sue, had ended in June; an ultimatum was issued - "It's me or the football!"

I was pretty sure I made the right decision at the time, even after England's disappointingly unjust and untimely exit from the tournament. Fitting all those matches in and around a busy revision and exam schedule had left little time for anything else.

I do have a nagging feeling that I could have skipped some of the matches. Watching Scotland's 0-0 draw with Uruguay or Russia beating Canada 2-0 was hardly the stuff of footballing legend. And Maradona's handball, which was the beginning of England's downfall, is something I think will leave a bitter taste for a long time to come.

But sitting with friends, drinking beer in tiny rooms watching games on miniature TVs had an atmosphere all of its own. Also, in the interest of fairness, I think I may possibly have painted Sue in a bad light here, what she actually said was, "I wish you'd spend a bit more time with me."

Then I got cross, and then we broke up.

The more I think about it, the more I realise that I may have been a little unreasonable and hasty. The momentary thrill of being footloose and fancy free didn't last much past Argentina's final kick of the tournament, and my hubris and stupidity (Yes, I'll own them) didn't let me try and make things up before the end of term.

Sue is studying English, I had met her at the start of the course, when we were all new and trying to sort out who we did and didn't like, and how we were going to get through the next 3 years. I liked her straight away, she was pretty and laughed at my jokes – but only ever when we were with a group of her friends. They threw a protective cordon around her which I soon found out was because she had a boyfriend at home, and they wanted to guard her from my unwelcome advances.

Nevertheless, I tried it on. Not just once or twice either, pretty much every time I saw her – flirting, making her laugh, and buying her drinks. I don't have much in the way of seduction skills, but I do have a great deal of patience and tenacity when it is called for.

We eventually got together towards the end of the first year. One of her friends from home had written to her to tell her that her boyfriend had been seeing someone else, the cad! Of course, I was there to comfort her, pass her tissues, agree that her now ex-boyfriend was a bastard - and get her drunk. Not taking advantage of her, just being generally nice and considerate.

It was in the summer term. We had some drinks at a party and kissed until our tongues ached. Then, before I knew it, it was summer and I went off to sell ice-creams. Many weeks of letter writing across the vast distance of the UK ensued, until a passionate reunion and a full-on relationship for the whole of year two - right up to the point where I couldn't see what an idiot I was.

Hopefully, when everyone else comes back to college, we can at least try to be friends; I regularly promise myself that I will try to be a better person and be more thoughtful about other people. I also regularly disappoint myself by not remembering to do either of those things. But every day is a new day, right?

Speaking of new days, this one is starting up now. Sarah and Lisa have been over investigating the painting materials while I have been eating in the kitchen. I join them and we start moving the tins around deciding where we want each colour to go. I am not particularly helpful at this, but nevertheless I feel free to offer my opinion.

Stewart and Jo come over in their dungarees (thankfully not matching, that would be too much – I would have to say something!) and together we work out a plan of attack. There is a prevailing theory that we will get more done if we are not in each other's way. So, we each take a set of painting materials and a pot of paint and go to a section of wall ready to get started. Except Stewart and Jo obviously, they are doing the same bit because they don't want to be apart. We move some tables to the side so we have something to stand on to reach the higher parts of the walls. It doesn't matter if they get a spot of paint on them, tomorrows' job is to scrub them clean and scrape the gum from underneath all the tables and chairs anyway.

I pop out for a smoke with Sarah, by the time we have finished the others have already spread out their dustsheets and started rolling their allocated paint colour onto their allotted section of wall. The room is deadly quiet as everyone concentrates on what they are doing. I can't stand the silence, I jog back to my room and return a few minutes later with my cassette player and a handful of tapes.

This results in work stopping and discussion starting about what we should be listening to. Sarah looks in vain for Donna Summer, or anything vaguely disco-ish, Stewart and Jo offer to go and get some Fleetwood Mac from their room, I push for anything from the 'Play Loud' tape boxes. Eventually Lisa picks out a Lloyd Cole and the Commotions tape which we all agree on, and we all set to work at last.

The paint goes on quickly, easily and messily. Before long we have made good headway on our allocated sections and the smell of paint permeates the room. The paint has managed to stay mostly in the areas it was supposed to, with the exception of the smudges on the opaque glass screens and some small splodges on the floor tiles which I have mostly wiped up with the edge of the dust sheet. There is also some on my jeans, my t-shirt, my shoes, my hands, my hair and possibly my face – hard to tell at the moment. I can't see how the others are getting on right now, but I expect it is similar.

Time passes quickly and at some point, with my not noticing at first, Easy Pieces is replaced with Madonna's True Blue. I suspect Sarah did the deed, sneaking back to her room to get it when she went for a toilet break.

Normally I would resist this, but I am engrossed with my painting, and secretly, but never admitting it publicly, actually don't mind Madonna that much. It has us all singing along and even having the odd shimmy here and there. My musical taste is, of course, impeccable. The fact that nobody else seems to like it says more about them than me – I think. Anyway, it was lucky it hadn't been Lisa popping out to the loo or we could have ended up listening to The Smiths.

Tea and cigarette breaks punctuate the work, and although it's going well, it also seems to be going agonisingly slowly. There is so much wall still to paint.

Eventually we stop for lunch. Everybody squeezes into the kitchen and a sandwich production line is established, I am in charge of the margarine. Soon we are back out on the grass, eating lunch and enjoying the sun.

Even though we haven't officially started our final year yet, talk turns to future plans. Stewart started it, "Me and Jo are going travelling next year." He says, smiling at Jo and holding her hand in his, "No need to be a wage slave straight away."

"We're going to start in India," added Jo, "then maybe go on to Indonesia or somewhere."

"There's plenty of world to see. "Stewart finished.

I am sure there is, I don't really know where Indonesia is and quietly wonder where they will get the money from and how they would manage it. I wouldn't even know how to start getting tickets, passports or visas. I'd only ever flown once before, and that was a school trip, so the teachers booked and arranged it all, I just turned up and had fun.

"Sounds great." I say.

Sarah thinks she will probably just work in her dads' pub until something more interesting comes along.

"Like what?" Lisa pushes her gently.

"Maybe something arty," Sarah replies, which makes sense as she is studying art.

"What about you?" She asks back to Lisa.

"I've applied for some postgrad courses, hoping to hear back soon."

Lisa is the brightest of us, one of the cleverest people I know. I'm not sure how she ended up at our small rural college when she could have gone to a university of her choice. I had heard rumours from someone in the year below us, who knew someone who went to the same school as Lisa, that she had been accepted into Cambridge but had decided not to go.

I did ask her once. Last year when she was helping me with some impossible coursework, that she made seem easy when she patiently explained it to me. As I was writing some notes from her essay (copying bits) I had said, "How come you didn't go to university? You must have got good enough grades."

"I can get a degree here, and cities are too big."

I didn't pursue it at the time, too busy trying to get my own half-arsed essay into good enough shape to be handed in, but now I think about it I'm sure that she wanted me to ask what she meant. I guess I missed that moment.

Of course, everybody knows what I'll be doing next year (if all goes to plan). I'll be doing what I've wanted to do since I was at school - go back to school! I am doing a teacher training course and hoping to start teaching next year.

It feels like it's been a long road from when I first had the inkling that it was something I wanted to do (after a week of evenings as a helper at a local youth club.) More of a whim really, I mentioned it to a member of staff who directed me to the school careers office.

When I found out I would need a degree I nearly gave up at the first hurdle. Going to college hadn't been the plan, nobody in my family had been to college or university, and my parents were anticipating that I would start paying my way. There was an expectation from me that I would start earning enough to move out and away from the bickering and sulking that had been a constant feature of my teens.

My friendly head of sixth form had talked me into it when I explained it to him. He guided me through the process of finding a course, applying and getting a grant. This had already been explained to everyone else, but I had bunked those lessons to play snooker as I wasn't planning on further study after school. If it wasn't for the lack of jobs (and my disinclination I suppose) I would probably have been working already.

So, I applied, got accepted and then told my parents, much to their surprise. After that I needed to put in some more study time instead of perfecting my cue technique, to make sure I got the grades. Since then it had been an uphill battle to keep myself on track and make sure I was passing. I'd managed two years so far, one to go.

Another cigarette, then we get our noses back to the grindstone. More paint is painted, walls are covered and gradually the seemingly endless acres of wall start to turn from the scarred, faded yellow it was to a bright clean palette of pale blue, light green, vibrant yellow and cerise. None of this is expertly applied, the best parts are Sarah's, who has had the twin advantages of having helped her Dad decorate once before, and studying art - so is therefore used to applying paint to surfaces. The best you can say for the rest of us is that we tried.

The day keeps getting hotter and hotter as it progresses, it is the kind of sticky late summer day when the air feels heavy and your shirt clings to your back and front. I had abandoned my tee shirt some time earlier and am busy splashing paint onto my skinny bare torso as I work. Stewart and Jo have also taken off their shirts and now look like extras from the video of Come on Eileen, with Jo showing an amount of side boob that is as distracting for me as it clearly is for Stewart.

Sarah and Lisa have both chosen to retain their modesty, but are obviously as hot and uncomfortable as the rest of us. The windows are all wide open, but there is no hint of a breeze to move the air around and we find ourselves taking more and more frequent drink breaks and standing outside in the sun letting the sweat dry from our bodies.

The sky is an unbroken blue, the stillness accentuated by the absence of the sounds of insects and birds. Not the sort of absence you notice straight away, but when you do, or when someone has pointed it out to you, it becomes louder and the quiet takes on a presence of its own.

Inside the common room the tape player continues to churn out a range of favourites, I have managed to sneak in one side of The Sisters of Mercy, I had been subjected to Dire Straits and we had all roared along with The Boss, who me and Sue had gone to see at Wembley last year – she's a mad keen fan. Stewart and Jo had also been, on a different night from us. Nobody objected to Bruce, and we listened to Born in the USA and The River, back-to-back as they were crammed onto one tape, one album on each side.

I keep working along the wall until the sudden realisation dawns on me that I have just started to paint over a clean and freshly painted area of wall. I stop and look around to find that everybody else is at a similar stage, the different colours merging in a not-too-jarring kind of way. I put my head in the kitchen to see what time it is. To my surprise it is nearly 5 o'clock, we have worked through the entire day and finished in time for some tea.

As we gather in the centre of the room to admire our handiwork, we breathe a collective sigh of relief.

"That's it then." says Sarah, "All done."

"Well done us," smiles Lisa as she moves to start tidying the various brushes, rollers and empty paint tins that are scattered around the room.

"Not quite" Stewart says as he picks up the tin of cerise paint and its accompanying brush.

We all watch as he walks over to the far wall, the bright yellow one. He takes the brush and carefully draws a six foot round red circle, bisects it and adds two downward sloping lines to make the peace sign used by CND. Nobody objected or moved to stop him. Lisa observed that, "Duddi won't like that."

Sarah countered with, "Fuck him, he's not here - and he was too mean to pay people to do it."

As we watch the red paint starts to run and drip very slightly on the not quite dry yellow background. It gives the sign a slightly sinister look and adds greatly to the overall effect. We all start to tidy up now, with Lisa directing us as to where everything should go, gradually the room comes back into shape.

We gather up our possessions and walk together back to our rooms to freshen up before we eat. It has been a long day, when I get into my room I lay down on the pile of crumpled bedclothes on the still unmade bed and close my eyes for 5 minutes, letting the heat of the day wash over me. I have left the door open and can hear the sounds of the others walking to and from the communal bathroom, knocking on doors to borrow hairbrushes and other sundries and calling to one another through the flimsy partition walls. The heat continues to build and I slip into a deep sleep.

Chapter 5
The walk

I am woken up by a knock on my door and Sarah putting her head round the door frame and announcing, "Come on, we've started cooking, we're going to eat then go out for a beer."

"Good plan," I mumble as I try to get my sleep addled head to organise itself into something resembling fully functioning. "I'll be right there." I get off the bed and walk to the bathroom with my wash bag. I clean some of the most obvious paint off of myself, soap under my armpits and spray some Turbo around. Feeling slightly more awake now, I retrieve a clean but crumpled yellow and white striped t-shirt out of my bag, pull it over my head and walk back to the common room with a cigarette.

As I walk the heat is still oppressive, the air is still and the silence is complete, until I get closer to the common room. Here the sounds and smells of cooking reach me long before I catch sight of the others. I walk in to the sounds of laughter and chat as my friends finish preparing the meal and start dishing up.

"Lazy bastard" says Stewart.

I shrug and smile.

"You're washing up, you know that don't you?"

I shrug again. I don't really care as there is a dishwasher that will make short work of it. If I was miffed, it would have been because it is not just the debris from this meal, but all of the cups plates, cutlery and pans from the last 24 hours. But right now I am most focused on eating.

Sarah and Lisa have moved a table outside, to go with the chairs we had sat on earlier. We take our plates outside and sit in the muggy heat of the early evening and eat. The food disappears quickly and easily and the atmosphere is relaxed as the conversation veers from subject to subject, punctuated by laughter and good-natured teasing, mostly about clothes and music preferences. I get my share of the flak as they gang up on me. Apparently, to summarise, I'm scruffy and the music I listen to is awful. I manage to take these things as compliments. It is true that I lack commitment to my studies at times, and that I resemble a badly dressed spider plant. I feel no real need to defend myself or my musical heroes – Kirk Brandon and Jeffrey Lee Pierce's music speaks for itself.

My post-prandial cigarette is lit and I am bracing myself for the trauma of clearing up. I lean back and blow out a plume of smoke. As I look up into the clear blue sky I see two plane vapour trails crossing one another. The image triggers a memory of the space shuttle Challenger that had blown up earlier in the year

The memory was clear for me, I had been on a school placement at the time, as part of my course. I had carefully planned and mapped out a unit of work based on space exploration for my class. I had used my own vague memories of the '69 moon landings, and a selection of books and posters as source material. It had stimulated some great creative writing, atmospheric art work and rocket building science experiments, as well as the history work it was based on.

The main highlight of the project was going to be watching the shuttle launch and collecting and collating the newspaper reports surrounding this. I had arranged for someone to video tape the news so we could watch it in class the following day. The project came to an abrupt ending at the suggestion of the teacher I was working alongside.

Undeterred, the children kept bringing in photos and newspaper cuttings showing pictures of the seven astronauts who had died, next to the vivid image of the single trail of steam and smoke splitting into two distinct parts, each taking its own crazily swerving courses towards their downward trajectory in the clear blue Floridian sky.

In the end the display started to look more like a shrine and was dismantled one evening by myself and the teacher. As we set up a new, hastily arranged, project about sharks I quietly hoped that none of the children had seen Jaws.

Other than that tumultuous event I rarely, if ever, watched news programmes or read newspapers. I am more Max Headroom and 2000 AD. Current affairs are not my thing, it takes events of truly world-shaking magnitude to get me to sit up and take notice. That, or catching the end of the news when I turn up early for Neighbours. In fact, I probably know more about what's happening in The Waterhole at Lasseter's than I do about what's happening in parliament.

My political views and understanding are still a work in progress. When I first left home I thought I knew everything, as you do. It was only after being exposed to a group of people who hadn't grown up in a small town in the West Country, where everyone and everything is both conservative and Conservative, that I realised there was more going on in this big world than I had understood. I am still evolving and learning in the swirling vortex of student politics.

I know that Margaret Thatcher is Prime Minister – we don't like her! I know that Ronald Reagan is President of the USA – we don't like him either. I know that between them they have decided that the UK is the ideal place for America to stockpile some of its huge collection of nuclear missiles.

I also know that Mikhail Gorbachev is the Russian leader, but is still quite preoccupied at the moment, trying to sort out the chaos and destruction caused by Chernobyl blowing up and melting down in April. That caught everybody's attention for a while - don't go out in the rain, keep an eye on the direction the weather is coming from, and don't eat the Welsh sheep. For a few weeks everybody thought that the whole of Europe would be laid waste and that the anti-nuclear lobby would be proved right all along. Perhaps now things will start to change.

I work my way through the piles of cutlery, plates, mugs and pans, feeding them into the machine and collecting them at the other end to stack in arbitrary piles on the counters. The job is soon done, I leave the piles where they are, I figure we're going to need them again soon anyway.

In my room I collect my wallet, my leather jacket and put on my DM's. I glance in the mirror to check that my hair is suitably untidy and see that I need a shave. I decide to leave the stubble where it is for now, no point going through all that palaver so late in the day. I head out into the corridor to where the others are congregating.

Sarah is wearing a clean version of the clothes she was wearing earlier. Lisa is in faded blue jeans with a white t-shirt, a sailor's cap and a large yellow bag hung over her shoulder, she looks pretty cool. Stewart and Jo are last to appear, both in collarless shirts and shapeless brown corduroy trousers/long patterned skirt respectively. They are both wearing sandals. Stewart has been reunited with his trilby and everyone has a jacket, coat or cagoule with them for the walk back, remembering how chilly it got yesterday evening.

As the village pub is not available, we have to revert to plan B. This is a walk down the lawn to the river, over a footbridge, along a stretch of abandoned railway track and over the embankment to a small country pub called The Fox and Hounds. It is quite a long walk and the heat of the day has not abated, meaning it will be a sweaty one too. That, I tell myself, is what will make the beer worthwhile.

Stewart and Jo walk off slightly ahead of us, chatting away to one another – probably planning their trip to Outer Mongolia, or wherever the fuck it was they were going. Sarah, Lisa and I walk together down the gentle slope of the lawn. We could have walked along the path at the side, but chose instead to follow Stewart and Jo straight down the middle.

It's called the lawn, but it's really more of a meadow at the moment. In the spring it is a sea of daffodils, in the winter when it snows it is an ideal toboggan run, but right now it has been left to grow into a murmuring forest of wild flowers and long grass.

Between them they throw a mixture of scents and seeds through the sun-filled air as we pass, and insects of various shapes and sizes hop and jump out of our way as we trample down the slope towards the river. The heat now seemed even more intense than it had been during the day, when we were working.

"My trousers are all sticking in my arse crack." Complained Sarah, tugging at the offending garments.

"So vulgar!" reprimanded Lisa, before adding "So are mine."

Mine are too, but I don't like to say, I change the subject.

"Is Duddi going to make us paint over that wall again do you think?"

"He'll probably tell us to." Sarah admitted, "But I'm not going to, I like it like that."

"It's our common room," Lisa added, "staff shouldn't need to come in there."

"No, but they do," I said, "you know someone will complain."

"Let them complain then," said Lisa, "if they don't like it, they don't have to come in. And anyway, why would anybody disapprove of nuclear disarmament or peace?"

I am sensing a feisty streak in Lisa. When we first met two years ago, she was quiet to the point of silent, and shy almost to the point of antisocial, having to be dragged out of her room for anything but lectures. She is also very funny, in a quick and intelligent way. She is always pointing out the ludicrous and bizarre things that might pass us by without her observations. Lastly, as I have mentioned before, she is ferociously clever. Clever friends are a real asset at college. God that sounds selfish doesn't it. It's not, I really like having Lisa as a friend, but I can't deny it has advantages for me at times, isn't that what friendship is?

"You know exactly who's going to complain anyway," said Sarah.

"Mature students," Lisa and I replied in near perfect unison.

For some reason I could never understand, the students who came to study later in life did not seem to share our joy de vivre or exuberance, preferring instead to go about the business of learning with an unsettling seriousness. It seemed to upset many of them that we found the time to have fun while they had to fit in their degree work around raising families. We did try to include them in things but they rarely hung around at the end of the afternoon and tended to cluster together during the day. Also, they regularly complained about the posters in the common room, honestly you would think they were in favour of fox hunting, fur coats and Margaret Thatcher.

We continue to chat easily as we head across the end of the lawn, following Stewart and Jo through the long grass to the river bank. It's more of a brook really, with flies skimming the surface of the water and the occasional splash on the surface as a fish takes an easy meal. The early evening sun flickers on the surface, dancing and flashing as the water pushes past rocks and branches and hurries its way out of sight. It is, I think, probably the most perfect evening ever.

The bridge, when we get to it, is more than a footbridge. There is no road leading to it from either side, only the track we had just walked along. Nevertheless, it is easily 8 feet wide, concrete with sturdy metal railings on either side. Someone once reliably informed me that it was to get cows from one side of the river to the other. As I had never seen cows in any of the fields around college I am dubious, but will reserve judgement until a better explanation comes along.

Stewart and Jo are sitting on the railings waiting for us. Stewart removes a long stalk of grass from his mouth and says, "Come on you lot, aren't you thirsty?"

I am. I am so thirsty. The heat hasn't abated one bit, it has become muggier and more cloying. The air is so thick and so still it feels like I am pushing my way through it. And the sun, getting much lower in the clear blue sky now, is still blasting out enough heat to make me wish the river was deep enough to swim in.

We carry on together, in my mind we are The Famous Five, off on an adventure and some derring-doo. Directly over the bridge we climb a well-established path down a low embankment onto a stretch of railway line. Weeds are growing up between the tracks and sleepers and it is deserted as far as we can see in either direction as it curves gently out of sight. The embankment is a blur of summer colours, everything still in full bloom and interwoven with brambles taller than me.

It is only a short walk along the abandoned track to the next break in the embankment on the opposite side. I'll be honest, my mouth is literally watering now, although only a short walk I am dripping in sweat, I can feel my socks damp inside my boots and my trousers were most definitely sticking in my arse crack.

We reach the crest of the climb and can now see the small pub that is our destination. This pub is in the middle of nowhere, it is hard to guess where its clientele come from, but there always seem to be people inside. There is a car park with a couple of cars in it at the end of a long dusty track running parallel with, but out of sight of, the train tracks.

Chapter 6
Another Pub

No beer garden for this pub, we go inside and find a table that's big enough for all of us, then appropriate an additional chair so we can all sit at it. Sarah has headed straight to the bar, and is already starting to pass over the first pints of beer while we adjust ourselves, light a cigarette and hang our coats (whose good idea?) on the backs of the chairs.

The Fox and Hounds is different from The Round Tree, but not much. Horse brasses dangle over a dark wood bar, the inside is a jumble of nooks and crannies interspersed with small tables loaded with ornaments and old books. The fruit machine dominates the main bar area but thankfully, no Chris De Sodding Burgh!

The first gulps go straight down, quenching my thirst, but doing little to cool me down. Everybody's first pint is finished in a short time, just long enough for Stewart to tell us a story about his summer: he had met with some of his friends from school and together they had driven to a local beauty spot for some recreational smoking. It had been a pleasant end to the evening but one of his friends had slightly overdone it. For 'friend' here I think it is possible you could substitute the word 'Stewart' – I am the suspicious type. Anyway, the 'friend' had felt sick in the car on the way back. He had decided not to make the driver pull over, but had been sick in his jacket pocket instead. It was only when they got out of the crowded car that they realised he had actually been sick into somebody else's pocket by mistake.

His story is met with a lot of laughter, a fair bit of disgust and revulsion and one or two questions about the fate of the jacket. If you are interested, it was binned. We then despatch Lisa to get in another round and some crisps, while I go to the toilet. I return in time to help carry the last pints to the table, sipping mine as I walk carefully through the maze of furniture. Once the crisp packets are laying spread-eagled and disembowelled and full glasses have nudged empty ones to the outskirts of the table we settle into the rhythm of conversation again.

Sarah confesses that she watched Prince Andrew and Sarah Ferguson getting married, she had spent the whole day with her parents and some of the regulars in their pub watching the excitement unfold on TV. I told them I had been to work, then to the beach and then to the pub and missed the entire thing.

"You're kidding," said Stewart, "even I saw some of it. I didn't mean to, it was just on TV when I was having my breakfast."

I look at him, "It was on in the afternoon wasn't it?"

Stewart shrugs, "Sorry mate, we're not all wage slaves."

Jo punches him on the arm and then leans herself against him,

"Well, I watched," she said, "it was beautiful, Andy was so dashing in his uniform."

"Really?" Stewart queried,

"Really!"

"A man in uniform eh?" he said, looking himself up and down and stroking his sandy beard. "What about you? A big meringue dress with a veil? Actually yes, you would look better with a veil."

This earns him another punch on the arm which he rubs in an exaggerated manner while I turn to Lisa.

"What about you? Did you waste time watching to see what they are spending our taxes on?"

The fact that none of us pay any tax isn't relevant at this point, not to me anyway, if they want junkets and jamborees they should do it at their own expense.

"No, I was busy." Lisa replies.

"What, at your woodland camp thing?" asked Jo.

"Sort of." She looks away and takes a gulp of beer.

"Volunteering?" I ask.

"Something like that."

Now we are all intrigued, Lisa is not usually evasive. Sarah asks directly,

"What were you doing?"

"I was at Greenham."

It is quiet for a moment as we assimilate this new piece of information.

"What? Greenham Common?" I ask.

"Yes."

"The women's camp?"

"Yes."

And now the floodgates open as Lisa fields the questions she is being bombarded with.

It turns out that Lisa's mum had picked her up from her volunteering on the Friday and driven straight to Newbury to meet up with a family friend. In the end they had met the friend plus a host of other people. Lisa described it as being like a camping party. They had a great time and had made several more visits that summer, with the car loaded with provisions.

I can't imagine my mum doing something like that, or how my dad would get along if he was left to his own devices every weekend – possibly he would enjoy it. I can't help myself from expressing my opinion about something that excluded men, so sexist! I say so, then wish I hadn't.

"Start your own protest then," said Jo.

Stewart looks upwards, holds his hands together in a prayer-like pose and leans back from the table, not wishing to get involved in the ensuing carnage.

Sarah tells me to "Shut the fuck up, stupid."

Lisa explains that it is women only because it was a group of women that started it, a Welsh group. Women had chained themselves to fences, blocked gates, organised several years' worth of direct action and been arrested and imprisoned. All this without men 'helping', it was built on the traditions of the woman's suffrage movement and showed that women were more than just mothers and wives.

As Lisa catches her breath I want to reply, to make a snappy comeback that proves my original point was valid. I can't think of anything.

"Yeah, well – ok."

Not the best I know, but you try coming up with something smart when you're two pints in and confronted with impeccable logic and fierce intelligence.

Stewart comes to my rescue – sort of.

"Never mind, as long as we've got Maggie in charge there'll be plenty of other things to protest about."

The mention of the Prime Minister brings an almost audible hiss from the group, like when the villain comes onstage in a pantomime.

He wasn't wrong though – Keith Joseph's plan to get rid of student grants was clearly misguided and wrong. The Students Union was pretty sure that with enough marches, demonstrations and petitions we could make sure that never happened.

There was still fundraising for sacked and wrongly arrested miners, opposition to the National Front and MPs sex scandals (yes, you Cecil!). There was plenty to protest about and a world to change – we were going to be busy.

More beers and more conversation. Three pints in and the chat is becoming louder and less restrained. Sarah tells a couple of filthy jokes, then I share a joke, told to me by my friend Simon, a few days previously, it got a good laugh. Jo adds a joke I've heard before, but I think it was on Hi-de-Hi!, so I don't admit to it, not cool. Lisa follows with a joke so corny it makes everybody groan.

I take the chance to visit the loo and get in one more drink before the bell rings. I push some empty glasses to the edge of table before we set into the final pint of the evening. Lisa and Jo both move to halves for the last round, I am feeling light-headed and wondering if maybe I should have too. Never mind, I have the whole walk back to clear my head. I get some change from the barman and stock up on cigarettes from the machine, as always alcohol consumption has a correlation with nicotine intake and I am running low.

Restocked and refilled, we regroup and laugh and slop our way through our final drinks. Stewart tells us another story, this one about 'a friend' of his who had accidentally set fire to his trousers when he was drying them over a camp fire and had to walk home in just his underpants. He got stopped by the police who felt so sorry for him that they gave him a lift home. Sarah asks him if he's sure it's 'a friend' and not him. Jo smirks and says nothing as Stewart protests his innocence so vociferously that I am left in no doubt as to who the real star of the flaming trousers story was.

The barman comes over and starts taking some of the empty glasses and abandoned crisp packets from the table. We take the polite hint, drain our glasses and get up.

Chapter 7
Homeward bound

We walk back to the break in the embankment, retracing our steps as we start out on our homeward journey. Everything looks different in the encroaching darkness, if it wasn't such a familiar route for us it would be easy to miss the narrow cut-through. As it is, we are up and over the bank and onto the tracks in the straightforward way that only tipsy teenagers can truly master.

Once we are on the level tracks, we follow the rails, trying with varying levels of success to 'tightrope walk' as many steps as we can, before overbalancing. Sarah sets the record of 13 steps. I am not even close to this, and the more I try to concentrate, the wobblier I become. I am so busy concentrating on this whilst counting that it takes me a moment to realise that the others have moved to one side, angling towards the path leading back to the bridge. As I adjust my own course Sarah announces,

"I just need to pee." With that she disappears into the gloom further up the track.

"Why didn't you go at the pub?" Stewart calls after her as we wait at the foot of the path.

"Didn't need to," Sarah calls back.

"Just a nature lover at heart." Shouts Lisa.

Sarah reappears, wiping her hands on her trousers legs in an exaggerated fashion.

"There's a train up there." She says.

"Where? Up the track?"

Sarah looks at me with a withering expression that I am too drunk to really appreciate.

"Seriously?" she says. "Yes, up there where I just came from. On the train tracks funnily enough."

Stewart has already started walking up the track to investigate.

"How far up" he asked.

Jo follows him and Lisa, Sarah and me look at each other, I shrug and we follow them.

By now the dark is settling faster and the heat has reached oven-like temperatures. The air is so thick and still that it feels is if I am swimming through it. I am so focussed on watching my feet and not tripping on the railway sleepers that I walk straight into the back of Jo.

"Sorry." I say.

Jo barely notices, she is too busy talking to Stewart.

"It's not a train, just a carriage."

"It wasn't there before."

"It is now."

"Yes, but how did it get here?"

His question remains unanswered as we all look at the flatbed railway carriage sitting in the middle of the tracks. It is alone and unremarkable, apart from the fact it is there at all, recently appeared in the middle of the night on a disused railway track.

As we are looking around Stewart clambers up onto the flatbed. Sarah and I climb up after him, locating a short step rather than struggle over one of the wheels as Stewart had done. Once up there we can see that the carriage is empty barring one small cylinder, maybe a meter long, sitting in the middle of the bed.

Lisa and Jo join us as we gather around the object. I feel a faint puff of wind and appreciate its brief coolness, maybe it will get a breeze going and it will feel a bit less humid.

The flatbed appears to have no visible markings that I can see, no numbers or any kind of recognisable words or symbols. The cylinder is rounded at one end and tapered at the other. It is bolted into place with two arms that hold it clenched tight to the centre of the carriage floor. It is a nondescript greyish blue colour; I can see this in the faltering light with the dim guttering of my lighter that I am holding up to it.

My thumb becomes too hot and I let the lighter go out, putting my thumb into my mouth. While I am doing this, Lisa reaches into her bag and produces a torch which she shines at the object. The only visible marking on its smooth seamless side is a short series of seemingly random numbers and letters.

"It's a Trident missile!" I whisper.

The others turn and look at me. I assume they are going to admire my acute and incisive deductive skills. They don't.

"Trident missiles are enormous," says Lisa, "as tall as a house."

"A small Trident missile?" I try.

Lisa shakes her head witheringly and looks back at the object. She then shines her torch in a complete circle, revealing nothing but empty tracks and overgrown foliage on the embankments.

Another gust of wind shakes the branches of a small bush as the beam of the torch passes it, nothing else moved.

"What's it doing here?" asked Stewart.

Nobody answers, because nobody knows. What is this mysterious object doing on this long-abandoned bit of railway track? How did it get here?

Whose is it? Why has it been left? Why is nobody watching it? There were no answers to any of these questions, we all stand on the carriage looking at it.

Stewart crouched to look at the fixings,

"Shine the torch over here Lisa."

She does, and he examines the arms that are holding the object in place. We can all see what he is looking at now, each arm is held in place with a single bolt on one side and a hinge on the other, no obvious locks or catches.

"Let's take it." Sarah says.

"Yes." I agree.

"Why the fuck would we do that?" asks Jo.

I am already examining the bolt that Stewart is not looking at. It may only be a bolt, but it's done up good and tight, there is no give in it no matter how hard I twist.

"Is yours moving?" I ask Stewart.

"No, tight as a…" he looks at Jo, "Very tight." He finishes.

I stand up as a stronger and longer breeze blows across me, cooling the sweat on my face.

"I guess we're not taking it then," says Sarah, and with Jo she turns towards the edge of the carriage.

"Hang on, hold this" says Lisa, passing the torch to me. Lisa dives back down into her bag, all the way to the bottom and her hand comes back holding on oversized pair of pliers.

"Will these do it?" she asks.

"What the fuck have you got those for?" I ask.

"You can cut wire with them," Lisa replies simply, as if the answer was obvious – which I suppose it is really. While we are talking Stewart takes the pliers, and with me lighting his way starts attacking the bolt. Everyone gathers round to watch. At first it is resistant to his straining, and then it suddenly gives a little. A slight readjustment and it turns some more until, with some effort, it starts to move more freely and Stewart finishes undoing it the rest of the way. He lifts the arm off the cylinder and passes me the pliers.

"I guess we're nicking it after all then." says Sarah.

It takes some effort, and increases the amount of sweat running off me, I grip the pliers tight and eventually the second bolt starts to come loose. Stewart takes over and with some persuasion we eventually lift the second arm, leaving the cylinder free.

We look at each other, unsure, until Lisa makes our minds up for us.

"Whatever it is, it can't hurt anyone if we've got it," she says, and with that we gather round and put our hands under the cylinder and lift.

It moves easily and is not overly heavy, but certainly not light. It is a dead weight and its smooth surface offers little purchase, nevertheless we lift it up and take it to the edge of the carriage where we put it down.

As we set it down a bright light flashes. Dazzlingly bright, illuminating everything around us, the carriage, the cylinder and the tracks and surrounding bushes. Simultaneously there is a loud crack, it booms in our ears making us jump in shock just as the first heavy droplets of rain start to hit us. A second flash is accompanied by a sonorous, heavy, rolling, rumble this time.

We look at each other and Jo laughs. Lisa holds her hands out, palms upward, and looks up at the darkened sky as the droplets of rain start to come faster. At least it will cool us down, we shrug on our coats and jackets and climb back down onto the tracks. The wind, only brief puffs and gusts previously, now starts to blow more consistently. Combined with the increasing rain the temperature starts to drop and instils a sense of urgency into our mission.

Between us we heave the cylinder onto our shoulders from its perch on the carriage. With Jo leading the way with the torch we start to make our way back up the tracks, carefully treading over them and occasionally slipping and stumbling in the dark. The rain starts to fall more heavily and is running into my eyes and down the back of my neck. It is starting to soak through my jeans. Everybody else is hunching down and pulling their collars up hopefully with their free hands as we turn towards the embankment and navigate our way up the path, still carrying the increasingly slippery cylinder.

As we reach the top of the embankment the wind cuts across again, this time bringing with it a stinging barrage of hail. I try to turn my back to the wind, but still the hailstones attack me. The flashing lightning strobe lights our way to the bridge and the thunder makes everything shake and reverberate as it assaults our ears.

We make it to the bridge and set the cylinder down as we all stop for a rest. My arms are aching from carrying the weight of it, the rain has started to fall again and I am wet.

Not wet like splashed, but wet like everything wet. Water in my boots, soaking underpants, jeans stuck to my legs front and back, and a jacket that was going to take days to dry out.

"I don't think we can carry it all the way up the lawn," I say. "It's too slippery and I'm wet."

"We're all wet," says Jo.

"We can't give up now," adds Stewart, "but you're right, I don't think we'll be able to carry it all the way up to the house."

"No need." Lisa says.

Jo shines the torch at her, her hair is plastered to her head and rain is streaming down her face. She has the same expression she uses when she explains college work to me, it is a kind and patient face that says 'I'm about to tell you something so obvious you should have all seen it, but it's not your fault.'

"We can go and get the trolley." She says simply.

I feel foolish for not thinking of something so simple. I could blame the beer, but that wouldn't be the truth. I wish I had thought of it, it would have cheered me up. But the reality is I didn't try to think of it, I figured if we just gave up I could return to my room and get into some dry clothes.

There was no discussion about this, the rain streamed down on us as the thunder started to move away, growing quieter and less frequent. We certainly weren't going to get any wetter than we already were, although the cool air that arrived with the storm, combined with the now torrential rain, meant I was now starting to feel cold.

Together we trudge back up the path alongside the lawn. Path may be a misnomer at this point, it bears more resemblance to a stream, water running freely over its rough surface, and washing leaves twigs and debris in a careless yet purposeful manner. I try to light a cigarette, but everything is too wet to make it easy and the gusts of wind whip at the meagre flame of my lighter with relentless enthusiasm. Hunkering under my jacket I eventually get it to light, where there's a will and all that.

Of course, if I had been listening to the radio or had watched the news in the last 24 hours I would have known this was forecast. I had been content to enjoy the warmth and sunshine without once considering the possibility that this would be a precursor to a series of violent storms that would sweep across the south of the country.

Many places were hit hard, with flash floods, fallen trees and lightning strikes that took out power cables and kept most people safely indoors for most of the night, which is where I should be. Instead I am squelching through the pitch blackness with rain plastering my hair to my head and causing my fringe to flop around in my eyes.

We arrive at the common room, guided by the lights that act as a beacon, leading the way out of the teeming rain and into the dry sanctuary. I stand dripping as we all look at each other, hair plastered to heads, clothes flat against our bodies, everything pooling on the floor around our feet. Outside the rain blows against the window and through the open door, adding to the water we have bought in with us.

Jo bursts out laughing. It's infectious and soon we are all joining in, shaking out our hair, squeezing water from our sleeves and trousers and squelching as we walk. For a moment I forget that we have to go back out in it, when I do remember I ask, "Shall we leave it there and go back for it tomorrow?"

"No, we need to get it now," says Lisa.

"But we'll get wet."

"We're already wet. Anyway, we don't all need to go, I just need someone to help me."

I'm not really all that macho and manly. I don't usually volunteer for anything that might inconvenience me, but Lisa seems so determined and I don't want to let her down. I look out into the pitch black beyond the pool of light reflecting off the falling rain and say, "Okay then, but it better stop raining."

"I'll do it too," says Stewart.

Jo and Sarah ask if they should come. The consensus is that there was no need for everyone to get wet again.

Unlike me, Stewart actually starts moving, he goes to the trolley and take the remaining items off and puts them in a pile on the floor, Lisa joins him and I have to force myself to start moving to catch up with them as they go back out into the night. It hits me like a wet sock as I too go back into the wind and rain, we start to walk the trolley towards the path to the river.

"I'll put the kettle on." Shouts Sarah as we disappear into the darkness.

Walking down the path is not too bad. It is slightly slippery and hard to see where to put your feet, but the driving wind is now at our backs, keeping the stinging rain away from our faces. Lisa is trying to light our way with the torch, but we are too busy looking down at our own feet and leaning against the weight of the trolley to get any real benefit from it. The low hedge to our right whips around in a wind-fuelled frenzy, making as much noise again as the wind howling around my ears. Every step I take it begins to feel like a worse and worse idea.

Just as I am kidding myself that it may be starting to ease off, the storm intensifies again, redoubling its efforts. The wind whips a fresh salvo of hail into my face and an ear splitting crack of thunder makes me flinch. In the white flash of accompanying lightning I see Stewart and Lisa also cower briefly, looking at one another as something is blown – or scurries – into the hedgerow.

Everything around us is just noise, the hail and rain lashing through the leaves, the near constant rumble of thunder and the wind rushing past us combine to make an unholy racket. We are not speaking to each other, and I suspect we would struggle to hear what was being said anyway. Instead I keep my doubts and reservations to myself, quietly swearing and grumbling under my breath.

Finally, the ground starts to level out and I can see Lisa is shining the torch ahead to the bridge. I wipe the rain from my face, only to have it immediately pour down from my sodden hair and back into my eyes. I can taste the cold water as it trickles down over my mouth, on its way to seep down the front of my jacket. It is as if I am standing under a waterfall that is defying gravity, hitting me from an impossible angle. It occurs to me that the wind will be blowing straight at us on the way back, going up the slippery hill, in the dark, with a heavy cart to pull. I think about giving up and going back up to the common room for a cup of tea, leave the others to it. But I don't, I carry on pulling the cart along the bumpy track to the bridge.

When we get there Lisa shines her torch to the place we left the cylinder. It is still there, glistening and wet in the rain, the water running under the bridge now a swirling torrent, the noise of its rushing competing with the howl of the wind and the beat of the rain.

I look in the direction of the railway cutting, the murk and rain make a cloak of near-perfect darkness. All I can see are undulating, unfocussed shadows competing for the honour of which patch can be most impenetrable. Another flash from the heavens illuminates it briefly, wet leaves glisten as they shake off the droplets. I can see no sign of the embankment from here.

Without speaking, Stewart and I bend down, slide our hands under it and look at each other before lifting. It starts to slip through my grip immediately, I slide my hands further under and lock my cold, wet fingers together as best I can. It stops the cylinder from falling; together me and Stewart shuffle, stoop-backed the short distance to the trolley and set it down with a decisive bump. I go to the front of the trolley, take one side of the handle while Stewart takes the other and we start to pull.

The trip back is not as bad as I thought it would be. It is worse. The path is slippery, awash with mud and covered in water. The light from Lisa's torch is starting to grow weaker, not that it had been that effectual to start with, and the wind is now driving sharp shards of water directly into my face, making me squint and turn my head to one side. It is a slow and steady trudge up the path, what had seemed like a not-too-heavy cylinder earlier now felt like it weighed as much as a small car. I grit my teeth, blow some water from my mouth and take painful, slow, steady step, after step, after step.

The cylinder rolls around in the back of the trolley, banging against the sides with a dull clunking sound, first one side then the other. Each time it does this it feels as though it is getting ready to tip the whole trolley over. Lisa moves alongside the trolley and leans over to hold the cylinder and stop it from moving about and we progress.

I keep my head bent, watching my feet as I navigate the trail of rocks and branches in the darkness. The storm is too loud to make any conversation possible, even if I had the breath to facilitate it. Any doubts I have are pushed firmly to the back of my mind as I concentrate on getting back into the dry, one foot after another. There are no proper landmarks in this dark and alien landscape and I am afraid that if I look up I will see how far there is still to go and give up. I adjust my grip on my side of the plastic covered handle and start to walk with renewed purpose, before I decide to quit completely.

When I finally do look up, I see the ominous shape of the mansion looming out of the rain and darkness. Stewart sees it too and mouths words I can't hear as he points to my right. I look across and see the lights of the common room shining out across the grass and dissipating in the rainy darkness. Now I feel better. I look around and see that Lisa has both hands on the back of the trolley. She is stooped over and still pushing even as I slow down to look towards the common room. I start moving again, and before I know it, we are directing the trolley back inside, both it and us dripping and leaving pools of mud and water around us on the floor.

Sarah and Jo have been busy while we were gone. They have changed into dry clothes, Jo is in a pair of cotton pyjamas with a dressing gown over the top and a towel wrapped around her head. Sarah is in track suit bottoms, tee shirt and a huge grey cardigan. They both have their coats hung on the back of chairs and are wearing trainers.

On the closest table are five steaming mugs of hot chocolate, I take mine and hold it in my shrivelled fingers, trying to warm my hands. I reach into my pocket for my cigarettes; the packet comes out visibly damp.

"Fuck, they're all wet, now I'll have to dry them out" I say, followed by, "Sarah…"

Sarah passes me her packet before I finish speaking, she holds out her lighter. I inhale, breath out and drip.

Meanwhile Jo is fussing over Stewart, she has taken the towel from her hair and is dabbing ineffectually at various parts of him, trying in vain to dry him off.

Lisa has hung her coat and bag over a chair and is sitting drinking her chocolate and staring at the trolley.

"What are we going to do with it?" she asks.

I look at the cylinder, such a small thing really. It shines under the lights as the water slides off its metal body. I don't know what we're going to do with it, I don't usually think too far ahead. The drink- fuelled ambition to relocate it had worn off, the alcohol being numbed by the cold and the wet and the amount of time it had taken to move it. I look at the clock, it is now 12.30, and there is no way we are going to do anything with it tonight.

"We should hide it somewhere," says Jo.

"Or bury it," adds Stewart – I look at him to see if he's joking.

"We could though," he insists.

"Except we have no spades and nowhere to bury it and it's still pissing down. Why don't we think about it in the morning?" suggests Sarah.

"Agreed," I say, I just want to get dry and go to bed now.

"Yep!" says Jo, and with that she gets one of the dustsheets from the pile of decorating equipment and starts to shake it out over the trolley. Stewart gives her a hand and it is quickly covered up.

"We'll decide in the morning. Come on, before you catch pneumonia." Jo starts to chivvy Lisa out of her chair and towards the door, we all collect our wet things and start to follow, we wait at the door while Sarah switches off the lights and joins us for the dash over to the stable block. I can't tell if it's raining more or less than it was before, it is still coming down in sheets. The bits of me that had started to dry slightly are immediately soaked through again as I trudge behind the others while they hurry along with their coats held over their heads.

In my room I start to peel off the layers of soaking clothes. First the jacket, it looks a sorry sight as I dump it unceremoniously on the floor, looking like a dead animal – which I guess it kind of is really, so fair enough. Next, I sit and unlace my right boot, I hold it up and water briefly trickles out of it. I pull my sock off, revealing white wrinkled toes. I squeeze the sock adding more to the puddle on the carpet then repeat the process for my left foot.

I now take off the final layers of wet clothing and leave them in a soggy pile on the floor as I rub myself dry with a towel and put on a dry tee shirt and boxers. I then sit on the bed, press play on the cassette player and seek out my least damp cigarette as the Sisters of Mercy continue to sing about 'a rock and a hard place' - where they had left off earlier in the day.

There is a light knock at the door, which then opens before I have time to reply. Sarah's head appears through the gap.

"Are you decent? Can I join you?" she asks, coming in without waiting for an answer to either question. She joins me, sitting on the edge of the bed and lights her own cigarette.

"Shit music," she says.

"Thanks," I reply, I'm not offended, not everybody's taste is as refined as mine. I turn it off and we sit in companionable silence, listening to the rain beating against the window as we finish our cigarettes.

Sarah stands up and starts picking up my discarded clothing from the floor and draping it over the back of the chair and on the cold radiators where it continues to drip.

"You are a messy bugger" she says.

I acknowledge this with a nod and a smile. Sarah looks at the bed, still just a heap of blankets and sheets.

"You still haven't even made your bed."

I shrug and smile.

"Mine's made up, come on in and we'll keep each other warm."

I will admit, I am surprised, for a moment too surprised to reply. Me and Sarah have been friends for ages, but never in a 'maybe we'll get together' kind of way. Then again, I'm not entirely sure that is what is being offered, I clarify, "A made bed and a warm cuddle then?"

"Yep, or stay here and get cold."

Sarah goes, leaving the door ajar. I look at the dishevelled bed, the sheets are damp where I sat on them to take my boots off and the smell of wet leather jacket and smoke has filled the room. I walk across the landing to Sarah's room and through the open door as she is folding her trousers, putting them on the chair with her other clothes and climbing into bed. I climb in beside her, snuggling up to her back and putting one arm over her as I pull the blankets up over my shoulder. She is right, this is warmer and more pleasant than being on my own. It is also quieter on this side of the building, with just a regular, monotonous splash of dripping water from a gutter somewhere nearby. After the evening's dark deeds this feels safe.

Later I am half-awake, or dreaming, or both. I listen to the splashing water and in the distance I hear the sound of a branch falling, a wrenching, tearing sound that carries over the howl of the wind. Underneath these sounds, very faintly I am sure I hear the sound of a dog barking, a voice calling and the distant thrum of a helicopter. I lay still for a moment, then close my eyes, snuggle up to Sarah and sleep.

Chapter 8
The morning after the night before

I awake again, draped over the edge of the bed with one hand resting on the floor and one foot sticking out from under the blanket. Sarah is already up, she must have disturbed me when she climbed over me. She is pulling on her trousers and heading to the bathroom. I get up and go to my own room to find some dry clothes. The room has an omnipresent smell of dampness. I spend as little time in there as possible.

Outside it looks grey and cloudy. I look out the window as I dress, everything is shining and clean, the storm has washed away the dust and dryness of the summer, leaving everything new and fresh. I light a cigarette and head down to the common room. Sarah catches up with me on the way and we arrive together.

The others are already there, sitting quietly with mugs of tea. I go to the kitchen and make two more, along with some toast and marmalade and a bowl of cornflakes for myself.

Balancing mugs, plates and bowls on a tray I go to the table where the others are congregated and join them in looking at anything and everything other than the trolley. Sarah takes a slice of my toast, I don't object.
"Thanks."

I'm certain the others know we spent the night together. Ordinarily that would be cause for some sort of comment or ribald remark. Today nobody mentions it. I finish my cereal and gulp down my tea, then collect up everybody's empties and take them into the kitchen. Sarah joins me, unloading the tray and putting away the clean plates, mugs and cutlery. Then she stands by my side, she takes my hand in hers and leans over to give me a kiss on the cheek.
"Thanks for last night," she says.

Before I can answer, or even think what to say, she has disappeared back into the common room and is starting to marshal the others into table scrubbing, gum scraping and tidying up mode. Between us we carry all the tables and chairs out and line them up on the path as the clouds start to break and the sun claws weakly through the gaps. Nobody brings a cassette player today. In the far distance the high-pitched whine of a chainsaw carries over the clear empty sky. We work mostly in silence apart from the splash of hot water, the scrape of knives and the scratching of brushes. I am preoccupied with my own thoughts:

'Why did Sarah thank me?'

'Was she scared of the storm?'

'Did she just want company?'

'Was it because I didn't try anything?'

'What are we going to make for lunch?'

'What time will we stop for lunch?'

'What are we going to do with that bomb thing?'

'Why did we take it in the first place?'

My thoughts are suddenly interrupted by a loud voice,

"You're doing a grand job here."

Ian the caretaker has walked through the common room and is standing in the doorway watching us work. He is probably watching Sarah, Lisa and Jo more than me and Stewart if I'm honest – he's a bit like that.

I glance behind him at the trolley with the dustsheet draped over it and wish we had hidden it more thoroughly, or at least somewhere less indiscreet than the middle of the room. There is no reason for him to look in the trolley, why would he? Still I feel as if we are about to be discovered. I look at the others and they clearly share my worry.

"Have you got everything you need here?"

Sarah answers that we're all fine and tells him we will be done before tea.

"Grand, will you sweep and clean the floor before you move the crap back in?"

We assure him that will not be a problem, Stewart is speaking and I notice his eyes flicking over Ian's shoulder. Lisa asks, "Who's back tomorrow?"

Tomorrow is Monday. The students, including us, are not due back until Tuesday and the freshers will begin to arrive at the end of the week.

"Office, catering, I'm expecting to be run off my feet with all the things people find for me to do."

We know Ian has spent a lot of the holiday supervising building and ground works, arranging decorating and making sure everything is as ready as possible for the coming invasion. He seems glad to see us today, he always has a smile and cheery greeting for the students. I think he enjoys being surrounded by us young, carefree, stupid lot, even though he complains loudly and constantly about us and to us.

"Oh, and Duddi's back tomorrow, you might not want to be around when he sees that, he's likely to blow a gasket."

Ian points back over his shoulder and for a moment I am certain he is pointing at the trolley and that he has known all along what we are hiding there. But he's not, I see he is pointing at the wall with the peace sign daubed on it. He is about to turn back into the common room and disappear back into the depths of the building. Before he goes, he calls back over his shoulder,

"Andy's coming in tomorrow to set up the bar."

He turns and starts back towards the mansion. I hold my breath as he walks past the trolley, then exhale as he passes and I go to the kitchen.

"Tea anyone?" I call.

The others follow me, obviously the abandoned and empty common room didn't offer enough privacy. Once we are assembled and the kettle is boiling with mugs lined up on the counter beside it, Jo asks in a hushed and urgent voice, "What are we going to do with it?"

Stewart opens his mouth to speak, but before he can say anything Jo turns to him and hisses, "If you say 'bury it' again I will bury you!"

Stewart closes his mouth and me and Sarah look at each other suppressing giggles. Lisa saves us,

"We could hide it in some of the woods or bushes round the site, there's loads of places we could cover it up."

This is true, there is a lot of land around the site, plenty of places to hide something.

"But nowhere that people don't walk, or gardeners aren't out and about," I say, "someone will find it sooner or later."

"We could take it back." suggests Stewart.

"What? All that hard work and effort for nothing?" Lisa answers.

Sarah pours the hot water onto the waiting tea bags, gets the milk from the fridge and says, "We could take it away from the college and dump it somewhere."

"I'm not carrying it miles and miles, even on the trolley, and none of us has a car. Besides, everyone will be coming back soon, we have to do something right now," says Jo.

We all take our mugs of tea outside and sit on the newly cleaned chairs as Sarah and I light cigarettes. Stewart tries to lighten the mood by picking up a newly liberated lump of hardened gum and holding it up to his mouth.

"I'm starving."

"Don't you dare!" Jo almost shouts at him, "you are disgusting."

Stewart laughs and flicks the gum over to the pond where it lands with a small splash and disappears, the green algae immediately covering the space where it landed.

"That's it!" exclaims Lisa, "nobody's going to look in there, we can hide it in the pond."

It takes me a moment to process what she has just said. Stewart is quicker, he picks up a small stone from the side of the path and throws it in. We all watch as the same thing happens, a small splash and then a fresh covering of green, hiding all traces.

"It could work," he says.

"We haven't got any other ideas," Sarah points out, "come on, let's do it while Ian's busy in the Mansion."

Sarah and Lisa both get up and move inside towards the trolley.

I'm glad we've got a plan now; I had no ideas at all and would probably have gone along with Stewart's idea of burying it, if I thought Jo would ever speak to me again. The idea of hiding it in plain sight in the middle of college seems quite audacious to me, but I have to admit the evidence of the pebble seemed pretty convincing. I follow the others inside and help bring the trolley out.

Together we move the trolley up onto the path. The cylinder is uncovered, looking as silently blank as it had the night before in torchlight. I check up and down the path to see that we are truly alone then take one end and, together with Stewart, we lift it to the side of the pond. Jo gives us a countdown from three as we swing it backwards then forwards, then we let go.

Considering how heavy it is we don't do a bad job. It makes it out a couple of metres before landing. Unlike the pebble before it, it makes a huge splash. Large droplets of water and green slime fly up at me as I turn away and cover my face with my arm.

When I look back, I see to my dismay that the size of the splash has meant the algae did not cover over the space. There is a sizeable hole in the surface of it, a long sausage shaped hole. I lean over to see if I can see the cylinder through the surface of the water. To my right Lisa is doing the same. I look over to her to ask if she can see anything, as I do her foot slips and she stumbles. I reach out to grab her arm and pull her back – but everything is inevitable and there is nothing I can do. Windmilling her arms and trying to get herself back to an upright position she falls headlong into the water, splashing me and showering me with pond weed all over again.

For a moment nobody says anything. Then, as Lisa stands up, soaked to the skin for the second time this weekend and dripping with green gobbets of slime, Sarah starts to laugh. That sets us all off, and soon everybody, including Lisa is laughing. Lisa pulls herself out of the waist deep water and spits out a mouthful of water. As she does this, I look behind her. The problem of the hole in the surface is resolved at least, there are now several holes rather than one single conspicuous one. Also, I am pretty certain that Lisa's unplanned swim has pushed the algae over, covering the part where I think the cylinder is laying.

Jo takes Lisa back to her room to help her get dry and changed. The rest of us set about the remaining chairs and tables with a renewed vigour, happy to have found a suitable solution to our problem.

When Lisa comes back in a fresh set of clothes, we stop for lunch. I eat with a healthy appetite and afterwards we all set to cleaning the last of the furniture, washing the floor as promised, and tidying everything away. By the time the shadows start to grow longer we have finished and everything is back in its proper place.

I don't feel like going to the pub this evening, neither does anyone else. We sit and raid the biscuit supplies and make cups of tea while the usual haggling over what music to listen to goes on, until Sarah produces a pack of cards from her pocket. The haggling now changes to which game to play, and which regional variation of the rules to adopt. We eventually settle on Gin Rummy and I lose seventeen imaginary pounds before we all decide to go off for an early(ish) night.

I surrender to the inevitable and make my bed enough to be able to actually sleep in it, then lie awake for a while thinking over the events of the last three days. I have a deep feeling of unease about the cylinder, a certainty that we will somehow get caught and a curiosity about what it actually was that we had done. My eyes start to droop and I fall into a deep but troubled sleep.

Again, I wake in the night. This time I am positive that I can hear the sound of a helicopter in the distance. I close my eyes again and the distant thrum gradually disappears into the darkness of my dreams.

Alice

The car drove across the open road. The undulating moors, splashed with purple heather, spreading like a green sea in all directions. The road leads to only one destination, a large building surrounded by a high fence, topped with razor wire. If you could look down from above you would see the building was in the shape of a letter H. It is largely windowless and painted a uniform grey colour, with little intention of blending into its surroundings.

As the car reaches the gate and waits for the guard to brush some crumbs from his uniform and open the barrier Alice looks in her mirror. Way back along the river of tarmac she sees a flash of reflected light as a second car begins its approach.

'Good,' thinks Alice. She always likes to arrive before Dan, she feels as if it gives her an edge in their daily war of attrition over who's the most useful team member. In truth, she knows they both bring different strengths and skills. This is one of the reasons they were both acquired at the same time. The longer they kept thinking they were in competition, the more they would keep trying to improve. She knew that this was O'Brien's plan, and she was okay with it, although she didn't think Dan had figured it out yet.

She swings her Ford Fiesta into a space in the largely empty compound, hurries briskly out of the cold wind and keys her code into the number pad then walks towards her office. Before she can get there a door opens and Mrs Baker leans out,

"They're meeting in room 18. Go straight in, Mr O'Brien's waiting for you." She disappears again, 'good morning to you too, yes I had a lovely weekend thank you!' She changes direction and goes to the room.

O'Brien is already sitting at the table, along with Mr Jones. Both men are wearing dark grey suits and are busy reading briefing papers. They look up as she enters and acknowledge her with nods of their heads and clipped 'good mornings' before returning their attention to their paperwork. She drapes her coat and bag on the back of the chair next to Jones, sits down and breaks the seal on her own pile of papers.

"Is Dan here yet?" asks O'Brien.

"I saw him on the road behind me; he'll be here in a minute."

Right on cue there are muffled voices in the corridor, Alice is certain she hears Mrs Baker laugh. There is then a brief pause before Dan opens the door and strides into the room. It's not that Alice doesn't like Dan, she thinks he's quite good looking, and knows he is fiercely intelligent and good at his job. But there's something she can't quite place, something in his attitude that grates occasionally. They nod to each other and Dan greets everyone before taking his own chair and opening his own pack of papers.

O'Brien finishes reading. He squares the pile of documents and puts it neatly down in front of himself, then waits patiently for the others to catch up. His face has a neutral expression that belies his astute and piercing observation as he watches the others skimming the text. As Dan reaches the final page O'Brien says;

"Tea and biscuits please Mrs Baker."

He speaks to no-one in particular. Nevertheless, Mrs Baker appears moments later with the desired items, almost as if she had anticipated the request.

Once the door has clicked shut behind Mrs Baker O'Brien reaches under the table and presses a small recessed switch.

"Ok, this room only. We have a problem."

The first document in the pack they had been given had laid it bare. With some redactions, it explained how a classified item had gone missing from a train siding on Saturday night. All tracks and traces had been removed by a summer storm, in what had clearly been a carefully planned and executed operation, with access to inside information, by 'persons unknown.'

"Do we know why the package was unattended sir?"

"No, the men responsible are our first line of enquiry. This is currently being conducted by a specialist team. In the meantime, Jones you're meeting up with Special Branch, they'll be digging into any known groups or individuals who are active in the area. Dan, I want you to scout out the locals, residents, shops, particularly anybody who lives or works near the Fox and Hounds pub. Alice, it's a long shot, there's a college nearby. It's still shut for the summer, but there may be staff around who saw or heard something. You all have full authorisation to pull in any and all resources you may need for this. Questions?"

"Why was it there in the first place sir?"

"It was being relocated, a reorganisation of assets before the talks start."

Alice knows he is referring to the ongoing international nuclear proliferation talks and guesses that 'reorganising' is a euphemism for 'hiding things'.

"But why was it left?"

"It was supposed to be a straight handover, the idiots delivering it decided it would be okay to leave it as the transport that was collecting it was on the way. Trouble was, the collection was delayed because of a technical hitch. When they got there the package was gone, it had been left unattended for nearly an hour by then."

"Do we suspect the carriers?"

"We suspect everyone at the moment. Like I said, a specialist team are following that line of enquiry. Okay, so we all know what we need to do now then?"

Alice is miffed, not that Jones has got the big job for this, he has the most experience after all. She is miffed that Dan has all the nitty gritty work that will support Jones and she has been side-lined to looking around a bloody college that is closed. Still, that's the assignment. As everyone gets up to leave O'Brien says;

"A quick word please Alice."

She remains seated.

O'Brien runs this centre, one of several dotted around the country, although Alice has no idea where the other centres are, or who works in them. She was 'acquired' by O'Brien in her last year of university. A glittering career in translating foreign text books and manuals had awaited her before he approached and asked if she had considered the civil service. She hadn't, and still wasn't, until O'Brien added;

"I worked with your father; if you're anything like him I think you'll be good at it. You'll enjoy it too."

Her quiet and unassuming dad had never mentioned the civil service. As far as she was aware, he was a retired army officer, he'd never talked about his work and she had never asked. He had died shortly before she started university and there had been nothing out of the ordinary in his life, death or possessions. Her curiosity about this, and everything else, made this the perfect job for her as it turned out. She always wanted the answer to everything, although so far she had found out little else about her dad. She waited for O'Brien to speak.

"You saw from the briefing that everything so far has been focussed on organised groups, they're drawing a complete blank. I know you're not thrilled about getting the college, but dig around. I think it may have been dismissed too quickly.

Alice considered rebutting his accusation, but decided better of it.

"Yes sir. If it doesn't pan out should I support Dan?"

"Call me first."

"Yes sir."

"Okay, get going, it's a long drive. Good luck."

It is a long drive. When she arrives Alice goes directly to the nearby hotel where Mrs Baker has rung ahead and booked a room for her. She leaves her belongings on her bed and drives to the nearest Post Office, which is in the village close to the college. She has a short queue amidst the crowded aisles, surrounded by bread, postcards, tinned goods and other sundries. She eventually proceeds to the counter, where she passes the teller a card with a four-digit number printed on it. He reads the number, then without saying anything, heads into the back room. He returns with a bulky envelope that he passes over. They smile politely and thank each other as Alice turns to leave.

Standing outside the Post Office Alice looks in the direction of the college. There is a long, straight, narrow road leading off towards some fields and trees. Beyond them, just visible against the mess of clouds are glimpses of the buildings that she has been charged with exploring. She sighs and gets back into the car.

In her hotel room Alice opens the package and starts to methodically arrange the bundles of papers that Mrs Baker has assembled for her. A full list of current students, a full list of staff, a list of tradesmen known to have been working on the site or making deliveries and the dates and timetables for the coming academic year.

Alice starts with the ancillary staff, in her opinion that is usually the best place to begin if you want to know what is actually happening somewhere. Besides, the academic staff were probably still all in Provence and the students were probably all still in bed. She slides her finger down the list and decides who would be the most likely person to contact. Bypassing the site manager, catering staff and administrators she eventually decides on the caretaker. She reads the sparse information she has on him, then she checks her watch and goes back to her car. As it is still early evening, she has time to stop and get something to eat on the way. Chips again, she really doesn't like being on assignment sometimes.

The caretaker, a nice man by the name of Ian, is very talkative as it turns out. She has chosen to visit the pub closest to his home and hit the jackpot, first time lucky. It is no time at all before Alice has bought him a drink and he has given her a full rundown of who was around college last weekend. It is a fairly short list thankfully, mostly the grounds team who were cutting up a fallen branch by the drive which stopped most people getting in and out all morning and Ian himself of course, he had checked around the site for any storm damage.

"Oh, and the kids."

"The kids?"

"Yeah, came to do some decorating. Clearing up their own mess for a change. Made a piss poor job of it too."

"Who organised that?"

"The kids arranged it with Dudman, he was too tight-fisted to pay for it to be done properly, serve him right."

Alice gets back to her room as quickly as she can. On her list of third year students she circles the names that she has gently pumped Ian for. She picks up the phone and calls O'Brien.

Chapter 9
Term starts

I am woken up by a heavy rumbling outside my bedroom window. It feels early, but a quick glance at my bedside clock shows that it's gone 9. I look out and see a large truck parked by the kitchen, numerous boxes are appearing from the back and are being wheeled into the open door on a sack trolley.

I look at the pond, overnight the algae has settled and spread itself back, covering the surface once more in all but a few small spots. I can hear the sound of Billie-Jean playing from Sarah's room and put on The Cure in my own room to drown it out while I get dressed. I rummage for my toothbrush and head to the bathroom to spray some Turbo and scrub my mouth.

When I return Sarah's door is open,
"Cup of tea?" she calls.

She has had the foresight to liberate the makings of morning tea so we didn't have to brave the kitchen, with its irritable manager who was even now unloading the van and packing things in their correct places. Doubtless he was complaining to anyone who will listen about the mess we made in his kitchen, even though we had taken pains to leave it pristine last night. It's best avoided really.

I throw my stuff on my bed and grab my cigarettes, joining Sarah. Lisa is already there, sitting on the bed talking about moving her stuff to her allocated room later in the day.
"I'll give you a hand." I say, I don't have to move, I'm in this building this term. Also, I don't have much stuff at the moment anyway.
"If you're giving Lisa a hand you can help me too," says Sarah.
"No problem, I have nothing to do, and all day to do it."

The music has changed to 'I'm in the mood for dancing' now, must be a mixtape. Fingers crossed for whatever comes up next. I take a sip from the mug of tea Sarah has passed to me, it passes muster and I take another slurp as I extricate a cigarette and light it. Sarah takes one from the offered packet, I look at the four remaining cigarettes.
"What time do you think Andy will be here?" I ask Sarah.
"Not till after lunch, you know what a lazy bastard he is," she answers.

Without Andy to open the bar there is no access to the cigarette machine, which will mean the long walk up to the village shop to get some. I am mulling this over when Lisa reads my mind and says, "I'll come up with you, I fancy a walk, it's a nice day and I need some chocolate."

"Need?" asks Sarah.

"Try seeing what happens if I don't get any," she responds. We laugh and there is a light knock on the door as Stewart and Jo crowd their way into the room to claim their own mugs of tea. The music changes to Bananarama and life is ok.

Lisa and I take the long walk to the village, it is a warm day, but not too hot, with a pleasant breeze. It feels good to have a down day at last, after the hectic activity of the last few days – and nights. I ask Lisa which elective courses she is taking next term, hopeful that there will be some the same as mine – a little help would never go amiss. It turns out we are doing mostly different courses. We are both doing the philosophy module, I'm not really sure why I selected it as I struggled badly with it last time round. Lisa is dreading the art module she has had to take. I offer to draw some pictures for her if she does some cognitive reasoning for me, I suspect this will not be taken seriously.

We arrive at the shop and Lisa gets some chocolate. I do too, and the pouch of tobacco I actually came for. I buy some ice-lollies to sustain us on the walk back, I thought I might have seen enough ice-cream to last me until next year – but apparently I was wrong. We eat them as we wander down the drive, past a pile of logs and sawdust and back into college.

Sarah meets us as we arrive back and beckons us to follow her, with some urgency, away from the common room. I assume the worst, and am not disappointed – Duddi's back! His car is in the car park, in amongst all the office staff who are getting ready for tomorrows influx, while simultaneously trying to sort out all the changes from clearing that followed the 'A' level results. He has been spotted wandering around, checking on what has and hasn't been done. He hasn't got as far as the common room yet and Sarah, Stewart and Jo had decided that it would be best to lie low for a bit until he is busy somewhere else.

We are gathered in a secluded area of the grounds where we sit, smoke and generally laze. I heave myself up into the lower branches of a tree, where I stand and look out across the campus. From where I am standing I can see the end of the drive, and I see a small blue car arriving. Even from this distance I can make out a distinctively shock-haired Andy sitting in the passenger seat. It passes out of sight and I climb down to tell the others.

Together we walk down through the grounds until we get to the bar. Andy's luggage is left in a pile on the path outside the bar and he has disappeared to the office to get his keys. We sit on the grass and wait.

Andy eventually ambles back, we all greet each other and he sits with us as we share Lisa's chocolate and everybody's news from the summer. We talk about which rooms everyone has been allocated, who has seen or heard from whom during the holiday and when we think various friends, acquaintances and course mates will be arriving tomorrow. I think this is largely guesswork based on the distance people have to travel and what transport they will be using. I think Sue will be getting back quite early in the day as her journey is relatively short and straightforward and she will get a lift from her parents.

We fill Andy in with what we've been up to at the weekend, well most of it – we omit one detail. Andy asks if we got caught in the storm and we admit that we did.

"You had to walk all the way down the drive in that?" he asks "You must have got drenched!"

He has assumed that we were walking back from the Round Bush, I do not correct him, neither do the others, but we do concede that we were indeed very wet by the time we got back.

As we are talking a brewery lorry rattles up alongside the bar.

"Shit!" says Andy, he jumps up and starts fumbling through his keys so he can open up and let the lorry deliver its precious cargo.

"Hold on!" he shouts to the driver as his panic rises and he attempts to get the right key to gain access to the bar.

Meanwhile Sarah walks over to the lorry driver,

"Do you just want to unload it here and we'll sort it all inside?" she asks.

"Thanks love," he replies and starts unloading crates and barrels from his inventory into a neat line along the edge of the path.

I think we have been volunteered for another job. Andy comes back and helps unload, checking the list the driver has passed to him and starting to organise the various piles of bottles and barrels into some sort of order depending on where they are destined – cellar or bar.

I start to carry the first of the crates up the short flight of steps to the bar. I step in and take in the red vinyl furniture and chipped Formica tables. Even though it has been empty for over a month, the smell of beer and smoke still lingers at the edges of the room. Posters from last year still adorn the walls and windows, invitations to the summer ball, an end of term disco and reminders not to perform experiments on animals. We should have decorated in here too, it is too late now, maybe Easter?

I get back down and the lorry has already departed. There is a chain of people, everyone is relocating everything to the correct places under direction from Andy. We all pitch in. Me and Sarah get all the barrels into the cellar. We are both quite short, so this is an ideal job for us. Once we have done this Andy comes in and starts joining the various pipes and tubes to the correct fixings and switches on all the pumps.

I go back upstairs where everything is being stored and stowed. There is a lot to do, but with six of us it doesn't take long. Andy starts to pour beer to make sure everything is connected properly. At first froth splutters and splashes up the side of the glass, gradually starting to run more smoothly and filling the glass.

He works methodically along the taps, lager, bitter, cider, Guinness. The glasses line up on the bar and Andy invites us to help ourselves or it will all be tipped away. We do not need to be asked twice and take some sips of the offered drinks as Andy finishes getting the Guinness under control and takes a big gulp himself.

"You're not wasting any time getting started are you?"

I look around and see that Duddi has finally tracked us down, there is no escaping, so I brace myself. But there is no dressing down, he says calmly,

"Good job in the common room, although I think that end wall will have to be repainted at some point."

I can see my relief is shared by the others, no telling off and the peace symbol seems to have a temporary reprieve. Andy offers him a drink, which he declines;

"It's too early in the day, and some of us have actual work to do."

He leaves, back on his rounds to do his 'actual work' and we finish off our drinks. Nobody can decide if it's okay or not, so Andy pours another round of halves.

"Thanks for helping with the delivery." He says, "That would have taken me all afternoon."

"No problem." I reply, rolling a cigarette. I sit at a table with the others and we pick up with the earlier conversation, finishing our drinks slowly before heading off to collect our keys. We spend the afternoon carrying luggage and belongings around the site and arranging new rooms. Posters are put on walls; book shelves are lined with folders and textbooks and wardrobes are filled. Unpacking my single bag is a swift affair, organising my few meagre possessions is similarly brief. I stuff clothes into drawers arrange my tapes alphabetically then lend a hand to Sarah and Lisa as promised.

I brave the kitchen to find that the kitchen manager has gone, but has left a note telling us there is a selection of salads and some cold meat in the fridge, and to make sure we clean up after ourselves. I can also smell the distinctive odour of jacket potatoes slowly cooking in the oven. I look in and am pleased to see that they are good-sized ones. I sit and wait for the others to turn up.

Stewart and Jo are the last to arrive, Jo is looking flushed, presumably from the brisk walk.

"Which of your two rooms are you going to be based in then?" asks Sarah, "I assume you've tested them both."

Jo blushes bright red and Stewart grins and winks as the rest of us laugh and then we get down to eating.

After clearing up, Andy tells us he's still a bit worried about the barrels we set up that afternoon and wants to check the connections. He invites us to come and help him. I am happy to assist and am soon sitting with a freshly poured pint in front of me.

Lisa moves first,

"I'm going back to my room, I need a bath and to rinse out my clothes again, they still smell."

She retreats, and before long the rest of us disappear for the evening.

I go back to my room. I lay on the bed smoking and trying to finish Angela Carter. I have The Danse Society on at full volume as I have no neighbours to annoy yet. Even though I am still fully clothed, with a full load of food and some beer on board I soon fall asleep. I wake again in the dark, it is silent outside, I climb under the covers and fall back asleep.

Chapter 10
Everyone comes back

I am woken up by the sound of various cars arriving and the campus around me gradually coming to life. From my window I can see the office staff coming back to work, along with the ancillaries, cleaners, cooks and grounds men. Some academic staff are already starting to arrive too, getting ready for meetings, checking timetables and preparing for the year ahead.

I make my way to Sarah's room and knock on the door. She is already up and dressed and is happy for me to make mugs of tea, which we take out on to the grass to drink while we smoke. We watch the college slowly become a living, breathing entity once more.

The morning is warming up slowly, there are patches of clouds up high in the sky and the sun has no real strength to it. There are still signs of the weekend storm around. Under some of the larger trees lie broken branches, clumps of green leaves attached to the broken ends of blown down twigs and detritus gathered at the edge of paths and around drain covers.

"Looking forward to the year then?" I ask.

"Bit nervous to tell you the truth, everyone says they really pile it on in the third year,"

"I'm sure they just say that."

"I don't know, last year's third years looked like they had plenty to do."

"I suppose there are finals to get ready for, but they're not until the end of the year, plenty of time until we have to panic."

"What, you think we should try and enjoy it for a bit first?"

"That was my plan."

"Sounds like a good plan to me."

Sarah raises her mug of tea and clinks it against mine.

There is a pause in the conversation, then I ask, "Do you think we should say something to someone about the other night?"

"Which thing? If you mean the sleeping together, I'm pretty sure Jo will tell anyone who'll listen, even though I told her nothing happened."

"No, I mean the other thing."

Sarah looks serious, she looks at me and picks up my tobacco to roll herself a cigarette, "I talked about it with Stewart and Jo last night," she says, "we think it's probably best if we don't say anything about it to anybody at all, not even talk to each other about it. God knows what that thing was, but I'm pretty sure someone will be looking for it by now."

I think of the dogs and helicopters. I'm sure they were not a dream, the whole thing was too vivid and real. I don't mention them, I just agree with Sarah.

"Jo's going to talk to Lisa this morning. I just think the less said the better."

"Still the other thing, not the sleeping together?" I check.

I get a good-natured punch on my leg for my troubles, just as the first fully laden car of the day, rear windows obscured by duvets, boxes and cases, drives past. The passenger is a friend of Sarah, on the arts course, she waves and we wave back as they drive on to the office to collect their keys.

Really, I want to sit here all day, I am waiting for Sue to return. I want to see her when she gets back. In my imagination she will run to me and forgive me and we will make up and go back to my room to catch up where we had left off in June. I know that this will probably not happen, given that we haven't spoken for 2 months, and that I may have to put in a certain amount of effort. But I can dream can't I?

Another car passes. I get up and stretch my legs.

"Well, things to do." I say. A lie, I have nothing to do really, but I know that if I don't move now I will just end up sitting here for the rest of the day. Sarah smiles and we part, I go back to my room determined to finish Company of Wolves. I get back and sit on my bed and read for an hour or so, listening to the sounds of cars arriving. I change the music to Alien Sex Fiend – loud, so people know I'm back. Before long there is a knock on my door, it is my partner in crime and neighbour, Paul. He comes in and sits down and we set to catching back up with all the latest gossip and filling the room with smoke.

Gradually, as tea time comes and goes, nearly everyone seems to have reappeared. There are still some people arriving in dribs and drabs, but mostly people are settling in, excitedly comparing notes from the summer and helping each other get organised in their new rooms. All around the site are open doors and windows, the sound of music and laughter as people get reacquainted, pop in and out of each other's rooms and get themselves unpacked and set up.

In the common room the drama students have returned and are holding court in their usual loud and flamboyant manner. I choose to sit with them, they are usually good for a laugh and certainly aren't going to bore me with stories of themselves on a beach in Cornwall with their parents. I am not disappointed; they are ostentatiously loud and ridiculous in equal measure and soon I am laughing along with them.

As the evening moves on I relocate to the bar and order drinks after claiming one of the tables as I settle down for the evening. I have temporarily lost both Paul and the drama students. As the beer starts to work its magic I circulate and am reunited with people who I have not seen for literally weeks, the excitement is palpable. As voices rise, the music gets louder. I bump into Sarah who is singing along with Marvin Gaye, then move outside to the lawn where people have spilt over, clustered into morphing, nebulous groups at regular intervals, occupying areas of the grass. I weave my way to Jo, Stewart and Lisa and a few other friends and clumsily sit down with them, splashing my beer on the way. As I touch down, I look over and see Sue. My spirits lift for a moment. Then I notice that she is once more surrounded by the phalanx of Laura Ashley bedecked friends that worked so hard to protect her in the first year, one of them scowls over at me and I realise that I am going to need to work on a more opportune moment for this. Sue doesn't see me. I finish my beer one sip at a time and try my best to enjoy the evening.

I go back to my room and start to formulate a plan. I'm pretty sure right now that it's a good plan. All I need to do is find a time when I can catch her on her own, smile nicely and tell her that…. tell her something. Then I could ask her…. Well something anyway. I don't know, it needs some revision, but at least I go to sleep happy in the knowledge that I have a plan.

*

The next morning, sober again, I realise that I don't have a plan at all. The corridor is busy with the sounds of people going to and from the loo or making their way downstairs and off to the common room. I follow the herd and end up in the common room drinking tea and eating toast. I have sat by myself at a quiet table under the new peace sign. This table is ideal for scanning the room for Sue's arrival. I have only taken one bite of my toast when I am joined by two course mates, they are carrying folders and files and clearly ready to make a start. They greet me with an enthusiasm that I attempt to emulate, although I still haven't really woken up properly. Also, neither of them smoke, so I am reluctant to light up while they are at the table. I am polite for as long as I can manage, before making my excuses and going back to my room to collect a notepad and a pen.

Again, I join a flock of students, this time heading into the lecture theatre for Year 3 orientation and welcome back. I find a seat near the back and am joined by Lesley. I had a brief fling with Lesley in the first year, when we were both freshers. I'm pretty sure she would still get back together with me if I wanted. I'm not sure I could manage her high-pitched Manchester accent, with an accompanying squeal of a laugh, in anything other than small doses. Also, it's Sue I want to get back together with, maybe I'll keep Lesley as my back up plan. It's good to see her anyway and we chat about the holiday and the course until the session starts, then we whisper and scribble messages instead.

Orientation finally ends and I go to the coffee bar where I know Sue usually takes her morning break, in the hope that I can 'run into her'. There are other people I know, who I sit and chat with, and some of Sue's friends sitting in a cabal at a table they have sole occupancy of, but no Sue.

The rest of the day passes. I am in and out of tutorials and seminars, being assured by all the staff that this year is going to be the hardest yet, and that I will need to really apply myself if I want to get the most from it. They really do labour the point, to the extent that I think it may be themselves they are trying to convince, not me.

By 3 o'clock I am done in, I go back to my room to sort out my notes and timetables from the day. I put on a mixtape of various bits and pieces I have recorded off the John Peel show and lay down on my bed to rest my eyes for a few minutes.

Alice

Things moved swiftly once Alice had made her phone call to O'Brien. More resources were diverted to the college and people were put on standby. As staff and students had started to arrive back the site had become busy, the need for absolute discretion made things more complicated. O'Brien had made it clear that nobody should move until they were completely certain of finding something. Alice's team needed to retain a low profile, everything as quiet as possible. Around the college, in car parks and laybys are a number of inconspicuous looking vans full of equipment and patiently waiting men in heavy black clothing.

The surrounding woodland and fields were dotted with men who watched, specialists. If anyone was walking in the woods, footpaths and fields they could pass within inches of them and be unaware of their presence. More people had been discretely inserted into the college itself, working in offices and kitchens. They had even placed someone in amongst the students. If there were any foreign hostiles involved and operating in the college, they would not even see the net Alice had woven until it closed around them.

Alice oversaw all this from a hotel room. They had now taken over the entire floor of the hotel. Discrete guards were stationed at each end of the corridor and the main entrance, and the tech guys had installed an encrypted phone system. While this was going on a search had been started. It seemed most likely that if the item had not been moved, and there was no indication that it had, it would be concealed in the wooded areas - possibly buried. Teams dressed as workmen and surveyors were working in the woods. They followed carefully plotted concentric circles around the perimeter, spraying occasional green crosses on trees to both mark their path and to give the impression they were doing something of some purpose. Alice looked at the aerial photos that had been taken over the last few days and marked the progress they were making on her map. It seemed painfully slow, but it was progress. If it was there, her team would find it.

Chapter 10
Everyone comes back (Continued)

There is a sharp knock on my door and I wake up with a start.

"What?" I call.

"Are you coming down to tea?" Paul shouts.

"Yeah, I'll be right there." I look at the notes, folders and timetable still spread out ready to sort. I sigh and then put my trainers back on and grab my denim jacket. I manage to roll and smoke a cigarette, lock up my room, catch up with Paul and walk to the common room all at the same time, who says men can't multi-task?

I make sure I am sitting with a view of the room as I eat and chat with Paul.

"You still not seen her yet?" he asks.

"Who?"

"Oh come on, you've been looking for her all day haven't you?"

"Suppose," I shrug.

"She's fine, I had coffee with her and Helen this morning." Paul is on the same course as Sue, I guess they grabbed a quick drink somewhere else between sessions without the hassle of queuing at the coffee bar.

"I told her you're back, she asked how you are."

I take that as a positive sign, it means she doesn't hope I'm dead in a ditch somewhere. Or maybe she does and that's why she's asking, I just don't know.

Paul has now started to list the books he is going to need to read over the coming weeks, together with the ones he tackled over the summer. I recognise the names of most of the books and authors, but haven't read any of them. I tend to avoid 'serious' books after a misjudged and ill-fated attempt at a Thomas Hardy novel a couple of years ago.

I manage to steer the discussion around to the Sherlock Holmes stories which Paul and I both read last year.

"I've got some Agatha Christie books with me. We'll give them a try if you like. She's from your neck of the woods, isn't she?"

I profess ignorance, but agree to give Agatha Christie a try, as long as there aren't too many pages – Paul assures me there aren't. We then clear our plates and head back to Paul's room and kill some time deciding who has which book to read first, while we wait for the bar to open.

Later I go to the bar. This evening I am taking it slowly, keeping an eye open for an opportunity to talk to Sue – if she ever turns up! I am so busy watching the door I don't notice Lesley coming towards my table until it's too late. She invites herself to sit with me and Paul and then proceeds to assault our ears, laughing/squealing at Paul's jokes – he's a funny guy, but not that funny! – and finding every opportunity to lean into me or put her hand on my knee.

I finally reach breaking point when Chris De sodding Burgh's Lady in sodding Red comes on over the sound system. I finish my drink, make my excuses and return to my room, where I listen to some more of my John Peel mixtapes and finish reading Angela Carter.

It is close to Midnight when there is a knock on my door, which is thrown open without waiting for me to answer. Paul stands there, swaying slightly,

"I saw your light was still on" he says, "have you got a cigarette I could scrounge?"

Of course I did. He roamed the room flicking through my textbooks and reading the spines of the cassettes while he smoked and he told me how it had taken him the whole rest of the evening to shake off Lesley, which he apparently blamed me for.

Eventually, after considerately rolling himself another cigarette from my pouch so he doesn't 'have to wake me up in the morning', he takes himself off to bed and I settled down for the night.

*

I am busy on Thursday, I meet back up with Lisa, Sarah, Jo Stewart and a number of others. We are part of the welcoming and induction committee for the brand new students that are all due to arrive tomorrow. The day was spent going through orientation packs, checking names against room lists and planning how, where and when everyone should be. I remember from my own first day how easy it is to feel a bit lost and a bit nervous. I am determined to give other students the same help and support I had. Also, there is a free lunch involved.

Eventually we are done and everything is prepared for the second influx of eager young minds. We have a late lunch together. I can't quite put my finger on it, but there is a slight sense of uneasiness between us. The conversation is stilted with not much humour from Stewart. Lisa is unusually quiet. We grab some cheese toasties and tins of Coke from the coffee bar and head to one of the outside tables to sit in the still warm sunshine.

Stewart waits until we are nearly finished and the already minimal small talk has started to dwindle, he says, "I know we all know this, but I thought we should all agree together. It's just that I don't know how you all feel about what we did, I'm worried we could get into trouble. If we just deny everything how could anyone know?"

"That's true," Lisa says, "as far as we're all concerned nothing happened, agreed everyone."

I agree, I had already started to forget, what with the busy couple of days we'd had catching up with everybody. There now seems to be a slight underlying tension to our group, the dynamics have changed and we are not as easy and relaxed as we were six days ago. The weight of the secret was already starting to buckle and bend the pillars of our friendship. I still wondered if just taking the cylinder back might be an option, but of course, it was way too late for that now.

We split up and go our separate ways. I find Paul in the Student Union and we play a couple of games of pool. We win one each so all's fair. I then hear a loud laugh in the distance. We look at each other and both mouth 'Lesley' silently to one another before slipping out of the back exit and off to find new things to do.

I wander aimlessly for a short while before deciding to pluck up my courage and go and find Sue, just to say hi. I turn towards her block, talking myself into this act of great bravery with every step I take. I arrive quickly and find the front door propped open so I let myself in and walk down to Sue's room.

As I approach along the magnolia painted corridor, I can see that the door is ajar and from inside comes the sound of laughter and voices. I can hear Dire Straits playing in the background and decide that maybe now isn't the best time. I can't face the group of disapproving friends, or the possibility that Sue might not even want to talk to me. I back out quietly and go back to my own room to listen to anything that's not Dire Straits.

*

The next day I am up promptly, lots to do today. Although it is quite warm already, I wear my leather jacket. It did dry out in the end, it has a slightly stiff and crispy quality at the moment, which I am sure will soften up eventually. I already have my favourite jeans and baseball boots, which just leaves my hair. I look in the mirror and decide yesterday's shave will suffice for today as well, I put some gel in my hair and pat and pull it around until it meets my expectations. Now ready, I go to meet with the others and prepare to meet and greet the new arrivals.

After this gentle start the day becomes hectic. Car after car arrives. There is a great deal of smiling and heaving of suitcases as people are led to halls of residence, given a hand with unloading cars and taken for short orientation walks so they can find their way to the most important places – Common room, bar, coffee bar, lecture hall, in that order.

I see Sarah walking towards me, she is with a new student – but not like the others I have met today. This student does not have his parents with him, he is dressed as though someone had bet him that he couldn't dress more like a student than anybody else. His long straight hair, button up long-sleeved tee shirt under a once-white collarless shirt and a pair of baggy brown corduroy trousers all look as if they had been slept in the night before. He smiles and waves as I pass, I stop and say hi back and Sarah introduces me,

"This is Trevor, he's not actually a first year, he transferred into our year."

"Oh sweet, where from?" I ask Trevor.

His smile gets even bigger, all teeth, and he answers, "Up north, I needed to be closer to home, family thing you know?"

I didn't, but didn't feel the need to say so, or to pry. Trevor carried right on, "I'm really looking forward to starting, it's good to be here, maybe I'll see you at the bar later?"

He waves his voucher and smiles again. The drink vouchers are the Student Union gift to new students, it entitles them to one free drink at the bar. 'Have a drink on us – have a drink with us!' It's to encourage new students to socialise and meet new people in their first week. It is also to try and persuade them to carry on spending a percentage of their grant at the bar during their time at college, as if they needed encouragement.

"Yeah, there most nights," I reply. And head off to meet my next new arrival.

*

I am waiting with Sarah.

"How's it going?" she asks.

"Okay," I reply, "nobody's changed their mind and gone home yet and nobody's cried, so it's a good start."

"Excellent! They're always quiet when they arrive, in a couple of days they'll be living it up with the rest of us."

"What about Trevor then?" I tease, "Will he party?"

"I sure hope so. He seems like a laugh."

I mull this over, he actually seemed like a bit of a dick to me, with all his over the top hand-woven, ethnic bollocks gear. Like Neil from the Young Ones. I keep my thoughts to myself, I am starting to become aware over the last year or so that not everybody is on the same page as me all the time. In fact, sometimes they even disagree with my judgements and opinions.

"Yeah, I'm sure we'll see him at the bar."

Two more freshers arrive, a mousey girl with her parents, and a boy in a David Bowie t-shirt, we take them on their respective tours and deliver them to their rooms.

Over tea we compare notes on the students we have shown round, nervous ones, odd ones, ones who seemed a laugh. There was a consensus with Sarah, Lisa and Jo that Trevor seemed really nice, my earlier decision not to like him seemed as if it was still best kept to myself.

Paul appeared and invited himself in to join us. Paul likes Lisa, and could usually be relied on to appear if she was around. He never did anything about it, or said anything to anyone else apart from me. I was sworn to secrecy and had to bear witness to his unrequited love on a regular basis. I'm not sure if Lisa knew or not, but she did always act a little differently when Paul was about. I wonder if I should take a leap of faith and try and get them to actually meet up with just each other sometime.

Stewart and Jo leave, then Lisa makes her excuses, and Sarah and Paul decide to go and play pool. They invite me, but I'm not in the mood, so I let them go while I return to my room and sit on the chair by the desk, looking out of the window and reading Agatha Christie's By The Pricking of my Thumbs, which was okay so far.

There is a tap on the door, and someone opens it as I am settling into my book. I turn around to shout to the tapper to come in. As I turn I see it is Sue, in spite of all the practise I'd had in my head of what clever thing I was going to say when I saw her next, the best I can manage is 'hi'.

Sue smiles, a genuine warm smile, and says "Hi, did you pop round to see me yesterday?"

"No," I lie. "I was just dropping round to see…" I momentarily struggle to think of a name to fit in with my story, then come up with "… Lesley, I needed to um, ask her something, I think."

Lesley! Why the hell did I say Lesley? I can't think of a worse name to use than the girl I was seeing before Sue, but now I have said it.

Sue smiles. Her face is framed by her long brown hair that bounces and flicks when she walks, and shines in the sun. I am distracted by her hair, she has started to speak and I have to catch up with my listening.

"…last year, her room is in a different hall now."

I knew that, of course. I have no idea how to extricate myself from the lie, so I nod and smile and offer a cup of tea.

"Well, I'm glad you offered," says Sue, "I was beginning to think you were ignoring me. We've been back all week and you haven't even said hello yet."

I want to point out that neither has she, I also want to point out that not speaking was just picking up where we left off. Most of all I want to make a heartfelt apology and ask her if she will please consider doing me the honour of considering the possibility of going back out with me, if I promise not to be a twat - again.

Before I can say any of that Sue leans across and picks up Angela Carter from my desk.

"You finished it at last, did you enjoy it?"

"Yeah, it was great. I liked the one about the tiger."

"Did you get the subtext and allegory?"

"Probably not, I just liked the story."

Sue laughs, and all at once it feels like we could get back to where we were before. Before I was an idiot.

"Can we get back together?" I blurt out, carefully considered words of healing forgotten. I still haven't got up to start making tea, Sue ruffles my hair with her fingers and says, "I'll think about it, give us a day or two to settle back in and I'll talk to you then." She picked up her book from my desk and left the room and I sit stupidly mute not knowing what I should or could say.

I decide this definitely needs to be a bar night, show the first years how to boss it! Well, given my near legendary inability to hold my drink and my outstanding ability to make an idiot of myself when drunk, maybe not showing anyone how to boss it. But I could have a drink or two with Paul.

I meet up with him at tea time and we sit together and eat. As we are sitting at the table rolling cigarettes and getting ready to leave, Lesley spies us and with a squawk and a squeak comes over. She sits next to me with her leg pressed against mine and does her best to join in with the conversation that me and Paul are just getting to the end of. She leans across me to reach the salt and pepper, only slightly- but enough for her to press her breast against my arm. I feel myself stirring and decide I need to go before I get all hormonal, I make my excuses, put out my cigarette and leave. Paul says, "See you later." and stays talking to Lesley as I leave to do whatever getting ready I might feel is necessary for a night of drinking.

In the end I decide that not much getting ready is necessary. A nap, a squirt of Turbo and a ruffle of my hair should do it. I grab my jacket and make my way to the bar via Paul's room. He's not in, rather than go by myself I decide that I will go over to Sue's and see if she's coming out. Then I could walk her over and it would be like the old days. As I start up the path to her building, I see Sue and her friends walking down the path in a gaggle. I immediately change my mind and turn back towards the bar, certain that I have not been seen this time.

It is predictably busy in the bar. By the time I have fought my way through to get served I have managed to spy Paul. He is still trapped by Lesley, who doesn't look as if she is about to leave any time soon. He also doesn't look too much like he needs rescuing, as far as I can tell from a distance.

Over the noise and perpetual motion of the crowd I have also seen Sue, still with her gang of friends, they are talking to Trevor. She is beautiful and sexy, I want to go and talk to her, to ask if she's thought about it yet. I know she said a day or two, but that was several hours ago. Also, she didn't say 'no', so that is a good sign, isn't it?

Still, I really don't want to run the gauntlet of her friends, and I certainly don't want to talk to Trevor, and why's she talking to him anyway? Pretentious prick! I get served at last and take my drink with me to the video game machine in the corner, where I am sure Sarah will be either waiting to play or playing. She is not. Eventually I find Lisa, she is sitting alone at the bottom of the steps reading one of the free papers that have already started appearing in piles in the common room and student union.

She puts it down when I arrive and has a sip of her drink before asking, "Not with Paul then?"

I guess we are usually together, but didn't realise that was what people had come to expect.

"Nah, he's upstairs." I reply.

"Lesley still chatting him up?"

As usual Lisa has pointed out the blindingly obvious, Lesley wasn't trying to get back with me –why would she after I broke up with her so abruptly, with no real reason and little explanation. She was trying to hook up with Paul, and I just happened to be in the way all the time.

"I guess, they seem to be set for the evening. Anyway, what are you doing down here by yourself?"

"Not really in the mood if I'm honest. Thinking of having an early night."

"No, stay for a bit, we'll need some help guiding drunk first years back to their rooms later."

"That sounds unmissable, but I may still pass."

She finishes the end of her drink and I offer to buy her another.

"No, it'll be midnight before you get through that scrum," she says "I'm going to bed."

She picks up her half-read paper and leaves. I am left trying to decide what to do next when Paul and Lesley appear, they say hi and then walk briskly off up the path towards Paul's room, Lesley has her arm around Paul and at the top of the path they stop and exchange a long passionate kiss, before disappearing into the night.

I wander back upstairs and find a group of people that I know. I hang around with them for a while, but my heart's not really in it anymore. I see mousey girl, she pauses to say hello when she passes, but seems quite keen to get back to the new group of friends she has been accumulating, I don't detain her longer than necessary. I also see David Bowie t-shirt explaining to everybody how great the Serious Moonlight tour was and how they really should have gone. Get over it mate, that was three years ago!

Finally, I see Sue, she is still talking to Trevor, the bloody hippy. I decide to finish up and go back to my own room where I can sulk in peace. I call it quits for the evening, and go back to listen to a bit of Joy Division, to get me in exactly the right mood for some maudlin self-pity.

I fall asleep to the distant sounds of people being disgorged merrily into the night and a much closer sound of high-pitched laughter, almost like a squeal. I bury my head in the pillow and go to sleep.

*

The next couple of days are all about getting back into the flow, adjusting and settling back in. Paul and Lesley have become a fixture, meeting up in the evening and spending the nights at one another's rooms on a rotating basis. I miss Paul when he's not there, but miss my sleep when he is.

Every time I see Trevor he seems to be hanging around with Sue, and I hate him! His range of hippy garb is extensive and revolting. My only consolation is that she doesn't seem to be actually going out with him. I am still waiting for Sue to decide if we are an item or not, I am waiting for an opportunity to talk to her on her own, but it never seems to happen.

I have also seen Trevor hanging out with Stewart and Jo, I gather from one of his many disgusting t-shirts that he too camped in a field in Somerset this summer and guess they must be sharing notes about their festival experience – man!

Lisa is nowhere to be seen and Sarah has disappeared to the art studio to get things set up for the year, she is wearing a trail between there and the bar and is always happy to stop for a chat, but always busy too.

Alice

Alice was meeting with the operative they had placed amongst the students. From her window she had watched him arrive in the hotel car park. A yellow 2CV covered in equal amounts of rust and stickers and belching a trail of blue smoke. He was now sat across from her, smoking a cigarette. He was dressed in an outfit that Alice could only think to describe as 'student stereotype.' Hand knitted cardigan, sandals, cords, hair in a ponytail. Alice doubted that any student ever had actually looked like this. In spite of this he seems to have made contact with numerous students, including the decorators.

He has placed five pieces of paper on the table, each one headed with a covertly taken photo and the name of each of the decorators. Beneath this, in neat handwriting, is a synopsis of everything he has managed to find out so far. It is fairly sparse, adding little to the information they already have. But Alice believes in the power of information, anything they can find might hold the key to unlocking this puzzle. This is why she has a file bulging with information about college staff, students and particularly the decorators. So far she has found no political affiliations, no foreign contacts, no previous attraction of interest or convictions, apart from Lisa.

Lisa was cautioned for trespass at the airbase this summer. She was part of a group of women who had tried to cut a hole in the perimeter fence, they had been quickly stopped by security and passed to the local police.

Frustratingly, this is the one person that the operative has failed to get close to or found out much about.

"She just hasn't been around that much."

"Where has she been?"

"Mostly in her room."

"Any idea why?"

"According to her friends she's a bit of a bookworm, I guess she's just getting down to her work."

"But you don't know?"

"Not yet."

"When then? She's our number one person of interest here, and you've found out practically nothing that we don't already have."

"I found out that she went on a demonstration last year."

"They all went on the demonstration. They're students, it was a day out. The demonstration was about education cuts, practically every student in the country was involved."

Alice draws a breath and exhales slowly.

"We need to find out more. The other teams are all turning up nothing, as of now the college is our best bet."

"She can't have done it by herself. This lot are so disorganised they barely managed to finish painting the walls."

"If they did it, we need to know. Which one of these is closest to Lisa?"

He pushes forward two of the sheets, one with a photo of a girl, she is laughing and her tumbling red-hair is tied back with a flowery strip of cloth. The other photo is of a boy with tangled hair lighting a cigarette. He points to the photo of Jo, "Everyone reckons they are best friends, but at the moment she spends most of her time with her boyfriend, they're all loved up." He rolls his eyes then puts his finger on the photo of the smoking boy. "He's good friends with her, but at the moment he's spending most of his time drinking and chasing his ex-girlfriend – who's too good for him."

"Spend time with them, spend time with him. Find out. This is taking too long, we need to rule them out or bring them in."

After Alice has watched the contact leave, rattling out of the car park in his piss-yellow coloured car, she falls back to detailed planning. Alice loves this part of the job, mapping out in detail possible actions, outcomes and contingencies. Making lists of possibilities and then providing a solution for each, along with a selection of worst-case scenarios. She regularly shares these with O'Brien, who evidently shares her passion for planning as he feeds back with helpful suggestions and clarifications.

Visitors come and go with updates. They are mostly military types in civilian clothes. Alice is addressed with a crisp attentiveness and respect. She is called Ma'am when she gives them instructions, sometimes it is all they can do to resist saluting. Alice prides herself on remembering their names, she thinks it helps build the respect needed for when people have to take orders.

The discrete search of grounds is still in progress, with no results yet. The team were working inexorably closer to the buildings. Alice picks up the new photos of the decorators and adds them to the pin board that has been installed on one wall of the room, alongside a detailed map of the area. The map is now a riot of colour, marking where everyone is stationed, which areas had been cleared and where all of the decorators lived. Although it is not central to the map, everything radiates from the quadrangle of grass and buildings at the centre of the college.

The phone rings, Alice picks it up and hears O'Brien's familiar voice. "Any news?"

"Not yet, nothing useful from the contact. How are the deep checks going?"

"The files will be with you in about....45 minutes."

"Thank you, anything I should be looking out for?"

"One has a brother in the military, apart from that nothing helpful that I can see. Maybe you'll spot something I missed."

Alice doubts it, O'Brien doesn't miss much.

"Okay, thanks again, I'll look over them. How are the other teams doing?"

"No news."

"Nothing at all?"

"No. I don't like it, but if we don't get something in the next 48 hours we're going to have to bring those kids in for questioning. If we can rule them out it will free up a lot of resources for the other teams."

"I understand sir, I've already got a plan for extraction in place, I'll prime it for tomorrow."

"Of course you have. Well, let's hope it doesn't come to it shall we?"

Chapter 10 (continued)

My really busy time doesn't start until the end of the week, when our first essay of the year is set. I am determined to get on top of things this year (I was last year too, but sometimes it just doesn't work out!) and so take myself to the library to make a start on the essay on the same day it is set, with the ambition of finishing it before the due date.

I am sitting at one of the large tables, with a moderate sized pile of books and a page or two of notes when I see Trevor come in, sporting a trilby hat and a Led Zeppelin t-shirt. He sits at my table, nods at me and says, "This okay?"

As he asks, he sets his stuff down and spreads it over his side of the table. To be fair, it is a big table with plenty of space, but even so! He is exaggeratedly quiet as he gets out his writing pad, books, pens and lord knows what else. If he knew how much he was pissing me off he would have sat somewhere else – or maybe not, maybe he was trying to annoy me.

We set to our respective work and I am actually getting into the flow of it when he whispers, "Have you got some Tippex mate?"

He can see I have Tippex, it's on the desk in front of me. How could he possibly need it already? He's only been working for 5 minutes. Why can't he just cross it out? I slide the Tippex over and he dabs at something in his notepad.

"Cheers mate," he says, sliding it back across the table. I nod and give a brief smile then look back to my books.

"Hey, aren't you one of the guys who painted that mural in the common room?"

I look up again. I assume he is talking about the giant peace sign, which technically was nothing to do with me. But then again, bragging rights, "Yes."

"Cool, it's a real statement. I like it."

"Thanks." ('cool' – who says cool?)

"Fancy a smoke?"

Actually, I do. I leave my belongings spread over the table and follow Trevor outside where I get out my cigarette papers. Before I can start rolling Trevor produces a pack of B&H and offers me one. I should retain my principles and my pride, but I don't. I take one of Trevor's cigarettes.

He talks enthusiastically about how 'cool' college is, how he really likes it here and how friendly everyone is. I try to listen, because I guess it's not easy starting over in a new place, and I'm not really an unfriendly person. I agree with him a lot, and just as I am finishing his cigarette he says, "Hey, someone told me there's a pub near here called the Fox and Hounds or something, down by the river. Do you know how to get there?"

For a moment I am flummoxed. I had tried not to think about the Fox and Hounds since the night of the storm. I certainly hadn't thought of going back there.

"I wouldn't bother, it's a bit of a trek. The Round Bush is much quicker and easier to get to."

"Is that the one in the village?"

"Yeah, it's got tables in the garden and more space if there's a group of you going."

"Ah, right, sweet, maybe I'll give that a try, it gets pretty crowded in the bar. Do you fancy coming along for a pint tonight, some of those girls in my hall will probably come along?"

Sue, he means Sue. I am torn, I should go and see Sue – also I could protect her from Trevor. But her friends would be there, it would be so awkward. Also, despite myself, I was starting to warm to Trevor a little bit now that I had actually met him.

"I've already said I'll meet up with someone else tonight I said, maybe another night eh?"

We finish our cigarettes and go back into the library. Trevor does a little more, then packs up and ships out with a whispered 'See ya!' I work on until I suddenly realise I am all alone. The rows of books on shelves are silently waiting for the building to be locked before the next troop of knowledge seekers arrive in the morning. I am hungry and it is tea time. I pick up my stuff, tuck it under my arm and leave.

I drop my books, pens and pads on the desk in my room and hurry down to catch the end of the evening meal. I sit near to the drama students, who are currently discussing whether the Cherry Orchard or Candide is the best option for their first performance of the year. I am just finishing my meal when I see Sue come in, alone. I watch as she collects some food and looks around, and I offer a little wave when her eyes settle on me. She starts to walk towards my table, slaloming around tables and chairs on an almost direct course.

As she arrives at the table she looks towards my empty plate and asks, "Are you just off?"

"No," I answer, "I was waiting to find out if they can decide what is 'The best of all possible worlds.'" I nod towards the dramatists.

"Ah, Candide," says Sue, taking a mouthful of salad.

Of course, she knows that! I was just repeating something I had heard them say, but Sue knew what it was.

"It's disgusting!" she tells me, before taking another mouthful of salad.

I assume she means Candide as she seems to be enjoying the salad.

"I'll take your word for it." But I won't, I tell myself I'll find a copy of it and read it and it will make me a better person, maybe.

I sit with Sue while she finishes her meal and we talk about how our respective third year studies have started out. Sue has been reading the same books as Paul, so I kind of feel like I have a head start in this conversation. I tell Sue a little about the essay that we have been unreasonably asked to do so near to the start of term, and the research I have been doing about Vygotsky. I think I manage to make it sound more interesting than it actually is. Sue finishes and we clear up and step out to the quad, where I light the cigarette I have been rolling.

"You should give up," Sue says.

"I should, maybe I will. Did you think about the other thing yet?"

"I did, if you take me for a drink later, I'll let you know what I decided."

"Won't your bodyguards throw a protective ring around you?"

"Shut up. No, they're all off to the Round Tree with Trevor, you should see them all rushing around deciding what to wear."

"They approve of him then?"

"I think they're all in love with him?"

"Why?"

"He's nice."

"He's not that nice."

"He asked me to go, if you're not scrubbed up and knocking on my door by seven, I'll join them instead!"

"I'll be there," I promise, as Sue turns and walks off towards her room.

I drop my cigarette end on the path and stub it. As I look down, I see a small, brown, dead bird lying at the edge of the gravel path, half hidden by some plants. I glance at it momentarily, then carry on back to my room for some Turbo and toothpaste. I have a good feeling about tonight.

I put on a clean tee-shirt and grab my jacket, then pop round to Paul to give him an update. I knock on his door and wait. I hear Paul cross the room, open the door a crack and look out. Over his shoulder I can see something with a floral print on the back of his chair. I'm pretty sure he doesn't have any flowery clothes, I am not always as daft as my actions would indicate.

"I'll see you up the bar later yeah?"

"Yeah, be up there in a bit."

"See you there," squeaks a voice from somewhere behind the door.

"Later," I call, as Paul closes the door and I wander off.

I don't want to hang around in my room, so I make my way to the back path, which loops up and around behind the main buildings and past the drama studio.

I expect it to be quiet and empty at this time in the evening and am not disappointed. The shady path running between double rows of trees does not lead anywhere that you can't get to quicker or easier from another direction.

Sue's corridor is a melee of noise and activity. Various people scowl at me as they offer insincere greetings and disinterested enquiries after my health. I answer them politely as I run the gauntlet to Sue's door, which is open. I knock and step in. Sue is applying some make-up in the mirror. She is wearing jeans and a plain white shirt. As I arrive, she finishes up, wraps a blue cotton scarf around her neck and pulls me out of her room and along the corridor, shouting goodbye as we go.

"It's mad in there," she says, "you'd think some of them had never been to a pub before. Mind you, maybe some of them haven't."

"Are they all going to the Round Tree?"

"I think so, quieter for the rest of us."

"And no guards for you."

"Yes, can we go somewhere and talk before we start drinking?"

I agree and lead the way back along the quiet path by the drama block, where we claim the first bench we get to. Our discussion is long and intense, I finally manage to apologise for my egregious behaviour, and Sue gracefully accepts my apology. She also gives me some reasonable suggestions for my future behaviour. I agree that these are good ideas, in spite of the fact that this means I will have to be more aware of what I'm doing and how it affects others. We agree that we should take it steady, not rush, just see how it goes.

Then, finally, we kiss. It is a long, involved, tonguey, spit-swapping sort of kiss, with occasional breaks to come up for air. We are now, officially, back together again and I am both relieved and happy.

We eventually pause and separate long enough for me to light a cigarette. Sue is adjusting her scarf, we kiss again, every bit as passionate as the last time, until we finally stop and move off, with our arms around one another, to the bar. We are lucky enough to find a table, where Paul and Lesley join us as we arrive. I get in a round of drinks.

It turns out to be one of those evenings when nothing goes quite as expected.

We have not been here long when the first year in the David Bowie tee-shirt comes over and joins us. None of us had really spoken to him properly since he arrived, although we'd all seen him around. Nevertheless, he sits down and starts acting as if we had all known each other all our lives. Most specifically he wants to talk to me. He has seen my Bauhaus badge on my jacket lapel and needed to know my thoughts on their cover version of Ziggy Stardust – which he thinks is a travesty.

We ended up agreeing to disagree, and I invite him to come to my room

some time and drop off a blank tape so I can record some Bauhaus for him, then he could make up his own mind about how great they are. Paul offers to put some Fall on a tape for him, this seemed to confuse things, so Paul helpfully starts to sing to him,
"Ooh ooh, ten times my age,
Ooh ooh one tenth my height
Our City Hobgoblins…"

This doesn't really help, although it makes Sue and Lesley laugh out loud. David Bowie tee-shirt wanders off to explain something to someone else. As he leaves, I realise I can't remember his actual name. I ask the others. There is a little confusion and uncertainty, but in the end we all agree it is Tom, or Dan, but definitely not Ron. I go and get some more drinks.

The evening wears on and more drink is consumed. The music is varied, from okay to awful – but at least no Lady in sodding Red.

I am on my way to the toilet when I see mousey girl. I say hi. She starts to reply, hiccups and throws up on the floor in front of herself – just missing my boots. Then she starts to laugh. She is not obviously with anybody else and I'm not sure that she can get herself back to her room, so I go and get Sue. Between us we encourage mousey girl to her feet, making sure she doesn't step in her pool of spaghetti loop and sausage chunk vomit, and we walk her back to her room.

This is hilarious, apparently. Mousey girl keeps asking where she is going, is it a party? She informs us that she has had quite a lot to drink. She then repeats the same things again, while leaning on my shoulder and being gently steered in the direction of her room by Sue.

We leave her in her room with a waste bin close to hand, and she assures us she will be fine. We leave, with mousey girl clutching the bin in one arm, waving with the other and singing some kind of bizarre goodbye song while trying to take her pixie boots off.

We emerge giggling into the night air. It has cooled considerably now and a puff of a breeze clears my head a little. I take Sue in my arms and we kiss, then she gives a little shiver as another gust of wind passes us by. I put my jacket over her shoulders and wonder if I should invite her back to my room. Is it too soon? Will she think I'm rushing? As we kiss she pushes herself up against me and I think that my unasked question is possibly being answered.

Another swirl of wind swishes through the branches of a nearby tree, and without warning it starts to rain. Sue pulls my jacket up over her head, grabs my hand and runs towards her block, pulling me with her.

We get to the porch and stop,
"Are you coming in?" she asks, "cup of tea?"
"Yes" I reply, "I'm not walking back in that." I indicate the rain which is only really a passing shower and is already slowing down to a spit.

We go in, past the doors of her friends. One door is slightly ajar and I can hear the sounds of several people talking. One of the voices I recognise as Trevor, as Sue goes into her room the sound of a guitar being strummed and tuned starts from the open door. I groan inwardly and quickly duck into Sue's room and pull the door closed behind me.

Sue already has the kettle on, and has draped my jacket over the back of her chair, I hold her in my arms and we kiss again, passionately and slowly with the muffled sound of Trevor singing Simon and Garfunkel songs in the background. When we come up for air Sue switches on her tape player to cover the noise. Janis Ian starts playing and I brace myself for the ensuing heartache, but say nothing. Luckily, I don't need to, Sue knows this would not be my first choice. She quickly changes it for Joan Armatrading, which rates slightly higher on my acceptable music scale, then finishes making the tea.

We sit and talk, about our summers (boring), about our families (awful), about our courses (too much work already) and about other people. We skirt around the topic of 'us', maybe it's too early to think about anything other than the right now. I also do not talk about the weekend of the storm. Sue does ask, once, how the weekend went. I am vague and change the subject after mumbling something about how hard we had all worked.

Eventually the tape finishes, the mugs of tea are emptied and decisions need to be made. I get up and stretch then say, "I'm just going to the loo, then I'll be off."

I creep out along the corridor to use the amenities. I walk quietly back past closed and silent doors to get my jacket. I open the door and Sue is standing by the bed in her underwear. Sometimes I don't get hints, but tonight I'm sure I'm reading the signals right. We kiss, we undress, and we go to bed in a fumble of frenetic passion that lasts long into the night.

Chapter 11
Everything goes wrong

I wake up the next morning with the duvet and Sue twisted around and draped across me. I feel ridiculously pleased with myself, and as I look at Sue I start to have thoughts about picking up where we left off when we fell asleep last night. I kiss her cheek and she opens her eyes and asks, "What time is it?"

As soon as she says it, I realise that there is too much light and too much banging of doors and movement in the corridor outside for it to be anything but time to get up. I look at her clock and see that it is fast approaching time for my first lecture of the day. I hate early lectures. I momentarily regret going out drinking on a week night, but can't deny that it was definitely worth it.

Sue does not have an early lecture and laughs at me as I hop around finding yesterday's clothing and attempting to put on my boots, jeans and jacket simultaneously. I am eventually victorious in my battle with my clothes.

"See you at lunchtime?"

"Yeah, coffee bar?"

"Okay."

"It was good last night, I'm glad we're friends again."

I smile and blow her a kiss as I hurry out of the door and she waves me away,

"Go on, before you miss the whole lecture."

I go running down the path, through the drizzle, towards the lecture hall. As I run, I wonder if I'll have time to rush into my own room to grab a notepad and pen, or if I should just wing it and see if I could borrow off someone when I get there.

As I approach the main building, I see the familiar figure of Lisa in front of me. She is also running late, but not actually running, more sort of ambling. She may be my saviour, she will surely have a pen and some paper that I can borrow, also we can go in late together and I won't have to face Dr Kevern's stink eye and caustic wit alone.

I catch up with Lisa, then slow down and walk alongside her.

"Hey, you oversleep too?" I ask.

"Yeah." She answers blearily.

"So much for fresh starts eh? Have you got a pen I can borrow? Mine's in my room, I don't want to be later than necessary."

"Sure." She takes her pencil case from her bag and starts to rummage.

"And some paper?"

"Sure" she says again. She is still searching for a pen.

I pause and turn to look at Lisa. She is pale and has dark rings under her eyes, she looks tired. She still hunts absently for a pen, but distractedly, as if she has forgotten what she is looking for.

"Are you okay?" I ask.

I put one hand on her arm to get her attention away from the pencil case. She looks at me, briefly making eye contact before looking right through me and answering, "No, not really, I'm feeling kind of strange. I think I might have the flu."

Now we are in the quad walking towards the lecture hall.

"Why don't you go back to bed?"

I glance at the last few stragglers going into the hall, I still think we might make it in time, as the doors close behind the last person. I look at Lisa again, she looks dreadful, pale and drawn. Now that I look, I notice that she has her shirt on inside out and has odd shoes, similar, but definitely not a pair. I am going to point it out, but Lisa is not looking at me, she is staring vacantly at the pond. The weed is now a custardy brown colour.

"Come on, I'll take you back and call the nurse."

"No, I'll be okay." She takes two steps toward the pond, the second quite tentative, then stops. She points at it as if she is going to tell me something, then simply repeats, "I'll be okay."

Then she's sick. Not blowing chunks like mousey girl last night, but a liquid stream that seems to pour from her mouth and cascade down the front of her shirt and trousers, splashing onto her odd shoes – and me. It is a dark red colour and feels endless, even though it can only have lasted a few seconds.

Lisa spits, wipes her mouth on the back of her hand then hands me the pen she has finally found for me. I take it, still staring at the bloody vomit drenching her. She follows my gaze down, looks surprised and then her eyes roll back in her head and she crumples to the ground, where she retches another salvo onto the gravel path.

I try to catch her as she falls, but only really succeed in simultaneously covering myself with more of her bloody sick and vaguely guiding her to the ground without her hurting herself. I look frantically around to see if anyone else is there to help. There is no one, the quad is momentarily deserted. I have an extraordinary amount of blood on my hands, my shirt and the sleeves of my jacket. I try unsuccessfully to wipe it off as I look down at Lisa. It's hard to tell, but there seems to be blood coming from everywhere now, soaking through the crotch of her jeans, seeping from her mouth and nose, all spreading like fingers through the damp gravel.

When I first left home, I thought I was an adult. Liberated, living my own life, having my own money. But right now, I feel useless, like I know nothing. I don't know what to do and would give anything for a grown up to come and make things right, to take over and help Lisa.

Someone appears at the corner of the bottom of the path and I shout, "Help! Hey, help – go to the office and call an ambulance!"

"What's that?" they call back, walking past the pond towards me.

Bloody idiot! Why can't people just do what you ask?

"An ambulance, go and call and ambulance."

They dither, and then finally seem to see Lisa and they get the message. They turn and run to the office.

By now my shouting has started to draw attention. People start appearing from the various buildings around the quad. They come over, slowly at first and then rushing when they see what has happened. Some stop short and cover their mouths with their hands, others come right over to me to ask what's wrong? and what happened? Somebody kneels down and starts adjusting Lisa, making sure she is on her side and trying to figure out where the blood is coming from. So much blood.

Duddi comes running from the office with a first aid kit and informs us that an ambulance has been called, he asks what happened and starts ordering people to 'move back' and 'give her space.' People are flooding out of the lecture hall now, I am forgotten and pushed backward along with the rest of the crowd. I turn and walk away.

I hold my hands out in front of me and look at them, still dripping blood, still holding Lisa's pen. I think of Macbeth with his ghostly dagger and throw the pen on the floor and carry on walking. I am telling myself that Lisa will be alright, I am telling myself that it's not my fault and I'm telling myself that nothing happened. But inside I know.

I find myself back at Sue's room where she is still organising herself for the day, she has dressed, washed her hair and is unravelling the cord from her hair drier. She is unaware of what has happened, although that news will travel quickly, it always does here. She looks at me and her mouth opens to say something, but nothing comes out. She comes to me, closes the door and guides me to the chair.

"What happened?" she asks, "What the fuck happened?"

I cry.

Sue shushes me, peels my jacket off and drops it in the sink before starting to wipe my hands and arms with the towel that she has taken from her hair. Mostly it just spreads the blood around, but gradually it starts to come off. I cry, large uncontrollable sobs that shake my body, and I keep apologising.

The rest of the day is a blur. I eventually let Sue go, she is back quickly. She has Duddi with her who has had people looking for me, everything is confusing right now, I answer questions and cry a lot. I don't tell anybody what I know. But I know. Eventually I am able to go back to my own room, where I strip off my clothes, which I leave in a heap on the floor, and run a bath where I try to scrub everything off of me. I keep on scrubbing long after the blood has all gone and the water has gone cold. Then I go back to my room. I lock the door, climb into my unmade bed and sleep.

I am eventually roused by a continuous knocking on my door and a voice calling my name. It's Paul, I get up and open the door to him. He doesn't say anything, just comes in, passes me a cigarette, lights one for himself and sits down. I feel a bit calmer now I have slept, but inside I am still panicking. I can't get rid of the feeling of uselessness, the feeling that it was all my fault somehow, and the image running through my head of all that blood.

Eventually Paul breaks the silence.

"It's tea time, do you want me to get you something to eat and bring it back?"

I realise I am hungry. I was too late for breakfast and slept through lunch. Paul leaves with a promise to get me 'anything' and goes out. He returns shortly after with a selection of food, he has also bought Sue back with him, she is holding my jacket.

Paul leaves the tray on my desk and I start to pick at it as Paul excuses himself and leaves us, with instructions to give him a shout if we need anything.

"He's been guarding your door all day you know?" Sue tells me.

"Really?" I start to pick at the tray of food.

"Yep, wouldn't let anybody in. I helped him, you seemed exhausted."

"Thanks. I was, I still feel drained now."

Sue passes me my jacket,

"I tried to get it clean, It's still a bit damp, but I did my best."

"Thanks, really thanks." I look at the jacket and it seems to be as clean as it normally is, if not cleaner. I look down at my other clothes, still blood-stained in a crumpled heap on the floor.

"How's Lisa?" I ask abruptly.

"Nobody knows, they took her away in an ambulance, nobody has heard since. Nobody even knows which hospital they took her to. What happened?"

I start to tell her about meeting Lisa on the path and how she didn't look well, but she interrupts me,

"Not that, everybody knows that now. What happened before that?"

For a moment I am genuinely confused, I try to think what else had

happened between me leaving Sue's room and meeting Lisa on the path.
"Before term?" she prompts.

The penny drops, I feign ignorance and tell her I don't know what she means.

"Don't be stupid. I know you don't always see me, but I see you. You've been avoiding Lisa and Sarah and the others since we came back. You lot are normally in and out of each other's rooms non-stop, now you're barely speaking. Something happened, just tell me."

"I can't. I wish I could, but I can't. Nothing happened."

More tears track their warm course down my cheeks. I feel pathetic and useless, and I really want to tell Sue. I want her to tell me it wasn't my fault, I want her to help me sort the whole sorry mess out. Most of all I want her to make me less scared.

Sue holds me. I pull away to wipe my eyes and nose on my tee shirt sleeve. I don't feel hungry anymore, and in spite of having slept all day I am tired again. I lay down on my side and Sue comes and lays next to me.

"Tell me when you're ready," she whispers.

"I will," I tell her, "I promise I will."

I realise that Sue is crying too, but I don't understand why. I am going to ask, but sleep seems to rush up on me like an express train.

I wake in the night. Sue is still there, she is curled up on the chair with a spare blanket draped over her. She is fast asleep in the dim light of the side lamp, which is pointed into the corner. It is highlighting the sheen of her hair draped across her shoulder and the curve of her breasts under the thin blanket, I am aroused but have other business to attend to first. I get up to use the bathroom, quietly leaving the door slightly ajar so the click of the latch doesn't wake her.

It is deathly quiet in the hall. It is the time of night when only those that have no choice are up and about. I take myself to the main door and go outside to the front step where I sit and roll a cigarette. It is chilly out here, I am only wearing jeans and a tee shirt. The ground is cold under my bare feet and I can feel the sharpness and texture of the concrete.

I breathe my smoke in deeply and exhale, feeling myself calming. I think maybe I have excised some of the horrors of the previous day, although this thought on its own starts to trigger the lucid and surreal memory of Lisa. I look up towards the stars, they are clear and bright in what is now a cloudless sky. The patterns and shapes they make are hypnotic as I look up and try to make sense of their far away existence.

I am disturbed by the sound of a car. In the silence I can hear it coming down the drive at a slow and steady speed, it stops and the night seems even quieter for the absence of the sound of the car. I listen to see if it will start up again, but hear nothing. I go back inside and gently wake Sue, she comes into the bed with me and we hurriedly draw each other's clothes apart to allow us to make love quickly and urgently before falling asleep.

Alice

The detailed plans are all in place, surrounded with coffee cups and spread out on the table where they have recently been shared with team leaders. Everything is set up, minimum disruption, covert and using some of their most experienced operatives.

This is not the first time Alice has had to arrange for people to be bought into centres, but it is the first time she has planned to do it to people she thinks are probably innocent. For the IRA suspects and political agitators she usually works with she has little doubt that she is protecting the wider public. For the decorators she cannot understand how they could have made such an important item disappear with such apparent ease, and with no obvious motive, backing or support.

She mulls this over again as she looks around the room. The pictures, maps, files and documents only go so far in disguising a room that is still a sterile journeyman hotel room with functional furniture and a bad reproduction painting on one wall. The bulky grey phone on the desk rings abruptly and Alice picks it up before the second ring. It's O'Brien;

"One of the decorators is ill."

"Which one?"

"The girl, Lisa."

"How ill?"

"She's serious, it looks like contamination. Right now these kids have jumped into our number one slot. Jones and Dan are on their way to join you, they'll give you all the support you need and as much manpower as you want. I want those kids out of there as soon as possible, without any fuss."

"What about the girl?"

"Already removed. We need the rest of the decorators out and the site closed down asap. Fingertip search until we find what we're looking for, it must be there somewhere."

"Yes sir, I've allocated each of the decorators to a different centre."

"Good, check if there's any further contamination, then close the site."

"Yes sir, I'll see to it."

"Thanks Alice, it's good you were quick off the mark with that caretaker, this would have caught us flatfooted if we'd been looking the wrong way."

Alice smiles to herself as she puts the phone down, it may have been luck, but it was her luck. She immediately starts revising all her plans to include health screening and full evacuation. The extraction plan is still in place, she moves the time to tomorrow night to allow for the new circumstances. The good news for her is that now they have a reason to flood the site with personnel, which will help make sure that the decorators don't disappear, and provide cover for the extraction teams.

By the time Dan and Jones arrive the amended plan is in full swing, the college is swamped with a mixture of medical staff and operatives dressed in white coats with stethoscopes draped around their necks. There are eyes on the decorators at all times, and so far none of the other students who have been checked over have shown any signs of sickness. Alice sends Dan and Jones off to reconnoitre the site, while she waits behind and collates incoming information on a new pin board that was put up this morning. A tally of the number of students checked, which is steadily rising, against an empty space ready to indicate any new cases.

On the other board, next to the map, she has put the plan. Each of the decorators was being collected by a different team and taken to their centre. Under her guidance the teams would be coordinated to remove targets simultaneously. Nobody is expecting any resistance, but a list of backups and firearms support for each target is included in the plan.

Dan starts looking through the plans.

"Do you want me to check these?"

"No need, but feel free to look through them."

Alice knows it is only a matter of time now before Dan starts making helpful suggestions, he's done this before. Unfortunately, he doesn't always look at the big picture. If you change one small detail you risk a chain reaction that can bring the whole scheme down like a house of cards. Right on cue Dan asks, "Could we change the centres they are going to if we needed to?"

"We could, but everybody is briefed for their own target, it would create a lot of work and potential confusion. Why do you think we should change it?"

"Oh, I was just thinking."

"Thinking what?"

"You haven't got any firearms teams accompanying the extraction teams."

"It's a college, they're kids. There won't be a need for firearms."

"Yes, but what if…"

Jones looks across from the map, which he has been studying closely and interjects, "Don't think Dan. Everything is ready, there are firearms teams standing by in the vicinity. All you need to do is what Alice tells you to."

Dan grumbles quietly and goes back to reading the plans. Having asserted his seniority, Jones looks at Alice and offers a brief smile as she mouths 'thank you' to him.

At 4 o'clock prompt there is a knock on the door and two senior army officers in civilian clothes come in. This part of the operation is being passed to them. Dan and Jones have left to give the extraction teams a final briefing, the army will be in charge of evacuating the site and starting the search as soon as possible. The college should be empty by mid-morning tomorrow, a cover story about Cholera has been agreed on and all local public bodies were being informed of this as soon as the decorators were gone, in the confusion nobody would miss them. By then Alice will be back at the centre waiting to receive their suspect, they are having the smoking boy. Transport is on standby to take her, Jones and Dan back as soon as she has finished this meeting. Other personnel would be charged with returning her car and belongings for her.

She finishes the handover and wishes everybody luck, then leaves the hotel by the rear exit where a helicopter is waiting. Dan and Jones are already inside as she ducks under the rotor that starts turning as she approaches, and climbs on board.

Chapter 11 (continued)

The next morning we wake up at the same time as each other. I still have a feeling deep in the pit of my stomach that nothing is right. But with Sue here things feel better. We kiss and she leaves for her own room to get fresh clothes. I am ravenous. I look at the tray of cold food on my desk and can see nothing that has survived the night in good enough condition for me to eat now, so I go to get breakfast.

Paul has been waiting for me to emerge and hurries out to join me. He catches up and walks alongside me.

"How are you doing?" he asks.

"Yeah, a lot better thanks. Starving. Have you heard how Lisa is?"

"No, nobody's heard anything yet. All the lectures are cancelled today and there's a lot of health people on site."

"Health people?"

"Doctors in white coats with clipboards, trying to find out what made Lisa ill I guess."

I didn't answer, because I was pretty sure I already knew. I was also pretty sure that someone would be looking for me soon, as I had been with Lisa when she collapsed. We arrive at the common room, there are only a handful of students there, and no hot food on offer as the kitchen has been closed, there is a large cross of yellow tape across the kitchen door.

Cereals and bread and jam have been laid out and I help myself to a generous serving of both. I have just sat down with Paul when Sue comes hurrying in. She has a clean shirt and jeans and has clearly rushed, her hair falling loose over her shoulders instead of her normal, careful plait.

"Did you hear? They've cancelled all the lectures today."

"I already told him," answers Paul as Sue sits down.

"What's going to happen then?" she asks both of us.

"I guess they want to find out what was wrong with Lisa," I answer.

"What do you think it was?" she asks.

I shrug.

"I don't know, but I hope I don't get it, she was sick all over me."

It's kind of true, I am worried. I think back to the night of the storm, who was closest to the cylinder? Who spent most time with it? How bad was it? What did we do? I take a spoonful of cereal and with my mouth still full ask if anybody else has been ill.

"Not that I know of," says Sue. "But I haven't seen Sarah, Jo or Stewart."

She looks meaningfully at Paul, clearly, they have been talking while I slept. They both look at me then, after checking nobody is close enough to overhear Paul says, "What did happen before term? You guys have been cagey as fuck. I spent all day yesterday thinking you were going to start spewing blood like the exorcist or something."

"Nothing happened. I can't tell you anything, you really don't want to know."

"Which was it?" Sue asks. "Nothing or something you won't tell us?"

"Nothing.".

"So, what can't you tell us then?"

I look at both of them and finish my cereal. Putting the spoon down I make a decision, I am going to tell them. If Sarah and the others aren't here, I really need to ask someone what I should do. I am torn between my promise to my friends and my need to unburden myself, to have someone to reassure me that I wasn't the one who made Lisa sick.

"You know the night of the storm?" I ask.

Paul nods and Sue says;

"Yes, the Saturday. It was awful, it blew down some trees around our way."

I continue,

"We'd all finished painting for the day and went over to the Fox and Hounds for a drink. We didn't know there was a storm coming, we just thought it was hot."

Both are now listening, no interruptions or questions, just Paul and Sue sat opposite me waiting to hear my confession. I am about to tell the whole story, to drag them into the mess I'd made. I can't remember whose idea it had been now, but I know I had played my part, it may even have been me who suggested it. I hesitate, not knowing how to continue without making myself look bad.

At that moment Duddi comes into the common room accompanied by two men in white lab coats. They look faintly ridiculous standing in the doorway, as out of place as they could possibly look in a student common room.

Duddi casts his eye around the room and it rests on us. He says something to the men and we watch as they walk straight towards our table. I have a bad feeling in my stomach. They get to the table and Duddi says, "These men need to check you're okay, because you were with Lisa yesterday. Probably all of you, if you spent time together since then."

"How is Lisa?" I ask. "Is she okay?"

"We don't have any information yet," he answers. "But she's in the best place to help her."

One of the doctors then speaks in a quiet, deep voice,

"We just need to do some simple checks to make sure you're all okay."

"Why what was wrong with her?"

"We don't know yet." But he says it with no conviction, I am sure that there is more to tell, but we are clearly not going to get anything from Dr We Don't Know. Sue asks what checks, and they tell her it will be quite straightforward, if we just come into the Mansion with them. Like lambs we get up from the table and follow them out of the room.

Inside the mansion it is busy with men and women in white coats who appear to have taken over the ground floor of the building. There is a church-like hush and the sounds of footsteps on the tiled floor seem too loud. We are met by a woman with a clipboard who comes towards us and asks our names. She checks her list and directs us to wait on a row of chairs half way up the corridor.

"What the fuck?" asks Paul, looking up and down the corridor.

"What do you think they want to check?" whispers Sue, reaching down to take my hand.

Before I can say anything, not that I had any kind of answer, Dr We Don't Know comes over and asks me to come with him.

"See you in a bit," I say to the others, getting up and following him.

My heart is beating in my chest as I go into the bursars' office, repurposed for the day as a makeshift medical room. I am convinced that they are going to start asking about the cylinder, that they know everything and are going to take me away in handcuffs in a police van.

Instead I am met by a young-looking, white-coated woman who smiles nicely and asks me to sit down.

"Nothing to worry about here," she says "We just want to give you a basic check over to make sure you're okay. How are you feeling today?"

"Fine," I tell her. It's true, apart from the blind panic that was threatening to surface at any minute. The almost overwhelming urge to confess, to blurt out everything and have done with it.

"Good," she answers, taking a thermometer off the desk and offering it to me. "Pop this in your mouth could you?"

I do this, and while I am mute she takes my pulse, counting silently as she looks at her watch. She writes a number on a chart on her desk then takes the thermometer out and records it next to the previous one. She then puts the thermometer in a glass jar of liquid and attaches me to a blood pressure machine. She pumps it up, lets it down and records that result, then starts prodding and poking around my neck, feeling the glands and asking to look inside my mouth. Her hands are warm, and apart from wishing I had brushed my teeth this morning, it is a painless and brief experience. I ask her if she knows how Lisa is, but she says sorry, she only got here this morning and doesn't really know what's happened. Her answer sounds rehearsed and slick and I suspect it is not quite the truth.

She finishes, then sits at her desk and writes some notes and asks if I will be leaving the campus today. Again, I sense an undertone to what she is saying, that she is actually telling me not to leave. But I guess I'm feeling a bit paranoid at the moment. She thanks me and gets up and opens the door. I leave, it feels like a reprieve, that I have not been discovered yet.

I go back outside to see if Paul or Sue has finished yet. I see no sign of them outside so I wander back to the common room to see if they have gone back there. As I am going in Duddi comes past with Dr We Don't Know and Sarah. She makes brief eye contact with me, but doesn't say anything. She looks about as calm as I felt earlier, I try to smile to reassure her before she is whisked away into the Mansion.

The common room is all but deserted, tables have been cleared and chairs straightened, leaving a few people at spaced out tables, drinking mugs of tea and working on essays or reading books. Nobody is talking and the huge peace sign looms over everything. It has a less optimistic feel to it now and I decide not to wait here.

I walk over to Sue's room to see if she has gone back there, but her door is locked and all the others are closed. I return to my own room, the corridor here is also empty and there is no sign of Paul. I leave my door open and sit on my bed listening to some David Bowie (curses, David Bowie tee shirt is right about how good he is though!) and read some more Agatha Christie.

I am deeply engrossed when Paul's head appears around my door. He comes in and we compare experiences in the Mansion. His sounds exactly the same as mine and I am reassured that I have not been singled out for special treatment.

"Have you figured out who did it yet?" he asks, indicating the book.

"The policeman," I answer, "it's always the policeman isn't it?" we laugh, and then Paul says, "You were about to tell us what happened."

"I'll wait 'till Sue's here too." I say. But that moment has already passed, my desire to unburden myself is less strong now, and I don't know if I want to add to the number of people involved in our misdeeds.

Paul nods, and then says he is going to meet Lesley and see if she knows any more about what's going on than we do. I suspect that if anyone knows it will be Lesley. I also suspect that Paul wants to catch up with more than the gossip. He leaves and I settle back to my book.

I'm only a few pages further on when Sue turns up. We have a similar conversation to the one I had with Paul about the doctors, as Sue sits next to me on the bed and snuggles up against me. I am suitably distracted, and before long we are kissing as if we'd not seen each other for a week. Sue is rubbing the crotch of my jeans, which are now stretched tight, and I have my hand under her tee shirt and am massaging her breasts.

I realise that Sue didn't shut the door up when it swings open. I sit up quickly and Sue is busy smoothing down her shirt and adjusting her bra as Paul and Lesley come in.

"Ah, should've knocked, shouldn't I?" says Paul. "Do you want us to come back later?"

"No, you're fine, come in." I answer, and they do. Lesley perches on the end of the bed, next to Sue, and Paul takes the chair by the desk. They report back to us that there is nothing much happening around college, everybody is either hunkered down in their rooms or huddled in small groups in various communal areas. The bar is blocked off with the same yellow tape as the kitchen.

Nobody has any idea what is going on, but there are lots of rumours and everyone has a theory. These range from 'the kitchen staff poisoned everyone', to 'somebody bought back a deadly virus from their summer holiday'. Duddi is busy with the white coats, rounding up students to take to the Mansion. He is working his way around the site summoning people.

There is clearly nothing to do, Lesley gets up and starts to rifle through my cassettes,

"Any U2?" she asks.

"No, sorry." I say. I'm not sorry though, I hate U2.

"This'll do," says Lesley, she puts on some Simple Minds, leaving the tape I had been listening to earlier on the side, out of its case. I can't for the life of me think why anybody would do a thing like that unless they are a sociopath? I get up as she sits down and put it away. I then ask if anyone wants a cup of tea, so they don't all think I only got up to put the tape away.

"I can do better than that," says Paul with a smile. He leaves the room and is back seconds later with a bottle of whiskey.

"Where's that from?" asks Sue.

"My bedroom."

"Right, smartarse. Why have you got it?"

"To drink."

Sue looks at me exasperated and I shrug and look at Paul, who helpfully furnishes us with the information that it was his birthday over the summer and his brother had given him the whiskey. I feel a bit bad, probably I should have known it was his birthday. I collect up some mugs and take them to the sink to rinse them out. Shaking out the drips of water I set them on the table next to the bottle. I am not normally a whiskey drinker, but then this isn't a normal day. Paul pours a generous measure into each mug and we all take a sip, I pull a face and look over to see Lesley taking a generous gulp of hers, while Sue and Paul take a second sip and agree that it is good stuff.

The conversation that follows veers from the surreal to the banal and deliberately steers as far away from any serious or current topic as it can.

Lesley proves to be as wonderful a source of gossip as I knew she would be. We are helpfully furnished with details of who's sleeping with whom, who's no longer sleeping with who and who's sleeping with someone who isn't the person they're supposed to be sleeping with. Paul and Sue talk books, who knew Gerard Manley Hopkins even existed, let alone is able to quote their poetry? Well, apart from Paul and Sue obviously.

Lesley has poured herself a third helping of whiskey, and we have all made good progress with our second and I'm feeling light-headed. This is either a very good or a very bad idea, only time will tell. Sue asks lightly, "What were you going to tell us earlier, at breakfast?"

I might have told them, but I knew I couldn't tell Lesley. It's not that I don't trust her, it's just that…well, okay I don't think I trust Lesley not to tell everything to everybody who would listen.

"I'll tell you later," I say, "I promise."

"I'll hold you to that." Sue says.

Paul disappears to his room again and returns with a pack of cards. Thus begins a game of cards that increases in volume and raucousness as the whiskey level in the bottle slowly goes down. Even I, with my antipathy towards whiskey, find that the more you drink of it the better it is.

Before we know it, the afternoon has gone. Me and Sue walk, laughing, together to her room. Lesley is slumped on my bed, close to oblivion and Paul has decided to wait there with her. We get back to Sue's room where we drink tea and listen to some Bruce. Sue asks, "Are you going to tell me yet?"

"I'll tell you everything tomorrow, when Paul's with us - and I've sobered up."

"Tomorrow morning then, that's a promise. The suspense is nearly killing me now."

"It's a promise."

The evening wears on and we drink more tea, listen to some more music and later in the evening we undress and go to bed, where we drunkenly fumble through the motions of making love before falling asleep, wrapped up in each other and the duvet.

Chapter 12
Things that go bump in the night

The sounds of movement in the room wakes me. There is no light from the landing, all is in darkness apart from the light of the moon seeping around the edge of the curtains. It's hard to tell how many people there are in the room. As my eyes adjust I see they are all dressed in white. White one-piece suits with white hoods. They have opaque plastic face plates that reflect what little light there is, only giving occasional glimpses of their features. Eventually my eyes used to the darkness and they resolve into three separate people, rather than one amorphous white mass.

Their voices are muffled, but they are telling us to get up. I am too surprised to refuse. I stand in my boxer shorts as Sue reaches from under the duvet to pick her clothes up from the floor. A female voice asks her name, Sue tells her, and the woman passes her dressing gown from the back of the door, which Sue gratefully pulls under the duvet and shrugs into.

"What the? What's going on? Who are you?"

"It's okay, everything's fine."

"What?"

"I just need you to come with me please," the woman tells Sue pleasantly.

There is a forceful quality to her voice, it is not a voice that is used to being argued with. Sue gets out of the bed. Her added presence is way too much for the tiny room, one of the other figures nudges a row of books which fall from the shelf with a clatter, and spread themselves across the floor.

The sudden noise breaks my paralysis. I grab Sue's arm, pulling her back towards me,

"What's going on, who are you?"

"It's just a precaution," says the muffled voice of one of the figures. "we think there's cholera here on campus, we need to check everyone."

"In the middle of the night?" I pull the curtain aside and look out into the darkness, I see more white suited figures moving like ghosts on the path by the window. I'm not a medical person, and I don't know much about cholera, but I know that is not what this is about.

"It's really important that you come with us so we can get things sorted," says the white suited woman. She puts her hand in the small of Sue's back and starts to guide her from the room.

"But I was checked this morning, I feel fine," Sue tells her.

Despite this she does not protest as she allows herself to be led from the room wrapped in her dressing gown. I let her go, and feel useless and exposed standing in my underwear in front of these strangers. I want to tell Sue not to worry, but I can't. I'm too scared of what will happen to me. I bite my lip and watch her leave, hoping that I have not put her in danger.

Once Sue is gone another white suit asks me if I want to pop some clothes on before I come with them. Like Sue, the fight has gone from me – if it was ever there in the first place. I put on my clothes, boots flopping unlaced and with my jacket slung over my shoulder.

I allow myself to be led from the room. The whole interaction has taken less than five minutes and appears to have caused no disturbance whatsoever, all the other doors are still closed and there are no sounds apart from our footsteps. There is also no sign of Sue as I am taken out into the dark, where an unmarked black van is waiting. I pause, and look around, hoping for someone to come to my rescue. I consider shouting, but everything seems to be happening so quickly, I am nudged gently forward by one of my escorts who tells me not to worry, this is normal procedure. I am corralled into the back of the van, it is like an ambulance on the inside, with trolleys and cabinets full of medical kit. One of the white suits climbs in with me, closes the door firmly and sits down, indicating I should do the same. I hear the driver's door opening and closing and the engine starts.

Once the van has started moving, I think of a hundred questions that I need to ask,

"Where are we going? Where's Sue? Who are you? Can I call my parents?"

The words start to tumble out of me and the white suit looks impassively through the faceplate of his hood, the light of the single, weak bulb is reflecting across his face and obscuring his features again. He leans over towards me, I lean forward so I can hear him better through the visor. Instead of answering my questions he touches my leg, there is a sharp pain and I look down and see a syringe in his hand. This is the last thing I see as a warm feeling starts to spread through me and I feel my eyes closing. I try to resist but it's hopeless, darkness.

Alice

The office is quiet. Alice sits at her desk, anxiously awaiting updates and information. Dan's intervention was enough to sow the seeds of doubt in her mind. The clock shows five past three, by now the extractions should be in progress. Four teams all working simultaneously to quickly and quietly remove their allocated targets. The only possible hiccup Alice could see was if the couple didn't want to be separated. She watches the second-hand sweep around in its never-ending circle, and waits.

In the end the couple had decided to sleep in their own rooms, so that problem was averted. There had been a concern when smoking boy had gone to his girlfriend's room for the night, but she had made no fuss and he had come easily. The best news of the night was that one of the decorators had panicked. In their confusion and fear they had blurted out an entire confession, including the precise location of the item. The pond! The bloody pond! Right in the middle of the whole college, the search teams were nowhere near it. The clean-up team were now ready to recover it the moment the site had been cleared tomorrow. It should be safely retrieved by tea time.

O'Brien phoned her when this news came through. His usual professional demeanour cracked for a moment,

"Brilliant Alice, absolutely brilliant. You are your dad's girl."

"Thank you, sir."

"No, thank you. You cracked this right open, it wouldn't have happened without you."

"So, is this the sort of thing dad did then?"

"Not exactly, but everything he did, he did with the same care and same results as you. I've got to go, reports to write, tomorrow we'll decide what to do next. Goodnight."

"Goodnight, sir."

Alice was pensive, so her dad didn't do this, she wondered again about what he actually did do. Thinking about this she goes to the cot in the corner of her office, where she will try to get some sleep as she waits for the transport to arrive.

She is woken by Mrs Baker bringing her a mug of tea,

"Incoming due in 30 minutes, everything is fine."

"Thank you, they made good time."

"Well there's not much traffic about at this time of the day is there?"

"I guess not."

Still, they must have been driving at a fair speed to get here this quickly, she hopes they haven't attracted any attention. While she is tying her hair back and washing her face Alice wonders if Mrs Baker ever sleeps or goes home. There has never been a time when Alice has been at the centre and Mrs Baker has not been here.

Alice takes her tea into the kitchen and helps herself to a yoghurt and an orange from the well-stocked fridge, she leans against the counter to eat and drink, then goes to the door where she waits for the team to arrive.

The estimated arrival time is precise, and Alice watches the van drive along the road, stop at the guard house then drive directly to the open doors where she is waiting. The boy who climbs out of the van looks dishevelled and confused, not uncommon for new arrivals. Alice looks at his eyes and sees the pupils are dilated, clearly he has been sedated for the journey. This was not uncommon for transit, some people even arrived strapped to the stretcher. Even so, Alice had been specific, no restraints or chemical coshes unless absolutely necessary, she doesn't believe this young man with his slight build who is training to teach 7-year-olds would have been a problem. Someone was going to get a bollocking, but that was for later. Now she invites him in and shows him to his room.

Chapter 12 (continued)

I gradually start to wake up again, my eyes are closed, but I can hear the sound of an engine and the vibrations of the moving vehicle. I had momentarily hoped that this had been a dream, but reality catches up with me quickly. When I open my eyes white suit is sitting across from me, I am on a stretcher with a blanket draped over me and a pillow under my head. I try to sit up, but white suit gently puts his hand on my chest and says, "Best not yet, it'll take a while for it to wear off." He then offers me a drink of water from a plastic cup, which I try to take a swallow of from my current position, white suit gently puts his hand behind my shoulders and helps lift me just enough to take some sips and wet my mouth without choking. I lie back again and look over at him. He has taken his hood off now, and looks like a perfectly ordinary man. The sort of man who might serve you in a shop or sell you a car, not the type that comes into your room in the dead of night and abducts you. Not that I know what that sort of man might look like. Well, actually I do now, but you know what I mean.

"I know you have lots of questions," he says, his voice firm but not unkind, "it's probably best if you wait until we get there, then someone will explain everything to you."

"Where?" I ask.

"Like I said, wait until we there, everything will be explained."

I am clearly not going to get anything from him, I look around the interior of the van. There are two back windows which have been partially blacked out, but there are thin gaps at the edges where daylight seeps through. We must have been driving for some time, most of it while I was involuntarily asleep. I have no idea what the time might be, or where I am, who I am with, or who else knows I am here. I lay back down and close my eyes again, gripping my hands into fists and wishing I knew what to do, how to make this stop. I listen to the sound of the van as it takes me to wherever I am going.

Surprisingly, I sleep again.

The next time I wake I am thirsty again. I sit up tentatively and look at the cracks in the windows, it is still bright daylight outside. The white suit man is still sitting watching me, he leans towards me as I swing my legs around to take up a sitting position on the stretcher. I feel slightly light-headed, but it quickly passes, I am passed a metal flask which I take gratefully. I anticipate steaming hot tea, but am not disappointed when I take the cap off and find it is full of cold water which I gulp down in big mouthfuls.

"Are we nearly there yet?" I ask.

"Not long now. Are you hungry?"

I am, now that I am awake I do feel hungry. I don't have to answer, the man has already reached into a small bag and passes me an apple. Better than nothing, I thank him and eat it. At least I'm not going to be starved during this kidnapping. I finish and look for somewhere to put the core, the man holds out his gloved hand and I give it to him whereupon he drops it into the bag it came out of. I get my tobacco out of my pocket, expecting to be told 'no'. He watches as I first roll then smoke my cigarette, leaning over to tip my ash into his bag occasionally.

"You should give up you know, it's not good for you."

I finish smoking it, then crush it out on the sole of my boot and drop the butt into the same bag as the core and ash.

All the time I wonder what is going on, where I am going and how much trouble I am in. So far it doesn't seem too bad, apart from being taken in the middle of night, drugged and driven off in an unmarked van. Nobody had tried to hurt me – yet, and I'd had something to eat. I take several deep breaths, maybe it's the after effects of the drug, maybe it's my usual reluctance to accept reality. I sit back and wait.

*

After an indeterminate amount of time, the van comes to a gradual stop. Outside I hear the sound of muffled voices, some laughter followed by a clanking, grating sound of something being moved. The van starts up again and starts to move off, it moves slowly and does not travel far before stopping again. I then feel it start to manoeuvre backward and forward, we are there, wherever 'there' is.

The van comes to a halt, there are more muffled voices from outside and then the rear doors open. They have been positioned so they lead directly to a waiting set of open double doors. I expected a reception committee similar to the group that had woken me a lifetime ago. Instead there is a single person, a woman in a smart pair of trousers and a plain white blouse. Her hair is tied back into a tight bun, showing a face that looked older than me, but not much. She stood straight and upright and greeted me with a smile.

White suit indicated that I should get out, so I moved forward and stepped down, there was barely any space between the side of the doors and the edge of the building. What there was, showed a long straight, grey single storied building with a glimpse of heath or moorland beyond. I only had the briefest of views before I was ushered into the building and the doors closed behind me, leaving white suit outside. I heard the sound of the engine starting, doors closing and the van driving off.

I look around the inside, I am in the middle of a long white corridor with doors at regular intervals, all a uniform dull red colour. A similar unremarkable corridor is ahead of me at a right angle to my current position. There are no markings on the doors or signs on the walls that I can see. As I look around the woman who had greeted me says, "Come with me, you must be tired after your journey. We'll get you comfortable and find you something to eat."

"Where am I?"

"All that later, let's get you settled first."

She smiled and led off down the corridor. I followed. There is a strong smell, like a swimming pool changing room, and everything is spotlessly clean, you might think it had never been used. There is a vinyl floor covering that seemed to absorb the sound of the woman's shoes, rather than making the clacking sound that I had expected. It is the only sound in the corridor apart from me sniffing and clearing my throat, but not actually saying anything – in truth I don't know what to say that might illicit some sort of actual answer. I don't know where I am, I don't know who these people are and I only have half an idea why I'm here. Well, I have a very good idea really, but I am determined not to let down my friends and talk about that.

We turn into another, identical, corridor when we get to a T-junction. About half way along the woman stops at a door and pulls it open.

"Go on in and make yourself at home, someone will be along in a bit to make sure you have everything you need."

I go obediently into the room and stop and look around. The room has white walls, a single bed, a chair and a desk. There are some shelves, one with neatly folded towels on, but otherwise empty. A small alcove with a toilet and a shower and a white curtain, currently pulled open, is at one side of the room. Other than this the room is bare and the option of 'making myself at home' does not really seem feasible. I turn back to the door just as it shuts with a click; there is no handle on the inside and I can't push it open. There is a metal grill with a small button inset in the plate next to the door, in one corner of the ceiling is a small speaker, in the opposite corner a small box which I guess houses a camera.

Still groggy from the drugs and the journey I sit on the bed, take my tobacco from my pocket and roll a cigarette. I light it and take one or two puffs before flicking some ash onto the floor.

"Please use the ashtray," intones a tinny metallic voice from the speaker in the corner.

Definitely a camera then, I look around and see that there is indeed an ash tray on the desk, I walk the two steps to pick it up, then return to the bed and carry on as before. There is no window in the room and nothing to give me a clue as to what the time is. I get up again and walk over to the grill by the door. I press the button and ask what the time is. The same metallic voice comes back from the speaker, "Someone will be with you shortly."

I press the button again and ask where I am.

"Someone will be with you shortly."

I decide that is probably going to be the answer to all my questions. I stub my cigarette butt in the ash tray and go and relieve myself. Having got all the amusement I could get from the room I take my jacket off, sit back on the bed with my back against the wall and wait. Thoughts race through my mind as the reality of my situation begins to set in. I wonder how much trouble I'm actually in, and what's going to happen to me.

After what feels like an age, but could equally be a short period of time, there is a tap on the door. It opens and a man stands in the doorway. He is wearing trousers, shirt and tie and carries a notebook in his hand. Before he can speak I ask again where I am.

"I'm afraid I'm not able to tell you that right now. I'm here to find out how we can make you more comfortable, would you like something to eat?"

"Like what?" I ask.

"Sausage and chips?"

"Yes please."

"Sure, I'll be back shortly."

The door closes again and I sit back down. I wonder how I am going to make sense of this. I look around the room again and notice a drawer under the desk which I hadn't seen earlier. I walk over and open it. There is a pad of lined paper and a pen which I take out and set on the desk. I then sit there with the pen in my hand, not writing anything while I mull over my situation and wait for my food. The room is deathly quiet, I start to hum but stop again quickly as the sound is enormous in the tiny room.

I come to the conclusion that I don't even know what my situation really is, I am sure it is to do with the cylinder, but I don't know how much they know or don't know. Whatever it is or isn't, it is clearly enough for them to track me down to Sue's room in the middle of the night, abduct me, drug me and take me to a secret location where they have locked me in a cell. However I try to arrange things in my mind I keep coming back to the conclusion, that I am in pretty deep shit.

While I am still thinking the door opens again. The same man from before comes in. He has his hair parted sharply to one side, like Prince Andrew. He sets down a tray of food on the desk. Sausage and chips, with the inclusion of some baked beans, ketchup and a tin of coke. He points to the writing pad and says, "Make a note of anything you think you may need, we'll try to get it for you. Somebody will be with you shortly, when you've finished eating."

I set about the food hungrily as he leaves the room. It has been a long day – I think. I wolf the food down in no time at all. I sit back light a cigarette and pick up the pen again; I start writing a list, the pen scratching in the quiet room.

- Some music – Theatre of Hate or Gun Club
- Some books - any
- Cigarettes - Raffles
- Clean underwear (boxers) and socks

This is all I can think of right now. I have the basic essentials for a sleepover. I put the pen down and tear the page from the pad. No sooner have I done this than the door opens again, not the man this time, but the lady who had met me from the van. She stands at the open door and asks, "Would you mind coming with me?"

"Where to?"

"Just some formalities, it won't take long."

"What formalities?"

"We need to check you're okay after the medication they gave you in the ambulance. Honestly, it doesn't matter how often we tell them to only use it if it's necessary, they seem to use it every time."

Every time? How often do they do this? Who else is here? Are Sarah, Stewart and Jo here too? And why did she call it an ambulance? It looked more like something from the A team to me. I follow her while these thoughts run through my mind. I walk behind her, absently watching her buttocks shift through the fabric of her trousers as she directs me to a new room. I am so focussed on her backside that I nearly walk into her when she stops. I realise that I have paid no attention to the direction we came or where we are in relation to my room. Not that it would have been useful knowledge, it is a mystery to me how she knows which of the unmarked red doors in the bland corridor she is taking me to. Nevertheless, she opens the door she has stopped by and holds it for me. I go in.

Inside is a windowless version of every doctor's surgery I have ever been in. There is a couch, a cupboard with various instruments and containers on top of it, and a desk with chairs on either side. On the far side of the room is a small sharp man with very little hair who invites me to sit on the chair facing him. As I step forward to do so the door clicks shut behind me. I look around and see that this door does have a handle on the inside, I wonder if I should try and leave. On some base level my instinct tells me that even though I haven't seen any guards there probably are some, and they were unlikely to just let me go after going to all that trouble to get me here. I sit.

On the desk in front of me lies a form and a pen.

"We'd like you to sign this please."

"What is it?" Thoughts rush into my head, is it a pre-typed confession? Me agreeing to be here indefinitely?

"It's just a standard consent form, so we can take some blood samples and complete some basic tests to check you are all tickety- boo."

I look at the form, and see that is exactly what it is. I sign it and push it back over the desk. The doctor picks it up with care and places it in a pile of its own, in the otherwise empty wire tray on his desk. He then turns to look at me over his glasses and asks in a serious and concerned voice,
"So, tell me exactly how you are feeling today. Please don't miss out any details, even if you think they're not important."

He leans on his desk as I start to answer his question and he nods as I speak, encouraging me to continue.

What follows is the most rigorous and extensive medical I have ever been involved with. At various times I am standing, lying, undressed, pissing in jars, blowing in tubes, standing on scales, being measured, having syringes poked in my arm and bending over. That last one is not one to remember, although I am sure I will have a hard time forgetting it. Everything is meticulously recorded, noted and checked; it feels like I have been here forever. Eventually the doctor gets up, walks to the door and opens it, thanking me as he does so. The woman is waiting by the door as it opens and leads me back to my room.

This time I pay a little more attention to my surroundings and a little less to her anatomy as we head down the corridor. It is more straightforward than I imagined, we take two left turns and are back at my room. I also realise now that I am paying closer attention that the doors are not unmarked, there is a tiny discrete number painted in red directly above each door frame. We get to my door, which I now see is number 3. The door is held open for me and I am asked if I want a cup of tea.
"Yes please."

I step into the room and see that my dinner plates have been taken away. There are also some new additions to the room. On the desk there is now a tape player and a small pile of tapes, there are also some books and a packet of cigarettes. On the bed is a neatly folded pile of fresh laundry. I move forward to examine them.

The books are all Agatha Christie's, including By the Pricking of My Thumbs, the one that I am currently reading. The tapes are Theatre of Hate – Live, Gun club – Miami and some Bauhaus and Killing Joke, all brand new. Whoever sorted these out knew what was in my pile on the shelf in my room, this selection echoed the mix of music I had there. Next, I checked out the clothes, plain tee shirts and straight leg jeans, all in my size, along with some underwear and socks as requested. My tea is delivered to me and I sit on the bed, light a cigarette and find my place in Agatha Christie.

I find it hard to focus on the book, the same thoughts keep running around in my head. Where am I? Who are these people? What the fuck's happening? I have decided that I am going to deny everything when they ask about the night of the storm. After all, that was what we all agreed. I worry that one of the others will tell all, and wonder how that will affect me. I wonder if the others are here, somewhere in this bizarre, silent building. I didn't see Sue after they took her out the room and don't know if she's here or still at college wondering where I've gone. I feel guilty for not having tried to protect her, although at least I didn't share the story with her. I recall with a shudder that I was going to the next day – or today as it is now.

I get up and cross the room to the door and press the buzzer.

"Where am I?"

"Someone will be with you shortly."

"Where are my friends?"

"Someone will be with you shortly."

"Can I speak to someone in charge?"

"Yes, someone will be with you shortly."

"What time is it?"

"Someone will be with you shortly."

"Can they bring me another cup of tea when they come?"

I don't wait for an answer, but go back over to the bed and pick up my book again. I stare at the page, reading the same paragraph several times before conceding that I am not going to make any progress with it today. I put it down and go back to the desk, where I tear the cellophane off the Bauhaus tape and put it in the player with the volume up high. I then sit back on the bed again with the music keeping me company.

I have not even finished listening to the second track when the door opens. Trousers lady comes in with a cup of tea. She puts it on the desk, turns off the tape player and swivels the chair to face me before sitting on it.

"I hear you have a lot of questions. That's fine, but I hope you will be patient and understanding when I tell you that I can't answer all of them right now, and neither can the control room staff," she points towards the metal grill. "Tomorrow you'll have a busy day and hopefully some of your questions will be answered then."

She smiles, and the smile seems warm and genuine. I want to argue and protest, but she has been so reasonable. Also, she's a grown up. In the small room I can smell her perfume, and now she is sat facing me I can see that she is attractive in a slightly-older-woman sort of a way, blue eyes and fair hair that seems to shine under the electric light, with just a trace of make-up. I nod and then ask, "Can I have something else to eat? I'm famished."

"Just press the buzzer and let them know what you want and they will get someone to bring it for you. We will do everything we can to make sure you're comfortable."

"Do you think I've got cholera?"

"You can go through that at your meeting tomorrow. But no, I think you're probably ok."

"How long will I be here?"

"I don't know, but I'm sure everything will be explained to you tomorrow, I know it's hard but try and get some rest."

For the first time I feel close to crying. I am alone and don't know where I am or what's happening. I look down at the floor and pick at my fingernails. The woman gets up and picks up my cup of tea which she brings to me, she puts it in my hand as she sits down next to me on the bed. I take it and she puts an arm around my shoulders. It is warm and comforting and feels good to have her next to me. I manage to stop the tears.

"It's okay. We're not going to hurt you. Everything will be sorted out and you'll be back to normal before you know it."

"Am I in trouble?"

"No, we just need to get some things sorted out. But I've already said more than I should have. Get some rest and it will all be explained - tomorrow."

She gets up and starts to walk towards the door. I want her back straight away, to feel her leaning against me again. She turns back and asks, "What do you want in your sandwich?"

"Cheese please."

"Someone will bring it in minute, try to get some rest."

Shirt and tie man duly arrives with the sandwich. He has also predicted my need for another cup of tea, which he places on the desk with the sandwich. He checks that I don't need anything else then leaves.

I try to take the woman's advice. After I have eaten the sandwich, I kick my boots off and lay down on the bed. Almost as soon as I have rested my head on the pillow the lights in the room dim. I close my eyes, pull the cover up and am soon falling asleep. I sleep fitfully, fully clothed, and toss and turn while the lights dim to almost nothing.

Chapter 13
In the belly of the machine

I wake abruptly. I don't know how much later, there being no clock to mark the passage of time or window to give clues about day or night. As soon as I stir, the lights start to gradually brighten. I get up and use the toilet, then splash my face with cold water in the sink. I ruffle my hair and look at myself in the mirror. I really need a shave, but no razor has been provided.

I sit on the chair, light a cigarette and wonder what the day is going to bring.

I don't have to wait for long. The door opens and shirt and tie man comes inside.

"How are you? Did you sleep well?"

"Fine, I guess."

"Would you like a cooked breakfast, or just some cereal?"

I wouldn't normally turn down a cooked breakfast, but today I feel slightly sick. I ask for Rice Crispies and toast with jam. Shirt and tie man takes my empty plate and cup from the desk, the door clicks shut and I decide the best way to face the day would be in some clean clothes. I am aware of being watched and go into the alcove where I strip off, put on some deodorant and clean pants socks and a red t-shirt. I put my own jeans back on and am sitting on my bed putting my boots on when shirt and tie man reappears with a tray carrying a bowl, spoon, toast and a cup of tea which he sets on the desk.

"Take your time. I'll be back when you're ready."

"Thanks."

I sit at the desk and eat my breakfast, my mind still swamped with unanswered questions. I finish the toast and light a cigarette, while I sit and drink my cup of tea. I have barely finished my last mouthful of tea and stubbed out my cigarette when the door opens again, shirt and tie man steps in and asks if I'm ready to get going. I can think of no other pressing engagements, so with some trepidation I get up and follow him out of the door.

This time I am more mindful of my surroundings and the room numbers, with no buttocks to distract me. We turn left then right. I am expecting us to turn right again at the next junction, in the same direction as yesterday, but we don't, we turn left and walk a short way down the empty corridor to what I see is room 17. Shirt and tie man opens the door for me.

"Go in and make yourself comfortable, someone will be along in a minute."

I go in and look around. Another windowless room, big like the doctor's room, but with less furniture. There is a desk set out from the wall with a chair on either side. In the other half of the room are two comfortable looking chairs with a low table between them. There is a large mirror set into the end wall and in the ceiling is the obligatory 'box with a camera hidden inside it' the same as the other rooms. It is as plain and unremarkable as the other rooms, with the same smell of cleaning fluid. This room also has a door handle on the inside.

I walk to the desk, pause then go back to the door to ask if I should sit at the desk or the coffee table. I open the door and look out, but the corridor is completely empty. Unsure what to do I go back to the desk and walk around to the far side of it, I sit in the bigger, more comfortable looking of the two chairs. I get up again and look at myself in the mirror, I ruffle my hair and rub the stubble on my chin which has now had several days to begin looking like a bad attempt at a beard.

I lean back in the chair and have hardly got comfortable when the door opens and a different man walks in. He is carefully balancing a tray with two mugs and a file on it, he pushes the door gently closed with his foot and walks over to the desk, smiling at me and putting the tray down with care as he sits on the free chair, with no comment about me taking the better one. He glances at the mugs and then slides one of them across the desk to me.

"Hi, I hope you slept well and have everything you need."

His voice is friendly with no discernible accent. He is taller than me, which doesn't mean a great deal, has a mostly bald head and is wearing a navy-blue shirt and grey trousers. Unremarkable in every way, just the sort of person you might see in any office. His face seems friendly, a small smile at the corner of his mouth and a look of genuine concern when he asked how I was.

"Fine thanks, are you going to tell me where I am?"

"There'll be plenty of time for that. I wanted to start by making sure we have all your details correct, is that OK?"

I bang my hand on the desk,

"Where am I?"

The man doesn't even flinch, and I think I may have gone too far by shouting.

He picks up his own mug and takes a sip, then puts it down and calmly opens the folder he brought with him. He then proceeds to read a list of details about me, asking me to confirm each one. To begin with it is very obvious things: name, date of birth, address, parents address, school attended. The sort of thing you might put on a job application. I confirmed the details as they were read out to me. But soon they began to become more oblique, my bank balance, names of friends, details of marches or demonstrations I had been on in the last few years.

"What is this?"

"We just want to make sure we've got all the relevant details we need."

"Why do you need to know all these things?"

"It just helps us, and it will help you get back if we have all the right information."

"It seems like you have all the information about me that there ever was."

"Okay, shall we move on?"

He sips his drink, and I mirror him, taking a drink from my mug of tea.

"Can you tell me if anything unusual has happened to you recently?"

"I was kidnapped in the middle of the night."

"Sure, I am aware of that, anything else?"

"Nothing really."

"What about the weekend you were at college? When you and your friends were decorating. Did anything happen then?"

I feign surprise, and then try to give the appearance of thinking carefully about the question. I take another drink of my tea and then shake my head slowly.

"I don't think so. It was a fairly quiet weekend really, apart from the storm."

"Can you talk me through what went on that weekend?"

"What do you mean?"

"Sorry, I wasn't clear, just tell me about what happened that weekend after you...."

He consults his folder.

"....Sarah, Stewart, Lisa and Jo met up at college?"

I drink the last of my tea then realise that I have left my tobacco back in my room.

"Can I pop back and get my cigarettes?"

"That's not a problem, if you hold on we'll sort that out for you. Start telling me about the weekend."

"Well," I start, "I got back after the others..."

At this point shirt and tie man comes in with a pack of cigarettes, a lighter and an ash tray which he puts on the desk in front of me then leaves. I light one and continue to relate the events of the weekend. I make everything as detailed as I can, only missing out a couple of details. As I talk the man makes notes in his pad. Once or twice he asks me to repeat something or to 'hold up' as he catches up with my tale. His note-taking is exemplary, he is certainly someone who I would borrow notes from if I had missed a lecture.

I finish recounting the events, adding some details and embellishments to give it authenticity. I am, in the end, pleased with myself for keeping to the plan and denying everything. I feel I have given a detailed account with enough truth in it to make it watertight. Blue shirt man quietly reads back through what he has written while I light another cigarette.

"Do you want another drink?"

"Yes please."

He does not do or say anything else, but a few minutes later shirt and tie man appears in the doorway with two mugs and a plate of biscuits. He sets them on the desk, takes the empty mugs and leaves without saying anything.

"Well, that was quite an interesting weekend, sounds like a lot of fun."

"It was."

"Can I ask you about the Saturday evening, the night of the storm?"

"What about it?"

He then asks if I saw anything or anyone on the way back from the Fox and Hounds, anything unusual or out of the ordinary? I go back over the same account I had given previously, it was dark, it was raining, I was drunk, we got soaked through to the skin. He nods as he checks that against his notes then asks if there had been anything odd at the pub. I can't think of anything that will distract attention away from us and briefly consider making up something preposterous, but quickly decide that this would lead to more questions so I leave it and shake my head.

"What about Lisa, how was she? Did she seem okay?

"What do you mean?"

"Well, you know her quite well don't you? Did she seem her usual self?"

"Yes, she was fine."

"No sign of her being ill then?"

"No, none at all, she seemed fine."

"Ok, that's good. Did she say anything about what she'd been doing in the summer?"

"Yes, she told us about the volunteering work she'd been doing."

"Yes, that's right. What about the other thing? The peace camp?"

I hesitate slightly, how much do they actually know? Surely they must know what happened, that we had done it. Or is he just fishing, hoping to get me to slip up. Well, I am determined to keep to our agreement. If none of us say anything how can they prove it? I light another cigarette.

"Yes, she did say about that. She went with her mum."

"Did she say anything else about it?"

"Not really."

"Did she tell you she'd been arrested?"

You really could knock me down with a feather at this point. I am truly flabbergasted. I shake my head and struggle to think of a response. Lisa, arrested? It really didn't seem possible or plausible.

"What for? How is she anyway, has anybody heard yet?"

"I'm afraid I don't have that information, I think she was arrested for trespassing."

He's a liar.

"Everyone will wonder where I am you know."

"I don't think anybody even knows you've gone yet."

"Sue knows."

I immediately wish I hadn't included Sue in this conversation. I wonder again if she is in a building like this, or maybe even in this very building. I ask if she is.

"I'm afraid I don't have that information either. But I do think it's just about time for some lunch."

As if on demand the door opens and Mr Shirt and Tie waits for me to come and join him. I turn back to Mr Blue Shirt,

"What do you mean, nobody knows?"

He just smiles, shuffles his papers back into the folder and leaves the room. Outside the door he crosses the corridor and goes through the door opposite, number 21. I catch a quick glimpse of a well-lit room with a bank of green filing cabinets, before the door closes and I turn and follow Mr Shirt and Tie back to room 3.

When I get back my clothes that I had abandoned on the floor are neatly folded on the end of my bed, which has been freshly made. There is a sandwich, some crisps, an apple and a can of coke on the desk and the pile of tapes has been added to. New additions are The Cure, Dire Straits and The Stranglers, I unwrap the Cure tape and put it on, cranking the volume up while I sit and eat my lunch. I am surprised that it is lunchtime already, although I am hungry enough to confirm it. I think about what Mr Blue Shirt has just told me about Lisa, she really is a dark horse – if it's true. I have no way of confirming that. But he did seem to know everything there was to know about me, so maybe it is true. I am also perplexed by his assertion that 'nobody even knows I'm gone yet.' Then I think of the times that people have gone away for weekends, visiting home or with friends, and nobody knew where they were or when they were getting back. Probably he was right, I could be gone for ages before anybody noticed.

This thought worries me, I lay down on the bed and close my eyes while I think about this and what it means for me. I am at their mercy, nobody knows where I am, nobody knows what happened and nobody knows or cares that I have been kidnapped. Except Sue, surely they can't have kidnapped her too? Paul? He would notice I was gone, he would ask questions. Or he would be very busy with Lesley and assume I was staying over at Sue's or that he was just keeping on missing me.

All this thinking is making me tired and I feel myself slide off into sleep as the music plays in the strange barren room, echoing off the walls and filling my head.

I wake and my heart is beating fast and I feel a cool sweat on my forehead. The tape player is still playing, so I have not slept for long, I get up and go to splash my face in the sink. I notice that there is now a razor in the small bathroom, I fill the sink, lather some soap, and shave. This routine activity helps calm me, feeling fresher I go back into the room and pick up Agatha. I try to read, but am still not really following the plot and my mind keeps wandering, going over the morning meeting and trying to make sense of what was going on. I put the book down and put on a different tape. I light a cigarette and press the buzzer to ask for a cup of tea.

While I wait I realise I have put on Dire Straits, it is reminding me of Sue. I quite like them, guilty pleasure, but they are more her sort of thing really. I put on some Bauhaus instead, which Sue hates, and wait for my tea. It is bought in shortly by trousers lady. She has also provided a plate of biscuits which she puts on the desk.

"Good afternoon, how are you feeling today?"

"Ok, apart from being locked up."

"Yeah, I kind of get that. The doctor wants to see you again later so that'll break things up. Is there anything else you need?"

"Can I get this weeks 2000AD?"

"I'll see if I can make that happen. Anything else?"

"Candide – by Voltaire."

She raises her eyebrows, but says nothing.

"And some high tops?"

I don't really know why I asked for them, I don't want to keep taking my DMs on and off, but could just have easily asked for some slippers – or walked around in my socks, it's not cold in here. Nevertheless, she tells me that it shouldn't be a problem and that she will see me later. I watch her leave, different trousers from yesterday, but still stretched pleasingly tight across her bum. The door closes and I let out a big sigh.

More time passes and the door swings open again. Trousers Lady is back. I get up and follow her to my appointment, hoping it is not as thorough and intrusive as it had been yesterday. We follow the route, which is now less disorientating; turn right, then right again and into room 16 where the doctor is waiting for me.

I have my temperature taken, various swabs and measurements and another few test tubes of blood. The doctor listens to my chest and tells me it would be a good idea to give up smoking. I think to myself that it would be a good idea for him to stop kidnapping people, but don't say it. When he sits down to write up his notes the door opens, it is Trousers Lady who appears to take me back to my room.

As we return I ask her what is in the other rooms. I am told that it is nothing I need to worry about.

"Are there other prisoners in them?"

"You're not a prisoner, and no, they're mostly offices, very boring really."

"What am I, if I'm not a prisoner?"

She laughs and opens my door, which we have now arrived at.

"Can I go out and get some fresh air?"

I haven't seen daylight for what feels like forever now, it is beginning to get claustrophobic.

"I'll ask, but don't get your hopes up, ok?"

I accept her answer and go into the room. There is a shoebox on the bed which I open straight away, a pair of Adidas baseball boots are inside – size 8. I sit down to take my boots off and notice a pile of magazines on the desk. Walking over with one boot on and one off, I find what looks like a years worth of 2000AD comics, a thick paperback book along with some more tapes. I sit on my bed to sort out my boots and put on my new trainers, then go over to investigate more thoroughly.

I put on some music and move the pile of comics to the bed where I prop myself against the wall with my pillow and get completely lost in the activities of Judge Dredd and Rogue Trooper. I am so absorbed that I jump with a start when the door opens. Trousers Lady lets herself in and sits on the desk chair, as she had done previously.

"Are those things ok?"

"Yeah, great. Did you ask about me going outside?"

"I did ask, it's not possible at the moment, but they will let you know when it is."

I shrug, I had expected as much.

"You look better now you've had a shave."

"Thanks."

"Do you want someone to come in and cut your hair too?"

I run my hand through my hair. Apart from me, nobody has cut it for over a year. I occasionally hack off bits that are bothering me, with whichever scissors come to hand. I don't want it cut, it has taken me a long time to cultivate this precise level of dishevelment. I shake my head.

"What's your name anyway?"

She looks at me, tilts her head at a slight angle and does the thing with her eyebrow again, one up, one down.

"I don't know anybody's names."

"You can call me Julia."

I suspect this is not really her name. I am okay with this, at least I have something to call her now. I decide that I will allocate my own names for the others.

"Thanks, Julia."

"You're welcome, I'll bring you something to eat in while."

"Thanks."

Julia leaves the room and I collect the notebook from my desk and start to make a list of all the people I had met so far;

- Trousers Lady
- Mr Shirt and Tie
- Doctor
- Blue shirt man
- White suits

I then start to give names to the people on the list;

- Trousers lady – Julia
- Mr Shirt and Tie –Andrew Prince
- Doctor - Doc
- Blue shirt man –Torquemada
- White suits – storm troopers

I am not sure about them, but once they were on paper they stuck in my head – so now everybody had a name. I keep the pad on my lap, turn the page and start to doodle small people around the edge of the page, stick people representing all the friends and family that I have been taken from. I wonder when or if I will see them again, I turn to a new page where I start to formulate a sad poem. I wonder, not for the first time, where the others are and if they are okay – especially Lisa.

Julia comes back later, with a tray loaded with roast dinner, a small gravy boat, salt and pepper and a tin of beer. I ask Julia if this means it's Sunday already. Now it is her turn to shrug. She tells me to enjoy my meal and retreats again. I do enjoy it, picking the bones clean and eating every scrap. I wash it down with cold beer, my first in a while.

The evening, if that's what it is, passes quietly and slowly. I start reading Voltaire, I'm glad it's in English but it's still quite heavy going. Eventually I give up and read comics instead. I spend some time trying to write anguished poetry and I smoke. Eventually I feel tiredness creeping up on me and surrender to sleep.

I dream of storms, lightning and thunder, with trees falling around me as I struggle to find my way through a forest. In the undergrowth and the shadows, eyes watch me. Under the sound of the storm are faint growling noises. Branches whip my face as I blunder blindly onwards and eventually come to a clearing. In the clearing is the cylinder.

It is calm in the clearing. The cylinder has grown to the size of a house and the storm seems to be emanating from its top, sending bright flashes and ominous rumbles of thunder out across the clearing into the roiling clouds in the darkened sky. Then it is raining, it pours and runs down everything in runnels and rivulets that reflect the near constant eye-burning flashes of light.

Lisa steps out from behind the cylinder. She sees me and takes a step towards me smiling, and then she stops as if she has seen something else behind me. I look back, but when I turn again Lisa opens her mouth to speak, and blood gushes out. An endless stream of crimson pouring down her front and mixing with the puddles on the ground. I turn and run back into the storm, closing my eyes.

When I open them again, I am in bed with Sue, she is caressing me and kissing my face. But her face keeps changing, morphing into Julia's face and then back. I reach out to touch her breasts, but as I do so her face changes again. This time it is Lisa's face that looks at mine, blood seeping from her eyes, nose and the corners of her mouth.

I wake up with tears streaming down my face and my heart beating its own tattoo. I kick the sweaty covers onto the floor and look for a drink. While I slept the lights had been dimmed to near darkness, as I fumble all I can find is an unfinished tin of beer on the desk. Instead, I go to the sink and put my head under the tap, drinking large gulps of cold water and washing my face. I get back into the bed, pick up the covers, pull them over myself and try to sleep again.

Alice

Alice has been watching the new visitor carefully, making sure he is settled, and not inclined to hurt himself. From what she has heard all of the decorators are now being cooperative and not making any waves. Also, thankfully, none of them appear to be sick. It is almost as if they were expecting this, like they wanted to be caught and were relieved that it has finally happened. Of course, smoking boy still hasn't actually admitted it, but that was just a matter of time, soon he would be confronted with the fact that one of the others had told them everything there was to tell.

It is customary, when visitors arrive, to give them names by which they will be referred in communications and reports. These are usually decided in advance, but the short lead-in time meant she had not yet allocated a name. Dan took one look at him in his ripped jeans and leather jacket on the CCTV and announced to everyone in the control room, "Look, it's Sid Vicious!"

By the time Julia had got him to his room the name 'Sid' had already been adopted by the team. It's as good as any, she shrugs and goes with it.

Her notebook is full of observations about what he has been doing, eating, asking and saying. What she has not been able to record is how lost and bewildered he looks. How he seems to be scared to death but is still trying to protect his friends, or himself, and is keeping himself busy between interviews.

She was amazed at how he has managed to make so much mess in such a short amount of time, and with so few belongings. The pile of comic books next to Candide is a striking juxtaposition, she wonders what the unfathomable reason is that made him ask for the Voltaire text. She reads what is written in his pad and is delighted to see that he has allocated names to everybody, it seems he is ahead of the curve on this. She will enjoy putting that in her report, some unintended retribution on Dan for lumbering him with Sid. She is also glad she told him she was called Julia, sparing her the indignity of a nickname.

She walks past the room again later and hears the music echoing around clearly through the door, it's awful. She doesn't know why he doesn't listen to the Dire Straits tape instead. She carries on to the control room where Dan is sitting with Bob, the tech guy, in front of a bank of TV screens showing various parts of the building. The main screen shows the interior of room 3, where nothing much is happening. Smoking boy is doing exactly that, sitting on his bed reading and smoking. Dan looks up as she comes in and taps Bob's arm.

"Here she is Bob, show her what you showed me."

Bob visibly blushes and says, "Nah, she won't be interested."

"She will, she's interested in everything this boring little specimen of hers is doing."

Julia bristles, but says nothing.

"Nah, it's nothing really."

"Maybe you should show me, I'll decide if it's important or not, he's my guest."

Dan giggles and Bob picks up a video cassette from his bench and loads it into a machine. He rewinds it to the start and then presses play. Alice is perplexed, all it shows is her and Sid walking along corridors. It is a compilation of the various short journeys they have made together. Then suddenly she sees it, now it is her turn to blush. Every step of the way he is in danger of tripping as he keeps his eyes firmly glued to her bottom. If it had been a cartoon his eyes would have been bulging out and his tongue would be flapping from the side of his mouth.

Dan laughs out loud and Bob shifts uncomfortably. Alice takes stock and watches to the end of the short tape then says, "I'll add it to my report, thank you gentlemen."

Now Bob asks if there's anything he can do, it reminds Alice of her actual reason for coming in.

"Bob, can you keep a close eye on him when he sleeps, when I was observing last night he seemed to be having nightmares, I don't want him any more unsettled than necessary."

"Probably dreaming about your cheeks," says Dan, still smirking.

"Shut up Dan. Can you do that tonight please Bob?"

"Sure, do you want me to wake you if it happens again?"

"Yes please, thank you."

She leaves the room and goes back to her office and writes up her notes, she makes sure she positions the information about 'Andrew Prince' at the top of a page, where she is certain nobody will skim past it. As she reads back through what she has written she is taken again by how composed he is in spite of his situation. She has had seasoned political activists and terrorists who have handled this situation with less composure or grace. True he's scruffy and untidy, but there's a certain charm there, an underlying gentleness and kindness that she sees in him.

Chapter 13 (continued)

A cursory knock precedes my door opening as the lights come back on. It is Mr Shirt and Tie – Andrew Prince– bringing in a cup of tea and putting it on the desk.

"Morning, sleep well?"

"So so."

I get up and light a cigarette, holding that in one hand and my tea in the other.

"What would you like for breakfast?"

"Toast, marmite, sugar puffs."

"No problem, back in a minute."

Andrew Prince leaves the room and I finish my cigarette and drink my tea. I am still sitting at the desk with the remains of my tea when he returns and puts my breakfast on the table.

"I'll be back shortly, you've got another meeting soon."

He leaves again and I eat my breakfast in silence then head into the cubby hole to wash up and clean my teeth before getting dressed. I am just lacing my new trainers when Andrew Prince comes back in.

"All ready then?"

I'm not really, I didn't sleep well. The edges of dreams are still clawing at my memory, trying to get back out. I have no desire to be interviewed again, I would rather be back at college getting on with my normal life. I am still committed to keeping up our cover story, nothing happened. But a part of me wonders, if I tell the truth will they let me get back to normal? Would they be able to sort everything out and return things to how they were? Or, more likely, would they keep me locked up here forevermore?

I follow Andrew Prince out of the door and back to room 17, where I am let in and asked to wait, as before. This time I go in and sit on one of the comfy chairs, my claiming of the desk chair yesterday now seems childish and unimportant. I slump back and wait.

I am expecting Torquemada to come in, but when the door opens it is not him. It is another man for whom the name Torquemada would have been even more appropriate. He is tall with a hooked nose, piercing eyes and grey hair. He has a slight stoop and glides over to the chair facing mine with file in hand. No cup of tea from this inquisitor then, I light a cigarette and wait for him to start.

"You gave us a very detailed description of the weekend you were decorating the college."

"Thank you."

"Just a few details I want to go over."

He opens the file, shuffles through some of the paper inside and then starts to ask a number of questions about how I got there, who arranged it, how come I had been involved and who else was around college at the time?

I answer these questions perfunctorily, we had covered them yesterday. He asks a peculiar question about what I was wearing on the night of the storm, for a moment I am disorientated, but I recover myself and do my best to recall exactly what I had been wearing. I think I have done a good job, it's not like I had many clothes with me to remember. I lean forward to stub my cigarette in the ash tray and he asks, "Why didn't you tell us you slept with Sarah that night?"

It was asked in such a casual way that it almost seemed like an irrelevance, but the implication that they knew more about the evening was clear.

"How did you know that?"

No answer.

"We didn't sleep together, we shared a bed, because we were cold."

"I'm sure, but why didn't you tell us that yesterday?"

"Because it's none of your business."

There is a pause; the man looks directly into my eyes. I find it hard to hold his gaze and look away.

"Everything is our business. Now, think hard, is there anything else that happened that you haven't told us?"

They know. They know everything. I don't know how, but they do. I try to think of how I can make this right, how I can sort out the whole mess. I sit and say nothing.

"Can we go back over the evening and add some of the missing details?"

I still say nothing. Torquemada 2 picks up his file and starts to read aloud the sequence of events on that night. He gets to the part where we stumble drunkenly out of the pub and start to make our way home, then stops reading and looks up at me,

"So, what happened then, on your way back to college?"

I still don't answer.

"You do know this is serious, don't you?"

I nod.

"Good, fill in the missing details for me, don't spare the horses. I'll give you a clue, there was a flatbed train carriage on the railway line that wasn't there earlier in the evening."

This is it, the game's up, they really do know everything.

"How much trouble am I in?"

"How much do you think?"

I look at my feet.

"How do you know it was us?"

"We just do, we know everything that happened. But it's really important that you tell it to me in your own words, the whole story - with nothing left out this time."

For the first time his voice has softened and he gives me an encouraging half smile, which I assume is the best he can do. I light another cigarette and ask, "Are the others alright?"

"Fine."

"And Lisa?"

"I don't know, if I did I would tell you."

I don't believe him, but I am relieved that the others are okay.

"It was nothing to do with Sue you know. She didn't know anything about it."

He nods slowly, gives me the same half-smile as before and says, "Just run through the details for us, maybe it will help if you start from when you were in the pub and go through everything from there, try not to leave anything out this time."

I resign myself to whatever is going to happen next, it makes me feel sick that I am about to betray the others – but I don't see any way out of this. I retell the whole sorry tale, leaving nothing out this time. Torquemada 2 does not interrupt me once. I try not to put any blame on anyone else, but also try not to implicate myself too much. It was a catalogue of collective poor decision making and I try to convey that in my recount.

Now there are questions;

"How long do I think we carried it for?"

"How long was Lisa in the water?"

"Did everybody touch the cylinder?"

"Where else did we put it down?"

I do my best to answer them. I come to a long pause in an answer, with nothing extra to add. Torquemada 2 abruptly nods, thanks me, puts everything back in the file and exits the room, leaving me sitting there, drained, wondering what I should do next.

The question is answered for me when Andrew Prince opens the door and says, "Come on then, lunch."

I am not hungry. I feel sick to the pit of my stomach. I don't answer, but just walk back to room 3 and let myself in, the door is closed behind me. I sit silently on the bed holding my head in my hands.

Minutes later the door opens again and Andrew Prince comes in with a plate of sandwiches, a chocolate bar and some fruit. He places them and a tin of coke on the desk and says, "Call if you need anything." Then he leaves.

A short while after he has gone, I go to get the drink from the desk. In spite of myself I am hungry, I sit and eat the sandwich, then polish off the rest before going back and lying on the bed with the ashtray balanced on my chest and a cigarette in my hand.

The afternoon brings another appointment with Doc. Julia takes me to him but makes no small talk. Things have changed since this morning, I'm not sure how, but they have. I hear a door closing in another part of the building, out of sight. The sound only serves to emphasise the pervasive silence.

Doc does his usual, thorough inspection. This time he takes some skin scrapings from various parts of me and takes several swabs from my nose and mouth, meticulously sealing them up and writing labels for their test tubes. He doesn't speak a word other than to tell me what I need to do to facilitate his efficient completion of his tasks.

When he is finished, I am taken back to my room. I ask Julia what will happen next,
"I don't know, I'm just here to make sure you're comfortable and looked after."

I suspect this may not be entirely true, I am sure her role is more significant than she is telling me. Everyone knows what I have done, and everyone knows what an idiot I am. I sit down, put on some Cure and read comics, only half concentrating on what I am doing as I run through the possible consequences of my actions in my mind. I am worried that I will be kept in this place forever.

Alice

O'Brien is sitting alone in room 18, Alice walks across the room to join him at the table. She sits down and waits for him to look up from his notes, which he does momentarily.

"Hello Alice, how are you?"

"I'm fine thanks, and you?"

"I'll be happier when this is resolved, you know why you're here don't you?"

Alice does, O'Brien wants to know what she thinks they should do with Sid. He had already spoken to Jones and Dan, now it was her turn to have a say.

"I'm putting a great deal of weight in your opinion. Partly because you've got to know him better than the rest of us, and partly because I trust your instincts, especially about people."

"Thank you, sir. Do we know what the other centres have decided yet?"

"They're all waiting for us to make a decision. Dan thinks we should lock them up and throw away the key. Jones said he would defer to you on this, he has a lot of faith in your judgement too."

Alice tries not to show her surprise, not about Dan, that was entirely predictable. That Jones should think she was best placed to make the call was unexpected, and flattering. Although she was certain it was not intended to flatter her.

"They had opinions of course, and gave me some useful background. But I really want to know what you think before I decide."

"Well, I think he's not an immediate danger to anybody at all. But what he knows could be dangerous at worst, embarrassing at best, if it ever got out. If we just send him back to where he was, there is a very real possibility that he will end up telling someone something. He needs a fresh start. If we prepped his family properly, they could support him."

"You've given this some thought, haven't you? Not that I'd expect anything less." There is a small smile as O'Brien says this, he waits expectantly.

"Actually, yes sir. I have had some ideas about how it could be done. I think it would be possible for him and the others to be relocated with very little fuss. It would require a lot of supervision. But if the others are like him, which I have heard they are, they have all had the shit scared out of them. They're young and adaptable and will be desperate not to be in any more trouble than they are already. If we provide them with cover stories and make sure they know we are watching them I think it's entirely doable."

"I assume you have a plan written up for this?"

"Yes sir."

"Good, pass it to Mrs Baker would you, we can all have a look over it before our next meeting. For what it's worth, I think you're right. I don't see a bad kid in those interview tapes, it would be a shame to make this any worse than it needs to be."

Mrs Baker takes the folder from Alice without asking what it is, she already knows. Inside the stack of paper are details of how the decorators could be safely moved out of the centres, how they could be supported financially and with new college placements, as well as what the potential risks are, and how to mitigate them. Alice thinks she has thought of everything. The only missing piece of the puzzle is how they can be given the emotional support they need. None of them knew about Lisa yet, although they surely suspected. There was no way of knowing how the trauma would affect them.

On her way back to her office Alice stops and looks into the control room to ask Bob how things are going.

"He's sleeping. Do you want me to turn his lights up so you can have a better look?"

"No, let him sleep, he's got a big day tomorrow. Let me know when he wakes will you?"

"Sure thing."

"Thanks Bob, you're a star."

She goes on back to her office and sits at her desk. The only decorative item is a small silver frame containing a black and white photo of her parents on their wedding day, both looking impossibly young, him in his uniform, her in a wedding dress. 'Is it what you would have done dad?' She likes to think it is.

Chapter 13 (continued)

There is a knock on the door. I assume it will be Julia with my tea. It is not, the door opens and Torquemada walks in carrying a folder. He steps over to the desk, opens the folder and places a small bundle of papers on the desk.

"I want you to read through this, when you have time."

"What is it?"

"It will be clear when you have a chance to look. It's important. Goodbye."

He leaves the room and, intrigued, I put down my comic and go over to have a look. The first page has the letters OSA printed in bold capitals, underneath this the words 'Official Secrets Act' are neatly typed. I feel slightly sick, of course I have heard of this. This is the special laws they have for spies and such. I know that there are things I can be jailed or even executed for, even now that capital punishment is banned. I can't imagine what I have done has breached this, I have never signed it. I sit at the desk and start reading.

It is a dense document that uses a lot of legal language that I struggle to understand in places. It takes some time and I have to concentrate hard. I buzz for a cup of tea which Julia passes in to me and departs quickly, then I sit and smoke my way through the remainder of the document.

Torquemada was wrong. It does not become clear to me. I get to grips with some of the basic ideas, like it is expected that you will not do something stupid or dangerous that might put the country at risk. It is not just for spies, it applies to everyone. I think I'm starting to get the point here, taking the cylinder could have been one of those things. I am still not wholly sure, and trying to make sense of some of the different sections is confusing and hard work. I put it back down on the desk, lean back and stare at the wall.

Now Julia comes and asks what I want to eat. I ask her if she has read the document in front of me. She nods. I ask if she can help me go through it.

"The boss will go through it with you tomorrow."

I wonder who the boss is, Blue Shirt or Torquemada. I ask for something with chips and Julia disappears off to organise it. I leaf through the document again, but I am no longer taking in the meaning of the jumble of words.

The rest of the evening was less eventful than the afternoon, if that's possible. When Julia comes to collect my plates and empty mugs she sits on the chair. It feels good to be in her proximity and I sense a slight softening in her attitude from earlier. She asks if I am ok.

"Not really. Will I be here forever?"

"I wouldn't think so. I think there are still some things to sort out though."

"What will happen next?"

"I think that depends, hopefully the boss will be able to talk about it with you."

"What then?"

"Honestly, I don't know. Try and get some sleep and see what he says tomorrow."

I don't think I will get to sleep, but I do. No dreams tonight, just restless tossing and turning that leaves the bed looking dishevelled and crumpled in the morning.

*

I wake up feeling barely refreshed and decide to shower and shave before having a cigarette. Some clean underwear and a fresh tee shirt help me to feel more awake and Andrew Prince arrives with a steaming mug of tea soon after I am done. He is as chatty as ever, leaving the room before I have even picked the mug up from the desk.

"Toast and Cocoa Pops?" he asks on his way out.

"Bacon sandwich please."

"Sure thing."

The door closes and I wait for my day to begin. For the first time my mind turns to my family, will I see them again? Will they start to look for me? And if so, when? This chain of thought leads me to think about Sue and I wonder when I will see her again, I sit and I wait and I chew at my nails when I'm not smoking.

Andrew Prince eventually collects me to meet the boss. I expected to go to room 17 again, but we walk straight past it, along the silent empty corridor to room 18. He lets me in to the room, where the boss is waiting behind a large wooden table and several chairs. The table looks like a dining table and is incongruous in the largely empty room. The boss, it turns out, is not Torquemada. He is a broad-chested man in a grey suit with a dark red tie. He has a round face with dark hair swept to one side and an expression that seems to veer between welcoming and threatening, without actually changing.

"Sit down," he says in a deep voice.

I sit in the vacant chair across the table from him. He is straight to the point,

"Did you read the papers I sent to you yesterday?"

I nod.

"Did you understand them?"

"I think so."

"Do you want me to clarify for you?"

"Yes please."

He then leans forward with both elbows on the desk and his hands clasped in front of him and explains, clearly and concisely, how the taking of the cylinder, which he refers to as 'our property', constitutes a breach of 'The Act' and how this could result in a prison sentence for me. Now I am scared, I never meant for any of this to happen. I certainly don't want to go to prison, being here is bad enough.

"Is there anything I can do to make things right?" I ask hopefully. Maybe I can get away with a fine or something? "Will this mean I'm not allowed to teach?"

The boss leans back in his chair and appears to give the matter some thought. He pours a glass of water from a jug on his desk and passes it to me, then pours another for himself, taking a drink and setting the glass down directly in front of himself.

"Here's the thing, there are some people who would really rather not draw any more attention to what has happened than is necessary. Do you understand?"

I think I do. I nod.

"In fact, there are some people who would really like to make it seem as if nothing has happened."

He pauses and looks at me, clearly expecting and waiting for a response.

"I understand."

I'm not sure I do entirely, but it seems like the best thing to say.

"So, this is what is going to happen."

He looks me directly in the eye again, to make sure he has my full attention. As if I would be thinking of anything else right now. I'm about to find out how much trouble I'm in and what my fate will be. I look at the table, my heart is beating fast and I have a dry mouth in spite of the water I had just drunk. I take another sip and answer, "Ok."

He clears his throat, takes another sip of his own water, and starts.

"There are a number of people who are very embarrassed about this whole incident. It is their opinion that the best way to make sure nobody ever finds out is to deny it. However, they can't do this if people that were there when it did happen are able to tell other people that it did. Are you following me?

I am, I nod. I have a terrible feeling that I am about to find out that I will be staying here, for some time.

"So, these are our options. One, we can just keep you here. I don't think that's ideal, it's costing us a lot to house and feed you and you would probably go insane through boredom, once you had finished all your comic books."

I detect a slight hint of condescension at this. Maybe some sympathy as well. I'm not sure that I'm really picking up all the unspoken signals here, I am confused, I'm sweating too much and my eyes are not quite focused.

"Two, we can send you to a regular prison. But then you will be asked awkward questions about why you are there, and as mentioned previously there are people who would rather that information wasn't out there. Which leaves option three. Option three is you go back to your ordinary life. You live just as you would have done if nothing had ever happened, and you never speak about any of this."

"Really? Is that an option?"

"Absolutely. There would be some conditions of course and your life couldn't be exactly the same. But basically, that's the offer."

"Okay."

"You really need to understand what you are agreeing to."

I consider the three options and only one of them seems to be in any way agreeable, I can't really see what the downside would be. I certainly don't want to stay here, wherever 'here' is, never seeing daylight again. Going to prison does not sound like a good option either, although I have no real idea what that would be like other than from watching the films Scum and McVicar. I am fairly confident that my decision is going to stay the same whatever the small print says.

"What am I agreeing to?"

"I'll tell you later, I need to check some things first. Let's go and get some lunch and we'll meet again later. It seems early for lunch, but who knows in this timeless place. Right on cue Andrew Prince opens the door and I follow him back to my room, where there are sandwiches and a drink waiting for me.

When the door opens again it is Julia. I am glad, I prefer her to Andrew Prince, she's prettier for a start, and also, she talks to me more. Today she is smiling again, I guess not as disappointed with me as she had been yesterday. I follow her, hanging back very slightly to catch a glimpse of her behind as we set off up the corridor.

"Am I going to see the boss again?"

"No, the doctor, just routine stuff."

"Will I see the boss after that?"

"I'm not sure, I'll see if I can find out while you are in with Doc,"

We are at the door now, I let myself in and am already in the room before I realise that Julia just used my nickname for the doctor. I may just be being paranoid, it is a common nickname for doctors after all. But I think she might have been looking in my notebook.

Doc goes through the now routine business of checking me over from head to toe. He asks me how I'm feeling, listing a range of possibilities such as nausea, dizziness, headaches and loss of taste or smell for me to consider. He takes all the usual samples and asks if he can take a bit of my hair. I agree and he snips off a small lock from somewhere near the back which he puts into a labelled test tube. He then gets me to perform a range of tasks, including an eye test, a balance test and some tapping of various parts of me with his hands and a small rubber hammer. Eventually he is done, he sits at his desk to write his notes up and Julia comes to the door to take me back.

"When will I see the boss?"

"Soon, he has some other things to do first. Go back and have a cup of tea and I'll be back shortly."

She sees me into my room, where there is a cup of tea waiting. I light a cigarette and sit down to wait.

It may have been no time at all, it may have been hours, it may have been minutes. I have no way of telling. Julia opens the door for me. My heart is beating fast as I anticipate the prospect of going home. I don't imagine it will be immediate, but it's happening and I hurry, walking briskly out of my room.

Julia leads me back to room 18. Inside it is sterile and windowless with bright tube lights casting a fierce white light over everything. The large table now has a row of chairs on one side and a single chair on the other, facing them. The chairs are populated by the boss, Torquemada and Andrew Prince, Julia walks around to fill the final chair and I sit facing them. I am now quite nervous. I had expected it to be just the boss again, not this panel. There are no smiles in the room, it is how I would imagine a courtroom to look. I cross my legs and await their judgement.

The boss has two small piles of paper in front of him, apart from that the table is empty. He clears his throat and starts to speak. He is all business now. He straightens the piles of paper, looks around to check that everybody is ready and then looks directly at me. His gaze is piercing, his face is serious.

"Did you have chance to think over what we talked about this morning?"

"Yes, I did. Can I really go home?"

"Yes, you can, we'd like that."

The others nod in assent. I smile, but nobody smiles back and I know that there's more to come. I take a breath and try to keep my voice level.

"Okay, and I'm not allowed to tell anybody about what happened."

"It's more complicated than that. There need to be some rules I'm afraid."

I nod. I can work with this, as long as I get out of here. I look at the two piles of paper and wonder if they are the rules. Both piles have a blank sheet on top, no clues there. Nobody else is contributing to the discussion. They are all deferring to the boss. He carries on,

"There will be some big changes. You need to be perfectly clear about this, there are other people who did not want to offer you this opportunity, but I hate to see a young life go to waste. If you can't keep to the rules you will end up back here, or somewhere worse."

"I understand."

I actually don't yet. I have the general gist, but can't imagine what they expect of me. How bad could it be? I shudder inwardly at the thought of spending more time here. I think I would agree to anything right now.

"First, you will be asked to sign The Official Secrets Act, just to be clear you have had a chance to read it, if you have any questions about any part of it you need to ask now."

I think of the folder in my room, currently residing underneath some 2000 AD comics. I'm pretty sure I understood most of it, the bits I read anyway. I don't think I really have that many official secrets to divulge, only the one.

"No, no questions."

"Good."

The boss removes the top sheet from the stack and slides the remainder across the table to me, I can see it is identical to the one in the folder in my room. He shows me a separate sheet. There is some blurb about agreeing to all and forthwith etcetera etcetera. At the bottom is a space for me to sign, and a space for witnesses to countersign. The boss is holding out a silver pen to me, I take it and sign. He then takes the pen back and adds his own signature, the sheet then gets passed along the table with the other people adding their own signatures. I try to see what their actual names are, but they are either too far away for me to see clearly, or indecipherable squiggles.

The paper ends up back with the boss who checks it over, squares it up, and passes it to Julia who leaves the room with it while everybody else sits in silence and waits for her to return. She comes back moments later and sits back in her chair, adjusting it slightly before settling. She looks at me and I think I detect the hint of a smile before her face resumes its previous sombre expression.

"Good, that's the first bit of business out of the way."

The boss now takes the second pile of papers and pulls them towards himself, turning over the top sheet. There is a page of handwritten notes underneath. The handwriting is not legible from where I am sitting, although I feel sure I am about to find out soon anyway, so I don't try too hard. I sit back and wait.

"Firstly, there are going to be some changes, as I said before. The first stipulation is that you will have no further contact with Sarah, Stewart or Jo. Is that clear?"

"What about Lisa?"

The previous silence in the room seems to grow an extra degree of quiet now. Nobody apart from the boss makes eye contact with me.

"Nobody will be making contact with Lisa anymore. I'm sorry."

I take a moment to process the implication of this. Did he really mean what I think he did? I remember that last time I saw her, wearing odd shoes and lying in a pool of her own blood, not moving or making any sounds. Was that really it? Was it my fault? I feel a tear trickle down the side of my face and I am struggling to hold back a tsunami. The boss nods to Julia again who leaves the room and returns moments later with a box of tissues, she puts them in front of me and puts an arm around my shoulder and whispers, "I'm really sorry."

The boss suggests we all take a short break and get a cup of tea. I am crying properly now, wiping away snot and tears with handfuls of tissues, I neither agree nor disagree with the suggestion. The others get up and leave the room, leaving me with the boss and Julia, who still has a hand on my shoulder.

"Everybody did what they could, but it was too late, there was nothing that could be done." says the boss.

"What the fuck was that thing?" I ask through sniffles and barely stifled anger.

There is no answer to this, Julia gives my back one last rub and resumes her seat as the others come back and take theirs. They bring back cups of tea and biscuits. I take the mug that is offered to me and take a sip as I recompose myself. Once everyone has settled again the boss resumes,

"That's the next thing, no questions. You can't ask anybody about the event, that's why we don't want you to contact the others. It is not a topic for discussion."

There is emphasis on the word 'not' which does not pass me by, I nod.

"As far as you are concerned, and as far as anybody else knows, nothing happened that weekend. I cannot stress this enough, there are people way more important than me who are quite clear on this point, nothing happened."

"Nothing happened? What about Lisa, what if people ask me that?"

"They won't. This is the most important thing for you to remember, rule one. Do you think that's possible?"

It feels wrong. It feels like I'm betraying Lisa. A part of me wants to say 'this is wrong!' But another part of me is scared. Scared of what will happen to me if I say no, scared of what might happen if I make a mistake, scared that the same thing that happened to Lisa will happen to me. I don't know if it's possible, but I say yes anyway.

"We know that this isn't going to be easy for you, we are prepared to offer you some help."

"What kind of help?"

"We'll keep an eye on you. We'll keep a very close eye on you. We'll make sure you're never tempted to tell anybody. This means we will be watching you. Whatever you may think about our ability to do that, forget it. We have extensive resources, our friends who want this kept quiet have made sure of that. You will be visited regularly and reminded of your side of the deal, and expected to cooperate fully with that."

He indicated Andrew Prince and Julia.

"They will become a part of your life. You will see them from time to time. Even when you don't see them, they will see you, they will know everything that you are doing."

Andrew Prince and Julia both look at me and nod with serious expressions. They are my new best friends. I had imagined that when I left I would never see any of these people again, but it looks as though Andrew Prince and Julia are in this for the long haul. I had thought their job was mostly about getting me food and taking me from place to place, I was wrong about that then.

The boss continues,

"You will have a contact number, you can ring it at any time. You need to let us know if anything out of the ordinary happens, if anyone asks you questions, if you are moving house, if you are travelling abroad. Anything you think we should know. You are now what we call 'a person of interest'."

He stops, seeming to have run out of information to give me. He looks up and down the table and asks if anybody else wants to add anything, they don't. He looks at me and asks if I have any questions. I am quite overwhelmed with what I have already been told. I think about it then ask, "Am I going to die?"

Julia answers, "Not according to the doctor, thankfully all of your test results came back okay. You are fit as a fiddle, although you may want to give up smoking."

I don't know what else to say, I look around at their faces. I want someone to tell me it will be okay, that I will be alright. I want someone to tell me what I should do. I want to go home.

"One last thing," says the boss, "nobody knows you are here, but some people will have noticed you were gone. To help you stick to the same story we have provided some case notes from a clinic. Tell people you were there, tell them you had an anxiety attack after what happened to Lisa, a mini breakdown if you will. Everybody will be very understanding. Keep to the same story and tell anyone who asks that you'd rather not talk about it."

He pushes a brown envelope across the table to me. Then he takes a business card, with a single phone number printed on it, from his pocket and places it on top of the envelope.

I nod, then sit in silence as the group stand up and leave the room at some unseen signal, filing out in a silent procession and leaving me with Julia who smiles for the first time.

"Not so bad then eh?"

"I don't know really."

"Come on, let's go and get you sorted."

I follow her back to my room, where a holdall has been placed on the end of the bed.

"Anything you want to take with you put it in there."

"Most of it's not mine."

"It is now, take whatever you need."

I rummage through the belongings I have accumulated. I put in the trainers, Candide, some of the comics that I have not read yet and one or two of the tapes that I don't already have at home. I leave the Agatha Christie books. I have had enough mysteries for now. I feel numb and my head is swirling, still processing the information I have been given. When I am done Julia asks if I want something to eat before I go, as it will be a long journey.

I have barely finished eating when Julia returns and tells me to come with her. I follow her down the corridor where the double doors are waiting. Julia opens the door and for the first time in ages I see daylight, it is bright afternoon daylight that dazzles me and makes me blink and look away as I am guided into the back of what looks like the same vehicle I came in. The same storm trooper who bought me here is waiting, no white suit this time, just a rugby shirt and jeans. He has a barrel chest and thick muscled arms. Again, I catch glimpses of golden moorland stretching out towards an improbably blue sky peppered with clouds, a gentle puff of wind brushes my face before I am in the back of the ambulance.

I look back at Julia,

"He's not going to drug me again, is he?"

"He'd better not or I'll have his guts for garters."

She smiles at me and the man. I think she may have been joking but I'm not sure. She passes me a packet of cigarettes that I put into my jacket pocket.

"For the journey, travel safe, I'll be seeing you soon."

With that she turns and walks back inside the building, giving me one last glimpse of her backside before my escort slams the doors shut and bangs on the roof of the van. The engine starts and we move off.

Chapter 14
No place like home

The journey seems to take an age. Without clocks and watches there's no way of telling, it feels interminable. I retrieve some comics from the side pocket of my bag and read; the escort just sits in silence. At one point I ask if we can stop to use a loo. He produces a plastic bottle from one of the cubby holes and politely looks away as I fill it. He then puts a cap on it and places it back in the cupboard as the van carries on its relentless journey.

At times we are driving along endlessly straight roads. Other times we weave and slalom as though we are on a roller coaster. As the journey progresses the sounds of other traffic changes from non-existent, to intermittent, to regular. All the while I feel a palpable sense of relief as I leave the prison further and further behind me.

Finally, the van comes to a halt. The escort gets up and opens the door, and the evening sunlight floods in, dazzling me. When I regain the use of my eyes, I see we are at the bus stop at the top of the drive.

"You don't want us driving you in for everyone to see do you?"

I don't, I don't want anybody to ask me any questions about where I've been. I would also quite like the chance to stretch my legs after so long without having anywhere to walk. I turn to the escort.

"What day is it?"

"Sunday, you're in time for church."

He smirks, gets out after me and passes me my bag before shutting the door. He then walks to the front of the van and climbs into the passenger seat.

"See you then."

The door shuts and the van drives off.

"I hope not," I mutter.

I sling my bag over my shoulder and start the walk down the drive. I expect everything to have changed while I have been gone, but it's still all the same. The fields are still bare and empty, the distant sound of the main road rumbles in the background and the closer sound of birds completing their early evening business surrounds me. The colours of the trees have started to fade, ready to turn to gold and red, but maybe they had been like that before, I can't say I noticed. I bask in the weak sun and soak up the fresh air as I light a cigarette and continue the walk into college.

As I approach the buildings, I realise that something is not right. There are no people walking around, no cars in the car park, no movement at all. It is like that first weekend, walking through a deserted landscape, one that should be bustling with people. I continue on into college towards my room, hoping to see someone on the way, but there is nobody.

I walk along the path towards the quad and see there are metal posts with yellow tape draped between them surrounding the pond. As I get closer, I see that the pond is empty. It has been scrubbed clean, the sides and bottom are a pale white cement colour. I shudder involuntarily and carry on towards my room.

The mystery is finally solved when I get to the outside door of my building. A laminated sign is pinned there.

URGENT NOTICE

ALL STUDENTS ARE TO LEAVE CAMPUS IMMEDIATELY,
THIS IS TO ALLOW FOR DEEP CLEANING FOLLOWING THE
RECENT CHOLERA OUTBREAK.
TRAVELLING SUBSIDIES ARE AVAILABLE, PLEASE KEEP
RECEIPTS AND TICKETS FOR REIMBURSEMENTS.
ANYONE WHO IS NOT ABLE TO RETURN HOME AT THIS TIME
PLEASE REPORT TO THE MAIN RECEPTION, WHERE
ARRANGEMENTS WILL BE MADE FOR YOU.
THIS IS A MANDATORY NOTICE.

There is a footnote that explains that students are expected to be able to return at any time after 10 on Monday morning. So, I have the whole site to myself. I feel lonelier now than I did in the previous days. I go upstairs to my room and let myself in. My room is spotless, everything has been cleaned and my bed is made up with fresh laundry. What clothes I have are all washed, ironed, folded and put away. It is certainly not how I left it. I drop my bag on the floor and lay down on my bed fishing for a cigarette from my jacket pocket.

As I take the new packet out, I see that someone has written on the side of it in indelible marker, 'there is food in your bag'. I unzip the bag and sure enough there are some sandwiches, crisps, chocolate bars and a couple of apples, thank you Julia. I put the food on my desk and unpack the other things, putting nothing away. I put on a tape, a compilation of old punk singles, lay back on the bed and light my cigarette.

Later in the evening, as it gets full dark, I go for a walk. It is eerily deserted. I walk to Sue's room, which is locked. I go to the mansion, which stands dark and threatening. I zip my jacket against the chill air and look down the lawn in the direction of the river. I don't know what I will tell Paul or Sue when they ask, what can I tell them? I promised them the truth, but now I will have to break that promise. I remember how I felt as we walked down the lawn that evening, sticky with sweat, Sarah being vulgar and making us laugh. I struggle to understand how such a carefree evening could have led to this. I think of Lisa with her bolt cutters and me and Stewart pulling the trolley through the pouring rain. My face is wet, I replay the last time I saw Lisa in my mind, and I don't know how I will be able to tell people nothing happened, because it did. It did happen, and it was my fault, or partly my fault. I go back to my room and go to bed in the silence of the empty building.

*

I dream again, it is a blur of corridors and deserted buildings. I keep seeing familiar figures standing at the end of the corridors. When I approach, they turn and walk around the corner. I follow and find myself looking down another corridor, first Sue, then Paul, then Julia, then the boss, and finally Lisa. She does not walk away, but as I get nearer, I can see that her hair is falling out in clumps, her clothes are covered in blood. She smiles, with gaps where her teeth had been, and walks towards me. I turn and run back down endless corridors, past firmly closed doors.

I wake tangled in the bedclothes, covered in sweat. Then I open the curtains to let in the morning light. I look at my clock and see that it is 7.30, two and a half hours before the others get back. I am looking forward to seeing Sue and Paul, although I have not quite figured out yet how I will avoid Sarah, Jo and Stewart. Nor have I figured out how I will answer any awkward questions, but I'm working on it.

I sit down and eat the final sandwich, left over from yesterday. It has been on the desk all night and is dry and curled slightly at the edges. But food is food. I follow it up with the apple, then get up to look out of the window to see if there is any sign of life yet. There are one or two staff cars in the car park and Ian the caretaker is walking along swinging his keys. I turn back to sit on the bed and as I do so I notice a brown envelope underneath my bedroom door.

I pick it up and look at the outside of the envelope. It is an official college letter with my name typed neatly on the front. I open it, pull out a single sheet of paper and read it. It is very succinct, inviting me to meet the principal at 9.30. This is a surprise to me, I have never actually met the principal, only seen him from a distance. He spoke to all of us when we first arrived, telling us to have a good time and work hard, or something like that. After that he retreated to his office.

I imagine that it is to do with the decorating weekend, and wonder if he is aware of what happened, probably not. So, then it must be to do with what happened to Lisa. Is he going to ask me questions? I run through, in my mind, what lies I can fabricate, but without knowing what he is going to ask me it is proving hard.

I look at the clock again, ten to eight. I decide to go for a walk and see if anybody has decided to come back early, a vague hope. I was right not to expect too much, the college is coming to life with cleaners, gardeners and lecturers in an echo of the final day of decorating weekend, when the work was done and we were contentedly waiting for the campus to be reborn. Then it was a time of expectation and optimism, now it is a different feeling altogether that grips me. I prowl and pace in a circuitous route that leads back to my room, where I put on some New Order while I read and wait.

The clock crawls. The sound of traffic and arriving staff increases outside. The knot in my stomach pulls tighter and tighter until eventually I can't stand it anymore. It is ten past nine, I grab my jacket, stub my cigarette in the already full ash tray and walk the short distance to the mansion, clutching my letter.

There is a quiet bustle of activity as admin staff move from office to office, nobody pays any attention to me as I walk up the grandiose staircase and turn towards the principal's office. The paint on the walls is mocking me, showing what could have been done with the colours of paint we had in the common room. It looks classy and adds to the dignity of the handsome, heavily wooded interior of the mansion.

I get to the office and knock on the door.
"Come in."
The principal's secretary is a smartly dressed woman in her forties. I don't know her name, but she reminds me a little of my mum. I get a pang of guilt thinking of mum, I should have called her last night to let her know I was okay, I just didn't think of it. I show my letter to the secretary.
"Hold on a moment please."
She presses a button on a box on her desk and announces that I have arrived. A staticky voice on the other end asks her to send me in please.
"You can go straight in." She indicates the door to one side of her desk and I open it and enter.

The principal sits behind a large desk, he is framed by huge windows that look out across the lawn and down to the river. From this height and angle you can see the scars in the landscape where the river and railway line cut through the valley. But this is not what draws my attention.

Julia is there, she is sitting on a chair to one side of the desk. Her hair is tied into a pony tail and she is wearing a blue jacket with shoulder pads up to her ears and a matching skirt. Her blouse has a high ruffled collar and some kind of a bow arrangement at the front. I had never imagined her wearing anything different from the trousers and shirt I had seen her in previously. Although, to be honest, I had never imagined her sitting in the principal's office either. The principal greets me and beckons me to sit on the chair facing him. I sit on it at an angle so I am half facing Julia too.

"I believe you already Know Doctor Morgan," the principal indicates Julia who nods at me and gives me a 'look'.

"Yes, we've met." I reply.

"Good then, it's good to see you're well, I hope you're feeling okay. It was quite a shock we all had."

"I'm fine thanks," I mumble, looking at Julia.

"Well, good news, your application has been approved. I have to say this is unusual for someone starting their third year, but given your circumstances, and what Doctor Morgan has told me, I think you have made a good decision."

"My application?"

Julia leans towards me.

"Do you remember you talked about moving to a different college, to help you recover from the trauma of what happened?"

I am on the verge of saying no, the look on Julia's face tells me this would be the wrong answer, I just nod instead.

"Where am I moving to?"

The principal names the college in my home town. I look at Julia, then back at the principal.

"What?"

"You recall," says Julia, "that we thought it would be best if you were able to have the support of your family at this difficult time."

"When am I going?"

"Today, your parents are on their way to collect you."

I want to object and protest, going back to live with my parents was not part of the plan - ever. I want to scream, to refuse, to say 'no I'm not going'. But Julia has fixed me with a hard gaze. I remember how easily they took me last time and how helpless and alone I was.

"I need to see my Sue and Paul first."

I look at the clock on the wall, 9.35, everybody will be coming back soon. I want to see them, especially Sue, to try to explain what has happened, as much as I can anyway. Now, apparently, I need to say goodbye too.

"You really need to go back to your room and pack your stuff first," says Julia, "make sure you are all ready to go."

It feels as though I am being dismissed, the principal stands up and comes around his desk to shake my hand and wish me good luck. Julia stays on her chair, still fixing me with her stare, but also smiling a sympathetic kind of smile.

Alice

This is the first time Alice has actually visited the college campus. All her prior information has been gleaned from photographs, maps and blueprints. Driving through makes her realise how much of a microcosm of society it is, everything you need, as long as you don't need much. She can see the attraction of this rural idyll compared to the large, grey, fogbound city where she had studied.

She climbs out of the car and her heels clack on the tarmac as she crosses the car park to the main reception. She finds it hard to not feel like an imposter when she dresses in a certain way, for a particular job, she feels uncomfortable in the ridiculous blue suit and flouncy blouse that is meant to give the impression of 'eminent psychiatric doctor.' She had scrutinised herself in her hotel mirror before she left and decided it would do.

After the administrators have finished fetching teas and coffees and introductions have been made, she talks with the principal. The conversation is almost verbatim the one she had with Sid's parents on the phone yesterday.

"He has suffered considerable trauma, witnessing his friend die is an event that is going to trouble him for a long time to come."

"I can imagine, we were all very shocked."

"Just so, his mental health and wellbeing has been seriously compromised. He needs a stable and loving environment to support him through this, and maybe a fresh start will help in the days ahead."

"Yes, I can see how that would be."

"I've arranged with his parents, for him to move back to his family home. The college there runs the same course, it will help his rehabilitation if he can transfer there straight away. I would really appreciate your help with this."

"Of course, I'll get onto it immediately."

In truth everything is already in place, but it doesn't hurt to let important people, like college principals, carry on thinking they are important, they may be useful one day. Similar arrangements are already taking place for the other decorators when their centres return them, but Alice's focus is on her charge. Everything is in motion, parents are on their way, there are funds to support him through the move and measures in place to ensure they keep track of him.

O'Brien has made it clear that she is to oversee every stage of this personally, for as long as it takes. He cited her attention to detail and commitment as the reason for this. What he didn't say was that he didn't think Dan would go all out to ensure that it worked.

When Sid is shown into the office, slightly early, he does not show surprise at her presence. In fact, he plays along admirably with the charade of her new persona. He seemed to take the news fairly well, as far as she could tell. The scare that O'Brien had put on him had obviously left its mark, as he didn't argue about what he was being told or get overly upset. The conversation was brief and after he left the room she thanked the principal for all his help.

"Poor lad, it really was the least I could do."

'Never a truer word spoken' thought Julia as she left the room.

Chapter 14 (continued)

I leave the Mansion and go back to my own room in a daze. They aren't really making me leave, are they? I look around at my things, then collect my duffle bag from under the bed. I am still standing holding it when there is a knock at the door and Julia lets herself in.

"Sorry, this is really for the best. I know you don't like it, but you need some space from the people who are going to ask you the most questions. This will make things easier for you. Are you okay packing?"

I look at Julia and reply, "All my friends are here, my girlfriend, everybody."

"I know, it's going to be difficult. We'll do our best to make sure everything goes as smoothly as possible for you though, I promise you that."

"This is not smooth. This is huge, it'll ruin my life."

"I think you're being a bit dramatic now. There are things that could ruin your life, but this definitely isn't one of them. Now, are you going to start packing?"

There is the undertone of a threat, more of a reminder really, to this last statement.

"I suppose."

"Good, I'm off now, I'll see you again soon."

Julia leaves and I start stuffing clothes into my bag. Followed by tapes, then books and folders. There is considerable overflow, even with the new bag from the prison. I am watching the clock inch painfully slowly towards 10 o'clock. Long before the minute hand reaches the zenith of its journey there is another knock at the door. I open it expectantly, hoping it will be Sue or Paul. It's not, it's my parents standing there. They invite themselves in.

"Oh good, you're all packed and ready then." Says my dad while my mum gives me a huge cringeworthy hug that I am glad nobody witnessed.

"We've been so worried about you," she says.

Dad starts to leave the room with my duffle bag and holdall.

"I can't go yet, I've got to see some people first."

"We've got to get going, the traffic was dreadful on the way up and dad has to get back for work this evening."

"Hold on," I say.

I run from my room over to Sue's. There are students starting to reappear in dribs and drabs, heading back to rooms and saying goodbye to parents in a re-enactment of last month. I knock on Sue's door but there is no answer, then I start patting my pockets in the vague hope that I might have a pen and notepad that I had forgotten about. There is nothing, all the other doors are closed and I walk disconsolately back hoping to see Paul.

My parents are waiting for me, my room is empty and there is no sign of Paul. My dad is looking at his watch, clearly keen to get going. I don't know what to do, so I follow them to the car, now loaded with my belongings. I climb into the back and we set off. We are heading in the opposite direction from everybody else, I keep looking out of the window, hoping for a glimpse of Sue, but we leave the drive and are soon headed off to the newly opened M25 motorway, that is going to make this journey so much quicker, for the final time.

I curl up on the back seat, next to my bag and close my eyes. From the front my mum keeps asking if I'm ok, so many times now it's beginning to get on my tits. I keep saying yes, but I'm not. I don't want to go home, I want to stay at college with my friends. I can already feel I am turning back into my 14-year-old self and I answer more curtly each time, until eventually I just pretend to be asleep.

We stop for coffee at a service station. I go inside for a pee, then come back to have a cigarette by the car. As I light it mum comes in for another hug, I hold it out of the way and suffer the embrace.
"I wish you wouldn't," she says, indicating the cigarette, then quickly adds, "but it's okay, you've been through so much."
"What have I been through?"
"Well, you know. Dr Morgan told us a bit of it. But she said you probably wouldn't want to talk about it."
"Yeah, well she was right, I really don't."

Doctor Bloody Morgan, who hasn't she talked to. After telling me not to talk to anybody, she's told the whole world. I wonder exactly what she has told people, that ridiculous story about the mental asylum. Right now I don't really want to know. I drop my cigarette end and obliterate it under my boot, then get back in the car and wait for the journey to recommence. I suffer the rest of the journey in silence, accepting the occasional boiled sweet that is passed back to me.

When we arrive home I decant my luggage from the car. I take it back to my childhood bedroom where I dump it with the rest of my belongings that have been neatly packed up ready for a journey that will never happen. I slump down on the bed and listen to the familiar sounds of my dad getting ready for his evening shift and my mum cooking a meal in the kitchen. My sister pokes her head round my door and says hi, then disappears back to whatever it was she was doing in her room, while listening to Madonna.

The evening passes in a kind of haze. I eat, I unpack a bit, I sit up late into the evening and write a long letter to Sue, trying to explain what has happened without actually saying what has happened and promising that I will keep in touch and visit soon. Eventually I give in to my weariness and go to bed. I sleep fitfully during the night, but in the morning I am deeply asleep when my mum brings in tea and toast.

"Time to get up, new college today."

"I'm not going."

"You have to, it's all been arranged."

She puts an envelope on the bedside table, next to the breakfast. I turn over and close my eyes again. Once she has left the room I sit up, drink some tea and start eating my toast while I open the envelope. There is a wodge of paper inside giving me details of who to see and how to register when I arrive. It also has details of my timetable for the coming term, and I see that today I have a full day of lectures and seminars. I finish my toast and close my eyes again.

I am eventually hustled out of bed by Mum, I get myself dressed then leave reluctantly for college, what else could I do? Although I have lived here all my life I have never been to the college before. It is a mixture of old and new buildings, clustered in a seemingly random manner, that presumably made sense to somebody at some point. There are halls of residence nearby and the usual melee of people moving from place to place, but mainly gathering in places that food, drink and tables are available.

I am, of course, late. I wander into the main office clutching my letter and looking dishevelled. My leather jacket is covering a creased 'RELAX' tee shirt and I am wearing my old ripped jeans that have clearly not been washed recently. I am warmly welcomed. They were expecting me and I am given directions to my first port of call, once I have finished signing various forms and pieces of paper that I don't bother to read properly.

The rest of the day passes quickly. I get lost twice, sit in the wrong room for ten minutes and am surrounded by groups of strangers, who all know each other. There are tutors to meet, some in offices, some in snatched time in corridors. They ask questions about my previous course, but nobody asks which college I have come from, I guess there is a memo somewhere telling them not to. They all seem happy with my answers, and welcome me to their courses. I am the outsider. A couple of people attempt to start conversations with me at different times, but I am not in the mood for making friends. I brush them off with vague answers and do my best to get through the day. On my way home I stop at the Post Office, buy a stamp and post my letter to Sue, then go home to be taciturn and uncommunicative there.

The next couple of days follow in a similar vein. I gradually get to meet a few people, sitting with them at coffee breaks and lunch time, and being suitably oblique about why I have just joined the course. I used the reason I remembered Trevor giving as my own. I needed to be closer to home, family reasons. It's amazing how nobody pushes further when you say that, they make assumptions about what it might or might not be, but don't want to pry.

By the end of the week I have made tentative friendships with several students from my study group. A large exuberant girl called Shelly, who only seems to own neon-coloured clothes, and her friend Grace. Grace is a riot of curly hair, deep brown eyes and a swathe of baggy jumpers and scarves. I decline their invitation to join them in the bar, choosing instead to go home and sit alone. I manage to catch up with work I have missed, and even get ahead with work that has been newly set.

Another surprise arrives at the end of the week. It is an envelope containing a cheque and a letter. The letter explains that the payment is a discretionary award to help students who transfer. It is a comfortable sum of money, more than I made selling ice-cream all summer. I put it to one side to pay into the bank.

The following week keeps to a similar pattern. I await a return letter from Sue, and write another epic to her, pouring my heart out. I also write a shorter missive to Paul, in which I ask after Sue, hoping to get some information. No replies come. At college I am, for the first time in my student life, ahead with my studies. I have taken to sitting quietly with Shelly and Grace at break and lunch times. It is good to have people to sit with, and they tolerate my near silent presence on the periphery of their group of friends.

This is my town. I know its secrets and its quiet places. Most of my friends are away at college, the ones who remained here seem disinterested in my reasons for returning. The nights out that I used to enjoy seem pointless now, I give up after a couple of attempts, my heart isn't in it. I walk through the empty streets and past the shuttered shops at night, wending my way to the beach and idling along under the strings of coloured lights. I enjoy the solitude and the time to think, although it's mostly the same thoughts that are circling around and around in my head.

Mum still fusses and clucks around me, but stops short at trying to discuss what happened, thankfully. She is attentive and provides regular meals that I often take upstairs with me to eat while I study – or mope. It depends what mood I'm in. Dad is jovial and tries to persuade me to 'get out a bit more, it'll do you good'. My sister pops in for an occasional chat, but is generally too busy with work and her own social life to bother me too much, apart from playing bloody Madonna non-stop in her bedroom.

Posters have gone up around college for a Halloween band. Previously I would have been first in line for a ticket, but now I am not really in the mood. Grace has asked me if I want her to get me a ticket. I have come to quite like Grace, she has a gentle way of including me in conversations without forcing me to join in, and always has a smile for me. I have been non-committal in my responses, but have started to think I may quite like a night out. The clincher comes one coffee break. Grace sits down opposite me and shows me two tickets to the Halloween bash.

"I got one for you, in case you change your mind."

"Do you know? I think I might come along after all, I need a night out. How much do I owe you for the ticket?"

"No, that's ok, it's on me." She gives me her quirky smile and I return it.

"Ok, I'll buy the drinks. I'm not dressing up though."

"Good, me neither,"

Shelly approaches the table with her coffee in hand. She nudges Grace along the bench seat and sits down beside her. As she sits she looks down at the tickets laying on the table and then gives me a wink, before starting an animated conversation with Grace about someone she had met the previous evening.

I have built up some surplus funds during my isolation, so buying drinks may not be as generous as it sounds. My meals had been provided at home and apart from tea in the refectory, chocolate and the new Mission LP I hadn't spent that much recently. In spite of myself and in spite of missing Sue, I am looking forward to it now. I kind of like Grace too, her name suits her and she is funny in a quiet way, and smart too. Just friends though.

The night of the band I can't decide what to wear. In the end I opt for the leather jacket, jeans and a faded tee shirt. I am nothing if not predictable. I run my hands through my hair and leave the house. I walk to the college and quickly spot Grace waiting in the throng outside, her long brown coat is wrapped around her to keep out the early evening chill, which is starting to bite at my neck and hands. Around her mill a crowd of ghosts, vampires and monsters. I keep my side of the bargain when we are inside and edge my way through to the bar, returning with two plastic pints of lager.

While I am doing this Grace finds us a table to sit at. Her coat is now draped over the back of a chair and she is wearing jeans and a furry striped jumper which is so big on her it could double as a dress. Her hair is tied back with a yellow and black piece of cloth. Her face is exposed, she looks incredibly pretty. Speaking loudly, over the noise and music we talk about our favourite bands and find there are two large areas of common ground. We are both fans of The Velvet Underground and Lou Reed, and we both have a singular dislike of Chris De sodding Burgh. She had spent her summer working in a shoe shop, where she claimed they played Lady in Red on a continuous loop. I kind of believe her.

I get more beer, as per the deal, and we carry on talking. Several people stop and greet Grace with shrieks, hugs and over enthusiastic delight at seeing her. Shelly comes over and is about to sit down and join us, then is distracted at the last minute and veers off to a different table, promising to 'see you later'. Most people extend their greeting to me, but it feels forced. They don't know me yet really, I haven't let them. I'm not even convinced that they would want to know me, if they knew what I had done, not that they ever will.

The band comes on as I return with fresh beer. We take liberal gulps to reduce the level of liquid and then carefully carry them into the massing crowd that has gathered around the stage. In spite of my reluctance to come out I find I am enjoying myself, the band is good, Grace stays close by me, pushing up against me at times as the mass of people around the stage move in strange eddies and swirls and I find that pint three has gone to my head. Maybe I am out of practise, I haven't been out much recently and drinking alone at home always feels like a pointless exercise.

By the time the encore is done I am sweaty and feeling in need of some air. While everybody else crowds back to the bar, to stockpile before last orders, I suggest we go for a walk. Grace agrees and we collect our coats and leave the building. Without discussion we start to walk past the rows of empty guesthouses towards the beach, ending up sitting beneath the sea wall, close to the ice cream shop where I spent my summer. The air is still chilly, but we are sheltered here, we sit and smell the salt in the air as the unseen waves splash onto the sand and the stars spread themselves across the sky.

Grace leans into me and snuggles up, in return I put my arm around her and hug her in close to keep her, and me, warm. Then suddenly, without any warning, she is kissing me. I am taken by surprise, I have a good track record of not reading signals well. I am also slightly tipsy. But it feels good and I kiss her back. To feel the warmth of another body pushing against mine, to have hands running through my ragged hair and an open mouth exploring my own is something I have missed and badly need. But I would rather it was Sue. The thought makes me tense up. Grace senses the change and stops.

"Are you okay?"

"Yes, well no. I'm not sure. I'm kind of seeing someone else really."

A space opens between us and Grace looks at me,

"Sorry, I didn't know, you never said."

"Well, not really, I haven't seen her for a long time and she's not answering my letters."

"Well, she's an idiot then."

I pause, what Sue doesn't know won't hurt her. She hasn't answered a single one of my letters in spite of my almost pleading tone, I even wrote her a poem. It was a gushing melodramatic epic that owed more to Joy Division lyrics than Keats, Shelley or Shakespeare. I assume she is ashamed of me. Or disgusted by what I have done. But now I have a fresh start,

Grace doesn't know what I have done, and isn't likely to. I make a decision. "Maybe she is, or maybe I'm the idiot. I'm sorry, I haven't really been myself recently. I'm not good around other people at the moment."

"You don't say?"

A quizzically raised eyebrow and a small smile assure me that I'm not being mocked. Grace leans towards me and whispers, "So, are we on or not?"

I answer with a kiss, some tight hugging and fondling and caressing through the layers of thick clothing.

In the distance, over the sound of the wavelets washing the sand up and down the beach, I hear the sound of a church clock striking over and over. Midnight is with us.

"Shall I walk you home?"

"That would be nice."

We walk, and I smoke, making small talk. Gossip and news about people that I am only just getting to know. It covers our mutual nervousness and apprehension. We get back to Grace's hall of residence and stand outside. She holds my hands and looks at me.

"Thanks for the beers."

"Thanks for the ticket, I had a good night."

"Do you want to come in?"

I hesitate.

"I'd better not, busy day tomorrow, early lecture."

"Fair enough, can we go out again?"

"Yes, I'd like that. Can we set something up tomorrow?"

"Okay."

We kiss again, a long, protracted kiss that makes me think again about the invitation to come in. Grace breaks off, smiles and says goodnight, then goes into her door with a quick glance back over her shoulder as the door closes behind her.

I watch her go in then start for home. I let events run through my mind as I walk. I hadn't seen this coming. Really, I want Sue. I want her to reply to my letters, I want her to tell me everything is okay, I want to hold her in my arms and take her to bed. I don't want Grace to be a Sue substitute, holding her place until things get back to normal. On the other hand, Grace is nice. She is pretty, funny and smart, and I don't know what normal is anymore.

I arrive home to find the lights still on. It's one in the morning, normally the house would be asleep by now. I have a momentary panic that something might be wrong. I let myself in and find Mum and Dad still up. They look up at me with tired eyes, I'm sure Dad has just woken up, he is slumped deep in his chair and his book is lying on the floor by his feet.

"Hello love, did you have a nice evening?"

"You didn't have to wait up for me you know."

"We didn't, we were reading that's all."

My Mum is such a crap liar.

"I'm not a child you know."

"We don't think you are, we just can't help worrying after....well, after everything."

I realise this is the first time I've had a proper night out since I got back. Dad finally joins in,

"So, how was the band?"

"All right I suppose."

"Do you want some cocoa?"

"No, I'm going to bed."

I leave them sitting there and go upstairs to bed. As I lie awake, I can hear them talking quietly to each other before making their own way up to bed. I wonder if I did the right thing coming home this evening, what the right thing was, and how I was supposed to know. When I sleep, I dream of Julia - as if things aren't confusing and complicated enough already.

I am in a panic the following morning. I oversleep, in spite of the parental alarm clock doing its best to get me up. I have a headache and did not get anything ready for this morning. I curse and crash around my room looking for a matching pair of socks and a clean tee shirt. When I sit down on the bed to put my trainers on, I just sit, holding one of them in my hand and looking at it. They are the trainers they gave me at the centre, not looking quite as clean or new now. They are real, they are a tangible reminder that everything was not just an awful dream or a terrible practical joke. I pick up my jacket from the floor and look inside the cuff. Even though Sue cleaned it, there is a patch of the red lining that is darker than the rest, much darker. This is where Lisa's blood spilt onto my arms, where it ran into my sleeves leaving its indelible mark. This is my proof that something happened. Something that was so terrible that I can't leave it behind and I can't tell anyone about.

I am sitting with my trainer in my lap, crying, when Mum comes in. She doesn't say anything at all. She sits next to me and puts her arm around me and I put my head on her shoulder and sob.

Finally, I am spent. I resume putting my trainers on.

"It will be okay in the end you know, things work out if you give them time. Are you staying home today? I'll make you some more tea. Or I can give you a lift in so you're not too late."

I hug her and kiss her cheek.

"I'm okay, just having a moment. I'll be alright. Thanks for the offer, I'll walk though, I need the fresh air."

I hug her again, finish putting my trainers on and collect up my things.

The walk in gives me all the fresh air I need. I am calm and my mysterious headache has gone by the time I arrive. My early lecture has also almost gone. I go straight to the refectory and get a cup of tea which I drink while I make notes from a book by Skinner. I have my head down in the book when a pair of hands clasp over my eyes, making me jump.

"Guess who?"

"Princess Diana."

"Close enough. Where were you this morning? You missed a great lecture."

"Really?"

"No. How are you this morning?"

"I'm fine, I just overslept that's all."

Grace looks at the queue that has formed at the servery and groans, then says, "Come on, come back to mine, we'll have a cup of tea there and I'll tell you what you missed."

"Will we get back in time for the seminar?"

"Nope, fuck it!"

I have no comeback to this. It won't matter to me missing the seminar as I wasn't at the lecture, so I follow Grace back to her room and sit on the bed and wait while she makes cups of tea. Grace is missing the seminar, she is doing it to be with me. She is yet another victim for me to drag down. When the tea is made I take it and have a big gulp, scalding my mouth.

"You know, you have a very distant look. Not just now, but always. I don't know what happened before but I think it was something bad."

"It was. I can't talk about it."

"That's fine. Maybe I don't want to know. But I like you, I enjoyed last night. I really want to be your friend, it doesn't have to be more than that."

I look at her; her face is earnest and beautiful. She looks as if she would do anything for me at this moment, but what might I ask her to do? And how would it end?

"I don't know if I'd be good for you."

"Why don't you let me decide that? I'm a big girl."

"I don't.... I don't know what to do."

"I know there was someone else, and might still be. If it comes to it, I'll back right off, disappear. But for now, why don't you let me in a bit? You might even have some fun."

I have no argument for any of this, I like Grace – really like her. I know this is a bad idea, but I put down my cup of tea, move over to her and put my arms around her. She puts her own tea down and starts to kiss me, covering my face and neck with small wet kisses and pulling my jacket off. I can feel her gently tremble as I run my hand under her tee shirt and slide my fingers inside her bra. I pause, but she whispers urgently to me 'don't stop', I slide my other hand up her skirt. There is an obligatory awkward moment when she asks if I have protection, as if any self-respecting leather jacket would not have a condom in one of its many zip-up pockets. It feels like no time before me and Grace are naked in the bed. I relish the feel of her against my body, the smell of her and the way she touches me. When we make love, it feels as if a weight is lifted from me at last, the absolution I have been waiting for.

"We missed the seminar."

"I'll ask Shelly if I can borrow her notes."

"Can I share them?"

"If you ask nicely. What's it worth?"

Her hand slides under the sheet, we miss lunch too.

*

Over the next few autumnal weeks, as the trees shed their final leaves and the wind blows in across the sea, we spend more and more time together. We spend a lot of it studying, in truth I have got into a good work routine and quite like the novel feeling of being ahead of my work for a change. We go for drinks, meet with her friends and spend time in her room together. Shelley seems to approve of me, and it is good to spend time with them. It starts to feel a bit like a new normal.

Grace has a small black and white TV in her room, I keep up with the news from time to time. Hostages in Beirut, Ian Brady confessing to more murders, helicopter crashes and Jeffrey Archer definitely not meeting with prostitutes. Away from the news Noel Edmunds has been killing people on breakfast TV and Arthur is getting deeper into trouble stealing the EastEnders Christmas money. It's all so grim. We usually resort to listening to music, Shelly pops in for cups of tea and to tell us who she is currently pursuing and we laugh and chat late into the night, more frequently now ending up with me staying the night and collecting clean clothes from home some time the next day.

We decide to go to the cinema one evening to break the bad news routine. We choose Platoon, which is good but doesn't really cheer us up that much.

Afterwards we go for a drink in one of the town centre pubs. There are other groups of students spread around, but nobody that we're friends with, so we choose a table by ourselves. Grace is talking when I notice someone sitting at a table behind her. It is a familiar face that I can't place. At first I think it must just be someone I went to school with, or have met fleetingly before. He is smartly dressed, not just compared to me, that's easy, but in comparison to every other student around him. His hair is cut short and he is having an animated conversation with the other people at his table.

Grace stops talking and looks over her shoulder in the direction of my stare, then back at me.

"Everything okay?"

"Yeah, who's that?"

"What the guy in the jacket and tie?"

"Yes him.

"A new first year, he joined late. I've seen him about, he's dressed like he's going to an office."

I continue to stare.

"What's his name?"

"I don't know, do you want me to find out?"

Just then he turns his head and makes eye contact with me. It's Trevor, its bloody Trevor. I mutter his name under my breath still staring. No hippy clothes or long hair, but definitely Trevor.

"Are you okay? You look like you've seen a ghost."

"I'm fine."

But I'm not. I collect up my jacket and get up to go, leaving my beer barely touched on the table. Grace hurriedly collects up her own belongings and follows me, trailing in my wake as I push my way through the milling people and out of the door. I don't know exactly where I'm going, but I know that I have to go somewhere. Grace catches me up at last and grabs my arm. I stop and look at her, she looks alarmed, I apologise.

"What happened in there?"

"I can't say. I'm not even sure."

"Are you sure you're okay?"

"I'm fine."

I'm not.

I am starting to calm down a bit now. But Trevor! What the bloody hell? We go back to Grace's and she doesn't ask any more questions.

From then on Trevor, who I find is now called Simon, seems to pop up regularly in the same place as me. The first time he approaches to talk to me I beat a hasty retreat, practically dragging Grace out of the bar, just like the first time I saw him.

"What is it with him? It's like you're terrified of him?"

"I'm not. I just don't want to talk to him. Ever."

"He seems quite nice, I was talking to him the other day."

"When? What about?"

"When you were in with your tutor, he talked about the course and how much he was enjoying it. He asked what the third-year modules were like."

"Don't, please don't talk to him again,"

"Why not? He seems harmless, a bit of a square. I'm not going to run off with him."

"I can't say, but please, for me?"

"What's it worth?"

We both know the answer to that one. I take Grace's hand and we head back to her room through the evening mist under the yellow lights that struggled to show the way.

Before I know it, Christmas is here. There is a Christmas ball and several parties, all of which Grace and I manage to attend. I am getting ready to go out in a good shirt and a tie I borrowed from Dad when Mum knocks and comes in.

"It's good to see you going out and enjoying yourself, we were worried about you you know."

"I know, thanks."

"So, when are we going to meet your young lady then?"

I still hadn't bought Grace back to the house, we always met at college or at her room. I hadn't even thought to invite her home. It still feels like a big step backwards to be living back with my parents, embarrassing really.

"I don't know, maybe I'll ask her to come round after the Christmas break."

The thought of bringing Grace here is excruciating, I am certain she will be horrified by my family. I think of Dad with his bad jokes and Mum with her 'hostess with the mostest' show. I am sure it would be a performance like no other.

"I'll ask her to come round for a cup of tea in the New Year, I promise. I'm off out now, see you later."

Two days later, the last day of term, everyone is meeting for drinks in the bar. I turn up late, with rain dripping from my jacket, I soon find Shelley and the others, but no Grace.

"Where's Grace?"

"She's still getting ready. She said to tell you to go to her room if you're here before her."

"Thanks, see you in a bit."

Shelly is already tipsy, as are the others. We are going to have some catching up to do when we get back. I go back out into the rain and hurry off to Grace's. When I get there, I knock on the door and open it. Grace is on the bed. She is wearing nothing but a black basque and stockings. She smiles, her hair drops in curls nearly to her shoulders, she looks stunning in the light of the candles she has set strategically around the room.

"I thought we were going out for a drink."

"You can go if you want, or stay here and open your Christmas present."

I rub my chin and pretend to think about it. I get a book thrown at me for my trouble.

"I only got you this."

I hold out a small blue parcel, inside is a tape of Iggy Pop's Blah – Blah - Blah.

"Oh, for fucks sake, lock the door, get rid of those soggy clothes and get over here."

I follow my instructions and spend the evening enjoying my festive, yuletide gift. We are woken in the early hours of the morning as Shelly and the others shout and clatter their way back to their rooms, doors bang, someone knocks something over and the smell of toast comes from the kitchenette. I can hear Shelly has someone with her, a man's voice, and good for her. We are awake anyway, so carpe diem as they say in wherever they say that.

The next morning we get going slowly. Grace is catching the lunchtime train home. I help her pack, and generally annoy and harass her until it's time for her to leave. Shelly comes in while Grace is in the kitchen.

"Have a happy Christmas you." She kisses me on the cheek and gives me a hug.

"You too, see you in the New Year."

"She's so much happier this year you know? You've really bought out the best in her. Don't hurt her."

"I wasn't planning to."

"Good, she's bought out something in you too, you're less grumpy than when you got here. Not so sad."

Grace reappears at this moment and there is lots of hugging and promising to have a good time and to see each other soon. Finally, it's time to leave. Like a gentleman I carry Grace's bag to the station for her.

"Don't go, you can stay at my parents' house."

I haven't checked this, but I'm pretty sure it would be okay, they are still trying to be nice to me, although I don't know if we would be allowed to share a room. My parents are a bit funny like that.

"I'm pretty sure my parents would kill me if I missed Christmas. I don't know whether my baby brother would be furious or delighted."

"I suppose, but if you change your mind…."

We kiss as the train pulls into the station. I help Grace lift her bag on board and watch as she settles into her seat. She breaths onto the window and draws a heart in the condensation, waving as the train creaks and squeaks its way out of sight. I stuff my hands into my pocket. I pull my right hand out again and hold up a flimsy scrap of lace and silk. Momentarily puzzled, I realize that it is the panties that Grace was wearing yesterday when I arrived, an extra Christmas present. I quickly push them back into my pocket and look around to check that nobody has seen, luckily the platform has already emptied. It is right now that I realise that I will miss Grace more than I will miss Sue this Christmas.

I have all but stopped writing to Sue. I have a Christmas card written for her and ready to send. Having not heard a word from her I have become resigned to not getting my chance to explain things. I feel like maybe I should admit that it is over between us. And I really like Grace.

I start the journey home, making a detour to get cigarettes on the way. When I get back there's a kit bag sitting in the hallway. It is stencilled with my brother's name and rank on one side. I head straight into the kitchen where he is leaning on the counter with a mug of tea, talking to Dad.

"Look who's home," announces Dad.

"I see, how are you? I thought you were at sea."

"We came back for repairs, we all got some shore leave while she's in dock."

"How long are you back for?"

"Why does everyone ask when I'm going back as soon as I arrive? Not long, we've got exercises starting in the New Year, we have to report back the day after Boxing Day."

"You've got time to come to the pub then."

"Always, but I'm getting changed first."

I look at his uniform.

"Why? You look dashing."

"Piss off!"

I start to whistle the music from An Officer and a Gentleman as he leaves the room and he flicks the v's to me as he goes.

"I'll get my shoes." Says Dad.

I wait on the doorstep with a cigarette until they are ready, then we all walk to the pub for an afternoon pint. My brother regales us with tales of life on the high sea, time passes quickly. It is several hours later when we return home. Mum has enlisted my sister's help in the kitchen, or should I say galley? Between them they have cooked up a storm and even managed to bake a cake. We sit and eat together, then argue good-naturedly about who is washing up. It ends up with Dad washing and me drying. Afterwards I go upstairs and sit down to write to Grace.

Chapter 15
Christmas

The Christmas break turns out to be busier than I expected. I have a lot of coursework that I want to get out of the way, so I busy myself with that. Then my school friends start to arrive back from whichever parts of the country they have been studying in. We catch up over drinks, but I find it hard, I have to be evasive when they ask why I have changed college. I am vague and only offer half explanations and reasons. Eventually I find it easier and less stressful to turn down invitations.

The other thing that keeps me busy is my impending school placement next term. There is lots of planning and preparation to do, lessons to prepare, files to write in and resources to cut out, copy and laminate. I am determined to be ready for this and to do the best that I can. My new found academic inclination has extended to all parts of my course; I am determined to give a good account of myself.

I am sitting in my room writing, it's a dull afternoon on the day before Christmas Eve. My sister is listening to the radio in her room. The Housemartins have got themselves a caravan of love, Jackie Wilson is being Reet Petite. I kind of don't mind it, so don't bother putting my own music on. The door opens and my brother comes in.

"A card came for you."

He passes the card to me and I take it excitedly. I don't get much mail, mostly it's from the bank, but maybe Paul or Sue have got in touch. I peel it open and pull out a Christmas card. It is simultaneously shiny and pastel coloured. The picture is a boy and girl, their backs to the artist. They are wrapped up warm against the winter snow. The message, written in gold lettering says 'Silence is Golden.' I open it and written inside, in neat blue handwriting it says 'Have a good Christmas – from Julia."

I put the card face down on my desk and stare at it.

"Okay?" asks my brother.

"Yeah fine."

"Not what you were expecting? You look disappointed."

"No, it's fine really."

"Mum told me about what happened. I'm sorry."

"It's okay, everything's alright really."

"Is it? You look awful. Do you need a drink?"

"No, I'm fine. I've got a bunch of stuff to do."

"Now I know something's wrong, working when you could be drinking."

"Yeah."

I smile and he puts his hand on my shoulder.

"Maybe later?"

"Definitely later. Hey, when you joined up did you have to sign the Official Secrets Act?"

"No, they just showed it to us and told us we are bound by it."

"So, you never had to sign it?"

"No."

"Did you ever read it?"

"What the contract?"

"No, the Official Secrets Act."

"No, not really, why?"

"Just wondering."

I want to ask him if he knows anything about secret missiles. About what might be in a metre-long grey cylinder that everyone seems terrified of. I know I can't. I know that if I do it won't just be me who will be in trouble, I don't want to keep pulling other people down with me.

"Anyway, give me an hour or so to finish this and I'll let you buy me a beer with all your shore leave money."

"It's a deal, but you can buy your own beer. I know how much money you students get."

On my sister's radio Chris de sodding Burgh has started to sing about spacemen. I quite like this song, but on principal put on Killing Joke and turn the volume up just enough to start a music war.

*

Christmas is great. Everybody is at home and it feels like it used to in the old days, before anything happened, before my world was turned inside out. Everyone has bought me a tie, or that's what it feels like. They are helping me prepare for my teaching practise, or so they say. They produce my real presents after I have politely thanked everybody for the beautiful ties. There is much laughter, and an early morning drink to toast the day as the turkey is put in to roast. I pass on going to church, nobody comments. My brother and sister go along to keep Mum happy, although my brother does draw the line at wearing his uniform. They all head off and I promise to peel the potatoes as my penance for not honouring the baby Jesus.

They have not been gone long when the phone rings. I have made a start on the potatoes and dry my hands on a dishcloth as I go to answer it. When I pick it up there is a pause and a click, I think the caller has hung up, but then Grace's voice comes through the handset.

"Hi, Happy Christmas, can I speak to…"

I interrupt her,

"Grace, happy Christmas, how are you?"

"All good, missing you though."

"Missing you too. Why aren't you at church?"

"I could ask you the same."

"Ok, truce then."

We talk on the phone for what feels like ages, news about families, news about pets, news about what we have been doing. It is so good to talk to her, but not good being so far away, not being able to touch or hold her. Eventually I hear a man's voice in the background call out that it's time for something inaudible. Grace apologises, we tell each other how much we miss one another again, then we end the call and the house seems too quiet.

I quickly finish peeling the potatoes and then prep the carrots and sprouts too, for good measure. The house is still too quiet, so I go upstairs and start looking through my pile of tapes. In an unmarked case near the bottom of a stack I find a tape I had forgotten about. It is a mix tape that Sue made for me. I can't remember what songs are on it, only that it was quite hippyish and not all my sort of thing. I recall there is definitely some Janis Ian on it, and she was sad about everything. There is also some Bob Dylan, who we never could agree on, and plenty of Bruce. I decide that whatever it is it might make a change, I put it on.

The first track is Dire Straits, Hand in Hand. The music starts and I am immediately taken back. I haven't listened to this song for what feels like a long time, it is beautiful and haunting. When I listen to it I can see Sue's face, 'If I've been hard on you I never meant to be' I really didn't mean for it to be like this, if I could undo it I would. Then I think of Grace and feel guilty and ashamed, I know I can't go on like this. I need to stop thinking about Sue, she has clearly forgotten about me. I take the tape out and drop it into the bin by the back door on my way out for a cigarette.

It's not long before the others return and Christmas starts in earnest with crackers, paper hats and too much food. We all watch little orphan Annie in the afternoon, I quite like a musical after a drink, Dad falls asleep and we all drift off to examine our presents. We reassemble for more food and a family game of Scrabble in the evening. Mum wins, I complain about my letters and my sister doesn't really try. I stay up late and watch Educating Rita before I go to bed. I sleep well. Before I go upstairs, I go to the deserted kitchen and fish in the bin for the tape. I find it, wipe it on the tea towel and take it back upstairs, where I return it to its place at the bottom of the pile.

Boxing Day comes and goes, before I know it my brother's leave is over and he is off, back to his ship. Mum cries, we all wish him well and he is gone again. It was good to see him. I can't remember when I last saw him. I certainly can't remember the last time I saw him that we didn't fight.

The rest of the holiday passes quietly, I turn down several invitations to New Year celebrations, choosing instead to see in 1987 quietly at home. In the end it turns out to be very quiet, as my sister and parents all have places to go. They try to persuade me to go along with them, but I'm really just counting the days until Grace comes back. I am nervous of saying the wrong thing to the wrong people, especially if I've had a drink or two. What might I tell them? What might happen if I say the wrong thing? I look at Julia's card, which stands next to Grace's more traditional one on my desk, and give an involuntary shudder.

Alice

Over the following weeks Alice keeps close tabs on what is going on, she is most worried about Sid becoming depressed. She had been serious when she had talked to the principal about his mental wellbeing. She knew from her background reading how damaging this sort of event could be, especially for young men - who were traditionally prone to bottling things up and not talking about their feelings. This macho, man-up attitude had a way of exploding if there was nobody to talk to about it. She had taken advice from a doctor who specialised in working with ex-soldiers, she had her number on hand if the situation needed her input.

Initially he seemed to be withdrawn and unhappy, natural she supposed. But more recently she had been pleased to see that he had begun to socialise more. He also seemed to have gotten a girlfriend, which surprised her, given the number of letters they were intercepting that he was still writing to his ex at her college address. Still, he did seem to be more settled now, so that was good.

In the first week of December O'Brien came by her office.

"Hi, how is everything?"

"Fine, thank you sir, busy as always."

"Good, that's what we pay you for."

Alice has known him long enough now to know that this is his attempt at humour, and smiles.

"How's it going with Sid?"

Alice also knows that he already knows the answer to this. She keeps him regularly updated with reports and notifies him of any significant changes, not that there has been much to report. She plays along anyway.

"He seems okay. He's formed an attachment with a girl and is socialising with a group of her friends, they've all been vetted, nothing flagged up for any of them."

"Good, good. So, you would say that it's all running smoothly then?"

"I would sir, yes."

"That's excellent, because I need you to take on another assignment. You'll be out of the country for a week to ten days, I'll ask Dan to monitor things in your absence."

"Yes sir, I mean thank you sir. When will I be leaving?"

"This evening, collect your briefing pack from Mrs Baker and pack a bag, you'll need a warm coat."

This feels like a big moment. The fact that she has been chosen for the assignment over Dan gives her a good feeling, followed by a smidgeon of guilt. She is sure that she will be able to leave things for Dan to supervise without him changing anything or needing to do much. She collects her envelope from Mrs Baker, who has it on her desk waiting for her, and leaves all the most recent updates for Dan on his desk with a note, then departs.

O'Brien was not joking about the coat. Alice spends the next eight days in Russia. She is part of a team, a small part, working with Russian counterparts to end the exile of Andrei Sakharov, nuclear physicist and disarmament campaigner. Between them they mapped out a pathway for enabling him to return to Moscow, and for the Russian government to use this as propaganda, an advertisement for Gorbachev's intent to follow through on the nuclear non-proliferation talks that were still in progress.

The work required long hours, and Alice's input was well received by other team members. Her eye for the detail and practicalities came in useful, although long nights in her hotel room reading classified background papers meant she had little time for anything other than sitting in highly decorated meeting rooms with men in suits. She did manage a whirlwind taxi tour with a colleague one evening before she left. Driving through the snow to see St Basil's Cathedral, magnificently lit up in the dark. The evening finished off with some vodka in the hotel bar.

She felt a great deal of satisfaction when she left to return home, everything was now in place for Sakharov to return to home in a few days' time.

It was late when Alice got back to the centre. On her return the first thing she did was report to O'Brien.

"Welcome back, how was the flight?"

"Fine sir, I just thought I'd let you know how it went."

"No need, I've read the briefings, I've also had positive feedback about your contribution."

She tried not to let the surprise show, she thought she hadn't done a great deal, just some suggestions. Anyway, she shouldn't really be surprised that O'Brien had been keeping tabs, she was his recommendation after all.

"Go and get some rest, it's business as usual here tomorrow."

"Yes sir, and thank you sir, for giving me the opportunity to go."

"You earned it, keep doing what you do."

She got up to leave, as she reached the door O'Brien spoke again;

"Alice."

"Yes sir."

"Now you know what your dad used to do. Goodnight."

So, a mystery solved. She was secretly pleased that her father hadn't been some kind of covert assassin or spy, she wondered how many places he'd worked, which people he'd met in the Forties and Fifties, all classified information that went to the grave with him.

The next morning, slightly later than usual, she returned to her office to catch up on work she has missed while she was away. There were numerous incidental reports and other projects that she gets out of the way before getting to Dan's update. She has saved this for last, it is her personal project, and she wants to give it her full attention. As she read Dan's report her face darkened, and as she got to the end she pushed her chair back with enough force to make it teeter on two legs momentarily before settling. She picked up the report and marched to Dan's office where she found him leaning back in his chair with his pen in his mouth.

"Greetings comrade," he says grinning. "How can I help you?"

"All you had to do was watch him."

"That's what I did."

"No, you didn't. You sent that idiot undercover operative back."

"We need to keep a closer eye on him, he's getting very close to that girl you know?"

"I know, it's helping him get over things."

"Best to keep tabs though eh?"

"But he already knows that man, he'll recognise him. I don't want to spook him."

Dan's grin never leaves his face.

"Oops, never thought of that. Perhaps he's forgotten him by now."

"You are an idiot."

Alice had been standing in the open doorway of Dan's office, and now O'Brien came out of his door to see what the noise was about. He walked wordlessly over to Alice and holds his hand out.

"May I have a look please?"

Alice handed him the report and retreated back to her own office to start to try and undo the damage that has been done, slightly embarrassed by the scene she has caused, but still furious with Dan.

Chapter 16
New Year Revolution

Finally, the holiday grinds to a halt and people start to reappear, ready for the start of term. I have no idea when Grace is likely to arrive, so I walk to her halls to check if she has returned. She is not here yet, but Shelly is back and unpacked. She invites me in to wait with her and makes a cup of tea. Shelly is pretty easy to talk to, she gives me the full run down on her Christmas break – including details of most of what she has eaten and drunk. She expects nothing of me in return, other than I listen, which suits me. She confesses that she has got back as early as she could because she has been writing to the guy she met at the end of term, she is pretty sure they are going to be an item.

The time passes quickly, I take my turn at making the tea and politely go outside to smoke, Shelly is a non-smoker and has asthma. It is while I am standing outside, wrapped tight in my coat (it has got really cold today) that I spot Grace lugging her bag along the path. I walk to meet her, she drops her luggage and runs into my arms, kissing me full on the mouth. Almost immediately she releases me and runs past me to throw herself at Shelly, who has come out to greet her. I go back and pick up her bag and carry it to her room for her.

When we are finally alone we have a longer, more extended welcome back. We resurface in time to go out for a drink with Shelly and some of Grace's other friends. While we were busy Shelly has arranged for her mystery man to join us in the pub. We order drinks and find a table away from the door, out of reach of the icy blasts of wind that find their way in whenever it opens.

We have been here for half an hour or so, and are just debating who's round it is next when Shelly's new man joins us. She jumps up and runs to greet him, making more colour, noise and movement than the pub has seen all evening. Then she brings Simon over to the table where he offers to get the next round in. I sit in mute horror and Grace grips my hand under the table and looks at me.

"Okay?"

"Not really."

Simon and Shelly are still at the bar.

"It'll be fine, he's quite nice really."

I can't answer. My inability to explain, my fear of saying too much, is paralysing. Shelly and Simon return with armfuls of beer and I sit in silence as everybody is introduced and starts to compare Christmas and share tales of drunken New Year excesses. I get up and go to the loo, leaving them to their outlandish tales.

I am just finishing off when Simon comes in, I see him in the mirror as I go to rinse my hands.

"You okay mate?"

I grunt and shrug.

"I'm not your mate, I know who you really are."

"You don't even know the half of it. Mate."

By now he is beside me at the sinks, he smiles a huge grin that makes me die a bit inside.

"Come on then, let's get back out there and have a good evening shall we?"

I manage another half an hour or so of sitting barely speaking before Grace announces, "I'm knackered after all that travelling, I'm going home. Are you walking me back?"

"Yes, I'll just finish this." I say, downing the tail end of my pint and standing up to put on my jacket. There are lots of goodbyes and some tentative arrangements for tomorrow before we go out into the frigid air.

"Wow! You've really got something with him haven't you? Are you okay?"

"Better now we're out here."

"What is it about him?"

"I can't tell you."

"Why not."

"I just can't."

"Can't or won't?"

"Can't. Trust me on this, if I told you, you wouldn't believe me."

"Maybe I would."

I don't answer. Grace is clearly puzzled and confused by my reaction. I want to tell her, to explain everything. But it's my secret to carry, and even now I can feel it gnawing away like a rat, trying to get out. I know what will happen to me if I can't keep my secrets. What I don't know is what will happen to the people I tell, maybe that is what scares me the most, although it is most likely my own self-preservation that drives me, rather than my altruism.

We walk back in silence. By the time we get to Grace's all I want to do is go home and be by myself. I apologise profusely and arrange to meet up tomorrow, then walk myself home. I sit at the desk in my room in the dark. I have left the curtains open and sit looking out of the window into the darkened street wondering who else is watching me. The couple that moved into the flat over the road before Christmas? The old man who walks his dog up and down our road each morning and evening? The next-door neighbours that we don't really talk to that much? Maybe it's all of them? Maybe it's none?

The next few weeks are bitterly cold, the wind howls in from the East relentlessly, freezing everything in its icy path. There is snow and the sun does not make an appearance at all, leaving the frost and ice to stay where it is in the constant sub-zero temperatures.

I manage to make things up with Grace, and being mostly too cold to get out and about for long we don't have many opportunities to meet up with groups of friends. Grace is consciously avoiding meeting with Shelly when I am around, as she usually has Simon in tow. Simon has charmed and disarmed Shelly and is a regular feature now, to her delight. Grace does not press me further, seeming content to let it go for now. Hopefully this will buy time for me to think of a strategy that is more sophisticated than 'shut up and leave.'

Because the harsh weather is so relentless through the whole of January, many lectures are cancelled as staff struggle to get into work. Much of the country has ground to a virtual standstill and we have extra time to spend together. Grace comes to meet the family one afternoon, as promised. A cake is baked especially for the occasion and the baby photos are bought out during the afternoon, to my disgust. Even my sister comes down from her room to cast her eye over Grace and give her approval, or otherwise, of my girlfriend.

I walk Grace home, we are wrapped in as many scarves, coats, gloves and hats as we can find.

"Sorry about that."

"What?"

"My family."

"They were lovely, they made a cake and everything."

"They were embarrassing."

"No, they were lovely. The baby photos were embarrassing though, cute baby butt!"

"They are definitely not lovely."

"Well, I liked them."

She stops and wraps her gloved hands around me and we kiss, icy noses rubbing together. Grace stamps her feet and starts to walk again.

"I might pop round more often."

"You won't!"

We continue the to and fro until we get back to Grace's tiny room, with its single bed and two duvets to try and keep the cold out. We won't freeze tonight, snuggled up together keeping each other warm.

*

Eventually the weather starts to warm up, and before we know it it's time for my school placement. Eight weeks of hell that takes me up to Easter. There are long days, and lots to do in the evening; planning, marking, writing up, recording. The only thing that makes it worthwhile is that it is such good fun working with a class of eight-year olds. There is never a dull moment - and never a quiet moment.

I am so focussed, I dominate mealtimes at home talking about what me and my class have been doing. I find myself forgetting to be worried, and remember why it was that I wanted to go to college in the first place.

Grace and I have become like ships that pass in the night. We barely see each other. The nights we do pass are fitted between our hectic schedules, and when I am too tired to do anything except collapse into bed at the end of the day. The weeks pass quickly and we both look forward to the end.

The final assessment of the teaching practise is a big deal. Everything you have done is scrutinised, graded and double checked. I am confident that I have got everything under control, but am still nervous as hell on the big day. When it comes it is anti -climactic. My folder does not look as if it has been more than flicked through, the assessor only spends a short time in my classroom. There is little or no conversation before I am handed a piece of paper with a summary of what this been observed and a grade. I have passed comfortably. The summary seems to contain some exaggerations of the quality of my work. I not going to argue about it though, I am glad it is over and I am glad that I passed.

Grace is also satisfied with her grade, and we arrange to go out and celebrate, along with Shelly, Simon and the others. In rare non-busy moments, I have been giving thought to how I can tackle the 'Simon situation'. Grace has not mentioned it again, but I know it troubles her. I hate Simon with every fibre of my being, but I also know that it will cause ripples that will become waves if I can't deal with this. My plan is simple, I am going to treat Simon as if he is my best friend ever!

Okay, I know this is not a brilliant plan overall, I'm not that good an actor. But I am determined to give it my best shot, I start immediately. The others are already in the pub. We are running late because we had 'things' to do before we came out, we are celebrating after all. I walk straight over and stand behind Simon putting my hand on his shoulder.

"Don't get up, I'll get these. Who needs another?"

Naturally, everyone does. I memorise the order, it is mostly lager so not too complicated. I ferry the drinks back to the table and share them out, then get the girl next to Simon to budge over so I can pull an extra chair in and sit next to him. I immediately start up a conversation with him.

"Where did you get your hair cut, it looks good?"

He looks at me quizzically, then he names a salon in town. Mine had been attacked by a local barber before my school placement. It was starting to grow back now to its normal untidy self. The haircut conversation is fairly brief, all the time my heart beating at 100 miles per hour as I sit with my nemesis. Even if I say so myself, I am good at this. I keep up a level of banal conversation, gently pumping him for snippets of information about himself and his life away from college.

"Where do you live?"

"No, not now, where are your family from?"

"How's your overdraft doing?"

"Really, mine too!"

I am vaguely hoping that I will gain some kind of advantage in our relationship. I don't know yet how that will help, but I have no better ideas.

The evening moves on, we all get a little drunker and I make sure that Simon doesn't fall behind on the drink quota. He tries to start a conversation with the girl next to him and I sense the tiny chink in his armour, he doesn't actually want to sit and talk to me at all. The girl is busy and he tries to talk to Shelly across the table. Shelly is deep in conversation with Grace, thanks Grace.

I turn the conversation to politics, specifically the impending general election. Personally, I think Neil Kinnock is going to be a vast improvement on Maggie, a chance to undo some of the shit things that have happened in the country in the last few years.

Simon does not think this, and can't contain himself,

"He'll ruin the country. The man's an idiot."

I should point out that this is not necessarily the best point of view to express at a table full of students.

"He's got ideals, he wants to make things better, and he wants to cancel Trident."

"Exactly, the man's an idiot. He'll leave the country defenceless."

Hah! Chink in the armour number two. Simon does not seem to be able to help himself from showing his political colours. If this doesn't ostracise him, I don't know what will. I change the topic to football, which I seem to be the only person on the table who has any interest in. Simon tries gamely to join in, but it's like he didn't even watch last summer's world cup. I am sure it doesn't go unnoticed. As he flounders, I quickly change the subject to music.

"What are you listening to at the moment?"

Simon reels off the names of some bands, like a list he's learnt. Some I don't like, I am at best apathetic to most of them. Simon mentions The Smiths. To clarify, I don't like them, but I read the NME regularly, I have a basic knowledge of them and their music. Simon, it turns out, doesn't. By now other people around the table have joined in the conversation, I sit back and let it happen. There are several diehard Smiths fans here (aren't there always?) who try to educate Simon as only the mad Morrisey brigade can. I withdraw from the conversation and happily watch Simon's life grow more complicated. Grace gives me a 'look', then smiles and turns back to Shelly. I sip my drink and am happier, now I have a strategy for dealing with Simon when he attaches himself to our group of friends. I will build on this success with my 'friend' Simon.

*

I am studying harder than I ever have before, which is not much to boast about, but is tiring. Finals are approaching, and there is coursework to complete. I am deep inside a book when Mum knocks and comes into my room with a cup of tea.

"Thanks Mum."

"That's okay, how's the work going?"

"Yeah all right, I think I understand this."

I hold up John Holt's Why Children Fail to clarify that it is work not leisure. I am busy finding and committing sections to memory, ready to make a point in an essay. It is full of underlining and scribbled notes.

"That's good. I know you're really busy, but if you have a minute do you think you could have a bit of a tidy in here?"

I look around. It is true that my study and work habits have changed in the last months. My organisation of my personal space has not. There are piles of clean and dirty clothes – not together, I'm not an animal. There are mugs and plates all over the desk, cassettes and vinyl records in various places around the room and even a couple of college boxes that I never got round to unpacking. These are ones that Dad was going to bring up to me, before things changed. It is mostly posters and student union stuff that I haven't needed, so have just left.

"Sure, I'll do it later. I need to take a break before my eyes start bleeding."

"Okay, try to do some – we're running out of clean cups downstairs."

I finish off the chapter I am reading and make a few more notes, then stop and look around the room, formulating a plan of attack.

Firstly, I decant the kitchenware downstairs, fill the sink and wash up. I leave the small mountain to dry, while I go back upstairs for phase two. This involves putting away clean clothes and another trip downstairs with an armful of laundry that I load straight into the machine and switch it on.

I think the room would be tidier if Grace ever stayed over, but I never suggest it. I rarely have the house to myself, and Grace has a perfectly good room that we can stay in. She has never complained about this. I spend some pleasant time organising and sorting my music into correct sleeves and cases and putting them away, before making my bed and finishing organising my desk. The last job is the college boxes. I am in two minds as to whether to just throw the lot in the bin or lift them into the loft to sort another day.

In the end my conscience, combined with my reluctance to return to John Holt, gets the better of me and I start unpacking them. The first box is entirely notes from student union meetings. Minutes, newsletters, agendas and other associated materials. I rifle through and find nothing that needs to be kept, so I carry the whole box down to the bin and cram it in on top of the other rubbish.

The next box is less straightforward. It has the posters that would have gone on my bedroom wall at college, if they had ever made it that far. I already have posters on the walls of this bedroom, which is why I never got round to unpacking it. I take out rolls of posters and sheets of folded images and look through them. Joy Division are there, looking mean and moody in an underpass. There is a print I liked by Salvador Dali, some swans/elephants on a lake. No kittens in flowerpots or tennis girls scratching their arses for me.

Also in the box are some letters from home that I received while at college. I pause to unfold them and catch up with some two years out of date family news. There is a small bundle of tickets from bands I have seen; Siouxsie and the Banshees, The Gun Club, Danse Society, Eurythmics, Bucks Fizz. The last one was Paul's choice not mine, although I have to admit to enjoying it - a bit.

There is a selection of unwritten postcards, I smile when I see them. It was a kind of joke. At the end of our first year we all agreed to bring back pictures of our hometown to share, so we could all have a bit of home in each other's rooms. Kind of stupid, but most of us remembered, even though it was one in the morning and we had been drinking when we decided it. I have cards from Sevenoaks, Carshalton, Norwich and Southend-on-Sea among other places. I pull them out of the box; each card reminding me of the person who had given it to me. Sue was the Southend-on-Sea card, showing the beach and pier, Newbury was Lisa, her card is a bridge that looks like it is joining two houses together over a river or canal. I feel a lump in my throat, my chest is tightening and I think I am going to cry. I go outside for a smoke and to get myself back together.

I have another surprise when I get back. I don't own a camera myself, so don't have any photos of my time at college. But from time-to-time people had passed me prints from films they had developed. At the bottom of the pile of cards there are three photographs, last year they had been stuck on my bedroom wall, together with the postcards and posters. I had forgotten they were there.

Now, here they are. First is a picture of me and Sue standing together outside the college bar. It is dark and the blackness of the night frames us. I am clearly drunk, grinning inanely as I wrap my arm around my prize, it was the night of the party when we had finally become a couple, having got past her phalanx of friends and her despicable boyfriend. Sue's friend had taken it and given it to Sue, she in turn had passed it on to me. I suspect that her friend just didn't want a photo of me in her album, her loss.

I look at our faces and think how young we look. I can remember the feel of the warmth of the evening, feeling Sue in my arms as we kissed and shared the joy of a carefree summer evening.

The next photo is a grainy group shot taken in low light. I am only just in it, in the bottom right corner. Paul, Lisa and Jo were there, along with some other friends. Sarah took the photo, she left it in my room one evening when she told me I should get a camera, then I could 'have beautiful pictures like this' in my room. It is not beautiful, everyone has red eyes from the flash, there is a pall of smoke, we all look slightly drunk. There is a clutter of glasses on the table and Lisa is looking in the opposite direction from everybody else. We all appear to be mouthing an obscenity to Sarah, whose standard photo instruction was 'say shit'.

The third and final photo is of just Sue. She is wearing a Halloween costume, a mass of black eye make-up and backcombed hair, she is grinning inanely. Ostensibly she is dressed as a witch. If you think of witches as being 19-year-olds with short black dresses, revealing black stockings and lots of cleavage, then she is. I think if that was really the case, witches would never have got all the bad press they have over the years. I remember that night, it was a good night and it ended well, witches are bad after all!

I stand the postcards on my desk, leaning against my pencil pot. I then tuck the photos inside the cover of John Holt. I put the rest back into the box and take it up to the loft. I go back to look at my room and admire the tidiness of it before grabbing my jacket and leaving to meet Grace.

Simon does not turn up at the pub this evening. Shelly is concerned and goes to look for him. The evening is slow and quiet and I am thoughtful, looking at the group of people around me that I have come to call friends, and Grace who I'm pretty sure I am falling in love with. They are good friends, but I am aware that I have been slow to let them in. All the time I have had my other friends that I have been missing. Finding the photos has reminded me of this and made me nostalgic at best, maudlin at worst.

On the way back to her room Grace asks if I'm okay.

"Yeah fine, a bit on my mind, you know."

"You can talk to me about it you know?"

"I can't, but it makes me feel good that you would listen if I did."

"Is it really that bad?"

"Worse."

"You are so mysterious, if you can't share whatever it is with me maybe I should try and make you forget it."

Grace does her usual sterling job of distracting me from what's on my mind, without being judgemental or impatient. This is why I think I am in love. We go back to her room and I let her spend the night distracting me.

The next morning I go back home, letting myself in and heading upstairs early to get the things I need for college. It looks wrong. It's not just the fact that it is not the tip it was yesterday, I'm certain it's not how I left it. I scan the room to see what it is that's different, but can't put my finger on it. I hear mum on the landing,

"Mum, did you get anything from my room last night?"

"No, I only looked through the door to see how far you got with the tidying. Well done!"

"Did dad go in my room?"

By now Mum is standing in my bedroom doorway with me.

"No, he's at work; he's been on nights."

"Did…."

"No, she stayed over at Claire's last night, watching some film thing on video. What's wrong with your room?"

"I don't know, it's like someone has been in here."

"Maybe the cat came in?"

I hold the doorframe in one hand and start clenching and unclenching my fist, I know that it is not right, but there is nothing I can pinpoint. Mum can see me looking around, she puts her arm around me.

"It's okay, we'll figure it out. Come on downstairs. We'll have some toast and a cup of tea."

"Yeah sure," I say, looking back over my shoulder as I am guided out of the room, then it hits me, nothing is wrong, nothing is out of place, nothing is left the way I would have most certainly have left it, even in the short time between tidying and going out. It's perfect.

I sit and eat my toast while I sip my tea and calm down.

"Are you sure you're okay? Should I call Dr Morgan, she said this might happen."

"God no! I mean no, I'm feeling better, the toast has done its job."

"Are you sure? Tell us if you want us to cancel this weekend."

"Is that this week?"

Mum, Dad and my sister are off for the weekend to a family wedding. I had cried off because of the closeness of exams. Or because it is only a distant cousin and I don't really want to go. You decide which excuse you think is the real one.

"Are you sure you'll be alright by yourself?"

"Maybe I'll ask Grace to come over and keep me company, we can study together."

"That's a good idea, you should ask her."

"I think I will."

I know full well I will. The house to ourselves for a whole weekend with nobody to bother us, why wouldn't I?

Later, when the house is quiet, I go down to the phone in the hallway. I take the card from my pocket and dial the number. In the still of the night I hear the phone at the other end ring. What am I going to say? Am I going to ask if someone was looking at my stuff? Have they been in my room? It starts to ring a second time and I quickly hang up and go back upstairs.

*

The weekend comes, and Grace arrives with her overnight bag, about an hour after my family have left. I take her upstairs to show her my room, where I have pushed the two beds together and borrowed the spare double duvet. It wouldn't feel right to use my parents' bed, for all sorts of reasons. Also, they have expressly forbidden me from doing so.

I have been to the shops to buy some food, and now show off my non-existent culinary skills to Grace. She quickly recognises my ineptitude and steps in, explaining the rudiments of basic cookery to me in much the same way she might explain a seemingly simple task to one of her classes of six-year-olds. I have also splashed out on a bottle of 'not the cheapest' wine. I busy myself with uncorking this, which I am capable of, and pouring it into glasses. The evening goes well, we eat, drink and end up in bed. Grace falls asleep and I watch her for a while. The curls of her hair spread over the pillow and she looks beautiful and peaceful. I feel like I should hold onto this moment, to capture it and keep it.

I come back from the kitchen where I have made breakfast. The sun has been up for a while, but we are in no rush today. As I walk into the bedroom Grace is sitting at my desk. She is wearing my Bruce Springsteen t-shirt and not much else, and is sifting through the piles of books and notes on the desk.

"What shall we read first today?"

"You."

"Seriously, we can't stay in bed all day."

"Why not?"

"Work to do."

"Can't we do some and some?"

I have taken a bite of my toast and started sipping my tea, which is still too hot really. Grace picks up John Holt and, to my horror, the photos spill onto the desk. She picks them up and looks at each one in turn as I chew my now tasteless toast, which I have to force down with my scalding tea.

"What was her name?"

"Sue."

Grace is smiling, she looks at the photos of Sue in the witch costume, then the one of me and Sue together.

"She's pretty. Is that who you were with when we met?"

"Kind of, yes, it's complicated."

I catch a glimmer of something in Grace's eyes, it is fleeting but it is there. I think it is hurt. She holds up the third photo and asks who the people are. I begin to name them, starting with myself. I almost do it too, but when I get to Lisa my voice cracks. I look at the grainy image of her face looking

172

away from the camera, I can't say her name and feel myself starting to tremble. Grace is quickly alongside me with her arm around my shoulders.

"It's okay, I'm sorry. I didn't mean to pry, they just fell out."

"No, I'm sorry. I found them last week, I'd forgotten I had them. I just didn't want them to get creased."

"You know it's okay, don't you? Whatever happened there is over, it's finished."

"No, it'll never be over."

"How bad could it be?"

"I can't tell you. It is bad, and if I told you, it would be bad for you too."

Grace gives me a look that is sincere, but at the same time disbelieving, if that's possible.

"What happened to her?"

She points to Lisa's face. I pull myself together a little.

"She's called Lisa. Was called Lisa. She died."

There is a dawning realisation on Grace's face that maybe things were as bad as I had been telling her.

"It was my fault."

"Was it? Or was it an accident?"

"It was an accident that was my fault."

"That's not how accidents work you know?"

"Can we change the subject? I'm really not supposed to talk about any of this to anybody. I'm sorry."

"Well, let's chuck this cold toast away and go make some fresh, and some hot tea."

"Good idea, I like that plan."

I give Grace a hug. She holds me tightly, but I can sense the space that has appeared between us. I owe her an explanation, but I'm terrified of what will happen to me. Also to Grace of course. But in truth mostly me if I'm being honest.

We have breakfast and a fresh cup of tea, both of us trying hard to stop the impending silence from taking over. I put some music on and sing along with Lou Reed. Grace gives a commentary on what she is doing. Between us we manage to fill the gaps until we settle to some studying. We sit comfortably on the bed together, lost in note taking, reading and asking one another about bits we don't understand. That last bit is mostly me.

Grace packs up her things mid-way through the afternoon and I carry her bag back to her room. We take the long route via the beach. It is still mostly empty this early in the year. We walk comfortably together, the awkwardness of earlier is now spent. We chat and even manage to find some things to laugh about. We kiss when we get back to Grace's room.

"Thanks."

"For the kiss?"

"Well, yes that, but also for being there - and for understanding."

"I'm not sure that I do, but I'll try."

Grace is abruptly requisitioned by Shelly, who is inconsolable having been ignored by Simon for the last week. I return home.

When I get back to the house the car is still not back. I had expected the family to have returned by now, but am happy to have a few stolen minutes of peace. I hang my jacket on the hooks by the front door and go up to my room.

Andrew Prince is sitting in the same place that I found Grace this morning. He is even sat in the same position, with one leg tucked under him. He is holding the photos in a fan, tapping them gently on the edge of the desk. I am too surprised to speak. I stand in the doorway wondering whether to run. I haven't done anything wrong – have I? Did I say something I shouldn't to Grace? Is this it, where life as I know it ends?

"You rang. Sit down before you fall down."

I obediently follow the direction and sit on the edge of the bed. Andrew Prince is still dressed in his tie-less work shirt and smart trousers, his dark hair is swept to one side and his chin is scraped clean of facial hair. He puts the photos on the desk and leans forward, looking straight at me.

"You rang us."

My mouth is dry and my heart is thumping in my chest.

"I wanted to know if anyone had been in my room."

"They have now, nice photos."

He taps the group photo with a neatly manicured fingernail.

"I didn't say anything, to anybody. I only said their names."

Everything swims in and out of focus. I am scared for me, scared for Grace. Andrew Prince talks soothingly,

"I know, but it was close, wasn't it? You nearly let the cat out of the bag."

I look around the room quickly, how the fuck does he know what I said? Is he listening? How? Does he listen to everything I do in here? Did he hear us making love? He seems to sense what I'm thinking.

"We told you we'd be watching. Don't bother looking though, you'll never find them. I drop in from time to time, I overheard this morning's conversation. You're getting very close to Grace, it's easier to make a mistake when you're comfortable with someone."

I guess that the 'them' are hidden microphones that I had no idea were even in the room. I also sense a hint of a lie about how often I'm being listened to. I wonder how long it has been going on, probably since I got back. I wonder how scared they are, to go to all this trouble to make sure I don't tell my story. Surely if it was this crucial they should have kept me when they had me. I guess that would mean locking all of us up. Maybe that would be too big to keep quiet. Andrew Prince grins at me. It is not a pleasant grin, I am convinced that he knows what I am thinking.

"The others all went too. They all got transfers."

"Where did they go?"

"I don't know, although I wouldn't tell you if I did, it's best you don't know."

"Why? Why is it so important?"

"There you go again, talking about things that never happened. Listen, I won't visit you again. If we have to speak again it will be back at the centre. You know how that goes. It's really important right now, and it's up to you."

I think of midnight abductions, sunless rooms, long days and enforced solitude, and I nod.

"Good, while I'm here you might as well have these."

He reaches into a black briefcase by the chair and pulls out a bundle of envelopes wrapped in a rubber band. I recognise them instantly, my letters to Sue. She had never received a single one. She never knew what happened to me, how I felt about her. She had never had a chance to give me the forgiveness I asked for. I take them and turn them over in my hand, flicking the edges with my thumb.

"Your grammar isn't always so good, but I liked the poem."

The last carries a hint of sarcasm, Andrew Prince gets up and picks up his briefcase. He walks past me and out of the bedroom door. As he is leaving, he looks back,

"No offence, but I hope I never see you again."

"None taken, it's mutual."

I stand shaking and watch through the window as he leaves the house. He walks down the short path and a blue Ford Escort pulls up by the kerb just as he reaches it. He turns and waves towards me as he is getting into the back of the car and then is gone. Seconds later the family car pulls up and everyone comes spilling into the house. I sit in my room looking at the bundle of letters in my hand and I shake, I throw them into the corner. As they hit the wall the rubber band holding them together gives way and the bundle explodes scattering the letters onto the floor.

Alice

Now she has got to 'play with the big boys' in Jones' words, Alice is called on intermittently for her input into other projects. She is called away to various locations and has to leave the centre, and her monitoring of Sid, to Dan each time she goes. O'Brien had words after the first time and has politely asked Dan to consult him before he acts on anything to do with Sid in the future. It is common knowledge in the centre that if O'Brien asks you politely for something, you make sure he gets it.

The situation with the undercover operative appears to have resolved itself. He was indeed recognised, in fact he almost seemed to have introduced himself. Sid dealt with it. Alice admired this, it must have taken some courage. She felt bizarrely proud of him for the way he managed the situation, as if he was her protege. She knows he still has bad days, and that not enough time has passed for him to feel anything but hurt. This intrusion on his recovery could have been a real setback. She is glad it wasn't. She has grown quite fond of him by now, watching his re-entry to the world with interest, she thinks he would make a good case study for someone one day, if the information surrounding him wasn't classified.

After one of her trips away, Zurich this time, Alice comes back to an ominous report. Dan has visited Sid. She reads through the report, frowning, then walks the short distance to O'Brien's office and knocks.
"Come in."
"Have you seen....?" Alice starts, then stops as she sees a copy of the report on his desk in front of him.
"I thought you'd be in soon, sit down. Do you want a cup of tea?"
O'Brien asks Mrs Baker to bring in some drinks and asks how Switzerland went. Alice had been at meetings where the ramifications of Willy Brandt's decision to step down as the leader of the Social Democratic Party in West Germany was being discussed. It was hoped he would be persuaded to lend his support and influence to the work being done to reunite the two Germany's.
"I think it was very positive, I can see it happening. Not yet, but soon. There's still a lot to iron out."
"Well, it's good it's still in the pipeline. Now, about this."
He sips his tea and taps the report with his free hand.
"I can't believe he did it."
"Which bit?"
"Any of it. Visiting was a terrible idea, giving all his letters back was an even worse one. It could be disastrous, he's still trying to adjust, this could really unsettle him again."
"I agree, you've confirmed what I was thinking. I'll deal with Dan, but I

want you to monitor carefully and closely for a while. Right now is not the time for anything to come out."

"I understand."

Alice has already cleared her diary, and moved Sid to her number one priority. They conclude their meeting and she goes back to her office ready to plan a trip to the seaside. Later, in spite of the thick walls and doors, she hears muffled shouting coming from further down the corridor. She shakes her head slightly and smiles to herself before finalising her arrangements.

Chapter 17
The Plan

Easter is approaching fast. I am still not over Andrew Prince's visit. I have spent the time since then studying, being with Grace and stewing over the injustice of things. I know I can't carry on like this forever, I have to do something. It is while I am sitting at my desk that it comes to me.

I have put my postcard collection in a line on the window sill. Each card shows me the hometown of one of my friends. I am pretty certain they will have all gone back to live at home, like me, somewhere they can be monitored and supervised. I don't have any home addresses of my friends, I am not much of a letter writer – apparently my grammar isn't that good. I did have an address book, but could never find it after I got back home.

But the cards would do it. I could visit the towns on the cards. I could look up people's names in their local phone books and track them down. If I could talk to somebody who understood, maybe I could figure out what to do, how to make things right. Also, I might get a message to Sue, to tell her how sorry I am. I get no studying done as I sit and think through what I need to do, and how I can do it.

Eventually I have the kernel of a plan, but I can't do it by myself. I will need Grace's help, and for that I'm going to have to be very careful. I'm also going to have to tell her a bit more. I am not suspicious by nature, but recent events have made me wary. I can't be 100% sure Grace isn't with them. I'm pretty sure she's not, I really like her and it would hurt to know she was not what she seemed.

I call for her the next day, she is pleased to see me, we have been too busy to get together for a few days. If she is betraying me she is doing a great acting job. I keep things as normal as possible while we are indoors, who knows where else is bugged? I suggest a walk to the beach. Grace is up for it so we put on our coats and go. I walk us to the far end where the cliffs start. It is deserted, there is a brisk breeze and only the most hardy, foolish or determined have come this far today. I sit on a rock and light a cigarette, Grace perches next to me and snuggles up. We watch some seabirds swoop and dive on the wind for a while, enjoying the sound of the waves, enjoying a quiet moment together. I flick my cigarette end away.
"I need your help."

Grace looks at me, I can tell she is intrigued immediately. I can also tell she is cautious.

"Okay."

"It's complicated, you're going to think I'm crazy."

"I already do, but I love you anyway."

This is the first time either of us has said this. I pause, not knowing how to respond. Then I hug her.

"I think I love you too. Although I don't know what you see in me."

"What I saw the very first time I met you. You were so handsome, but you looked so sad, you had the weight of the world on your shoulders and I wanted to make it better."

"I was a charity case then?"

I get a punch on the arm for my trouble. I deserve it.

"No. you looked like someone who didn't know who he was. Does that sound weird? From when you first talked to me it was like you didn't expect me to be anybody but myself, and you never have. I nearly didn't come back to college after the summer this year, I know it sounds stupid with so many people here, but I find it lonely. Then there was you, and we could be lonely together which made it seem better."

Grace has never looked more beautiful, with the wind blowing her hair around her face and her brown eyes looking into mine. I realise how much I have to lose and nearly back out. Just let things lie, get on with life and move on But I can't, there is unfinished business that I have to at least try to make right.

"You helped me find my place too, thank you for being you. I wouldn't want you to be anything else. I need to talk to you, it's important. We can only talk here, there are people listening everywhere else."

I expected this to be met with some kind of snigger or dismissal, but Grace merely nods at me to continue.

"I have to do something, I have to try and sort some things out, but there are people who will try and stop me."

Again, I get a nod to carry on.

"I want us to plan for me to come and visit you this Easter. We need to make the plan in my room so they know what I am doing. I need them to think that's where I'm going."

"They?"

"I honestly don't know, but they are listening and they need to know what I'm doing. Or think they know."

"So, you're not coming to visit then?"

"No."

"That's a shame. My mum would really like to meet you."

"If it all goes tits up you may never see me again."

Grace looks genuinely alarmed at this. I am not sure if it's the prospect of not seeing me, or the fact that I am clearly unhinged. I carry on and explain the plan about visiting towns and trying to make contact with people.

"Why are you doing this, if it's so dangerous?"

"Me and my friends did something stupid last year. It turned out it was pretty dangerous too, in lots of ways. It's best if you don't know what. I was at least partly to blame, and Lisa died. There are a lot of people that I never got to apologise to. If I don't at least try I know I will regret it."

"You are so fucking mysterious sometimes, I don't know what you did, I'm not sure I want to. If you have to do this I'll help. But I wish you wouldn't."

"I have to."

"Will you see Sue?"

"I need to let her know that I didn't mean to hurt her, or anyone."

Grace looks at me. I'm not sure what she sees, but she seems content. She holds my hand and kisses me.

"We'd better go back and start planning then. Of course, if you can think of anything else we can do while we're busy making plans, let me know."

"I can think of lots of things."

"I'm not talking about playing games on that stupid ZX Spectrum."

"Oh, okay, I can only think of one thing then."

I run my cold fingers up the inside of her thick woollen jumper and squeeze her breast. She shrieks at the sudden coldness of it, but she doesn't stop me. She pulls closer and kisses me, sliding her own hands into the waistband of my jeans, which makes me jump.

"Before we go back, tell me, is Simon one of 'them'?"

"I think he is yes. He was at my old college, but had a different name."

"He hurt my friend, anything I can do to get back at him will be my pleasure."

She grins an evil grin that I have never seen before, and am not sure I want to see again, especially not if I am the intended recipient.

"How did you know?"

"He seemed alright at first, but the effect he had on you, and the trouble he went to get close to you was weird. He was always asking Shelly questions about me and you. And he never really fitted in, he just seemed to be trying too hard."

The plan is not complicated, we have conversations about when I am going to visit Grace when we are in our rooms. We wrap up in woolly jumpers and warm jackets and walk to the end of the beach when we want to talk in private. We are sitting there now.

"You can still stop this if you want, it's not too late and I won't think badly of you."

"I know, I may just actually come and stay with you. If I can't find anyone and don't get caught, I may come anyway."

"That would be good, I have to warn you though, my parents are mad."

"That's what I told you about mine, but you seem to get on with them."

Since her first visit Grace had become a regular visitor at home. Mum and Grace got on really well. She would turn up with armfuls of books and laundry. I wouldn't get to see her until she'd had a cup of tea and been regaled with all Mum's gossip. She even got on with my sister, sometimes I wouldn't see her alone until an hour or so after she arrived.

"Your parents are lovely…. Look out! Spy dog!"

A spaniel lollops over to where we are sitting, it drops a piece of tooth-marked, sea-worn driftwood at our feet while jumping and barking. The dog's owner keeps calling it. But it takes no notice. Eventually it seems to get bored of us, it collects its stick to take back to its man. A flick of a tail and a spurt of sand and it's gone. We walk slowly back up the beach.

*

I have no reason to be in college right now. It's Easter break and everything is closed and locked. I am here anyway. Something about the familiarity of the buildings and the association with friends settles me. It is quiet here, the rest of town is waking up for the incoming flood of tourists and day-trippers, but here is an oasis of calm. I spend time contemplating what's ahead while looking at the green buds on the trees and the yellow daffodils surrounding the trunks. I walk home along the alleys and back roads.

A few days have passed since Grace left for home. I am upstairs packing a small bag. Some overnight things, a couple of books, an envelope of cash from the building society (many years' worth of birthday and Christmas money) and a small Atlas of the British Isles, with my postcards tucked inside. I go downstairs where Mum is folding laundry.

"Are you off love?"

"Yes, on my way now."

"Well, you have a good time, give Grace my love."

"Will do, I'll see you in a few days."

"Okay, hug for your mum?"

I give the required hug, painfully aware that it could be the last, then head off to the station.

I have decided my first stop should be to try and find Paul. He was not directly involved, so probably won't be being watched. He also has an unusual surname, which may make him easier to track down. Hopefully he will have some other addresses or phone numbers that will help me on my quest.

The journey to London is long, the train is busy and I spend most of it squashed between the dirty window and a large, uncommunicative, man. I am trying to read my book, but am far too preoccupied to concentrate on Tom Joad or his family. I look out of the window as the train approaches the city and watch the urban landscape unfold before me.

I navigate my way across the city to find London Bridge and from there the train that will take me to Sevenoaks, I pay for my ticket and go to the platform to wait for the next train. There is not long to wait, I soon find myself heading back out of the city, into 'the garden of England'. It is green and open and I try to relax, watching the fields flashing by. I am not sure what is going to happen when I get there, the basis of my plan is to find a phone box, hope it has its phone directory intact and start ringing any possible numbers. I have a pocketful of change and some hopeless optimism. The train eventually crawls to a halt at Sevenoaks station and I collect my things and join the other passengers, stepping out onto the platform.

I look up and down, in the hope that there is a phone on the platform. My eyes sweep past a woman sitting on a bench, then snap back. The woman is waving to me. I look behind me as the train starts to pull away, there is nobody else there. I look again, more closely this time, it's Julia. My legs turn to jelly, I look around for an escape route, half expecting burly men to appear, ready to bundle me into a van. I won't go without a fight this time. I look again, Julia beckons and pats the bench next to her, I resign myself to whatever this is and walk over and sit down, lighting a cigarette as I put my bag down.

"Still not given up then? You really should you know."

I look at her, I don't know what I expected her to say, but it wasn't that. I say nothing, but carry on smoking and looking anxiously up and down the platform. There is nobody who doesn't look like a regular passenger.

"It's okay, It's just me "

I look at her again, she is wearing a navy dress and has her hair loose, I guess this is why I didn't recognise her straight away. I still say nothing. Julia smiles at me, a kind smile that could be real.

"You're looking well, have you put on some weight with all that home cooking?"

I'm having trouble with this, I can't think of a thing to say.

"I hear your studies are going well, you've been working hard. That's good."

I crack,

"Thanks, I guess."

"You know why I'm here don't you?"

I nod.

"To take me back to the place I was at before."

I still glance up and down the platform, looking for the best way to try and escape, I think over the tracks, then over the fence on the other side would be my best bet, I'm not even sure if I could make it. But I could try. If it came to it, I would try,

"No, we don't want you back there. We want you back at home, studying, living a life, being happy with Grace. You need to go back, go home or go to stay with Grace, but don't carry on. It won't end well."

"It's already not ending well, I need to do it."

"You don't, not now. This is the worst possible time for you to stir things up."

"But nobody knows where I went, I need to see people, to speak to them."

"Listen, I can only advise you, you are on the wrong track here. You have moved on, they have moved on. There will be time, one day, to mend things if you still want to. But not now."

"Why not now, what's the difference between this month, next month, Christmas?"

"Things are happening. If everything goes to plan later in the year, I will find you, I will explain as much as I can. Things will be easier then. But now, now is not the time."

"How did you know I would be here anyway?"

"We know. The boss told you we'd be watching, I thought you would believe that by now."

I can feel tears coming now, frustration, or of anger? I can't tell, probably both. It takes me by surprise when Julia slides along the bench and puts her arm around me and pulls me close. The tears run freely, I turn my head away and use my sleeve to dry my face, as well as you can with a leather jacket.

"You know, I told the others you would need more support before you left. It must be really hard not being able to talk about it to anybody, especially about Lisa. They're all so full of their macho bullshit, they think you'll just forget it, forget her. I'm glad you haven't, it shows you have a heart and a soul and people will love you for that. All your life people will see that in you and love you for it."

"But I killed her."

"No, you didn't. Look at me."

Julia gently turns my head so I am facing her. We are so close I can smell her perfume, I am looking straight into her eyes.

"You didn't kill Lisa, we did. You were just there and it was unfortunate, but it wasn't you it was us. If you never believe anything else that I tell you, and I won't blame you, you need to know that this one thing is true."

There is something in the way Julia is speaking, something in the tremor in her voice and the pierce of her gaze, which starts to convince me. Now a tear appears in the corner of her eye, small and barely there, but a tear.

"We did something wrong and your friend died for it. Everything I know about Lisa tells me what an extraordinary, intelligent and brave girl she was. I'm truly sorry you lost your friend, she must have been very special to you."

I nod. Julia lets go of me and smooths the front of her dress as she regains her composure.

"Anyway, it's up to you what you do next, there's nobody else here right now. There will be later, when they realise you didn't turn up at Grace's, right now you're free to make a choice. Please make the right one."

"You'll explain it to me?"

"I promise."

I stand up, resigned, and go to look at the timetable to work out how long I will have to wait for the train back. Julia stands up and follows me.

"I'll tell them you got the wrong train. Good luck."

She smiles and nods then slips an envelope into my hand. With that she turns around and leaves the station, with me watching the sway of her buttocks through her navy dress the whole way. Old habits.

I look at the envelope, it has the words 'travelling expenses' printed on the front in blue ink, and I can tell from the feel and weight of it what it contains. I stuff it into my bag and sit on the bench again to wait for my train.

Alice

The lengths that Sid goes to keep his plan secret are quite endearing. Useless, but endearing. Alice listens in to the conversations and has people watching on a daily basis. She is impressed by the efforts he is making to protect his girlfriend, clearly he is still aware of what the repercussions of his actions could be.

As the plan takes shape, she shares it with O'Brien.

"Do you think he'll go through with it?"

"I'm pretty sure he'll try, he seems determined."

"How do you want to handle it?"

"I could confront him before he attempts it. But I think that would just delay it, I'm sure he would still try."

"Probably right. What then?"

"I thought an interception. That way he'll know that we know everything. The only trouble is, we don't know where he's going first. It could be any one of five or six places. But if I can meet him at his first port of call and turn him around, I think he'll get the point."

"I'm inclined to agree with you. Keep tabs, get some watchers and have a van standing by in case he doesn't take the hint."

"I think he will."

"I hope you're right."

Long before he steps onto the train to start his journey there is already someone on board keeping an eye. Alice is monitoring everything from a small airfield in Surrey, with a helicopter standing by to take her to the location, once they have confirmed it.

It feels like a lot of time and effort for just one boy. Although keeping him locked up would be inestimably more expensive than this. The potential cost of him spreading his story could be even more costly, so all in all Alice thinks this is the best option, and O'Brien agrees.

The first part of the day passes slowly as Sid's journey begins, the helicopter pilot drinks tea and makes small talk, Alice can't decide if he's being friendly or flirty. Once the message comes through that he has taken the train into Kent things change. The pilot becomes all business, checking into one of his planned flight routes and readying for the journey to within a couple of miles of the station, where a car will be waiting to meet them.

After a short but exhilarating ride, the pilot is definitely flirting, Alice arrives in plenty of time and settles herself onto a bench on the platform to wait. When the train pulls into the station she watches the other passengers get off while she waits to catch sight of Sid. As she expected, he is one of the last to alight, cautiously looking around the station before setting off. He has a look about him that Alice hasn't seen before, optimism?

Purposefulness? Happiness? She is loath to burst his bubble, but knows it has to be done. When he looks in her direction she waves.

After Alice has left the platform she does not look back or wait around, she knows what he is going to do, and it hurts her. She wants to make it right for him, make things better, but doesn't know how yet. She gets back into the car and returns to the airfield.

Chapter 18
The start of Summer

Me and Grace are on the beach again. I am sitting on the sand wearing a dress shirt with a bow tie dangled around my open collar. Grace is on the sand next to me in a blue gown with my tuxedo jacket draped over her like a blanket. She has her eyes closed, but is not asleep. Her curly hair is in the sand, I wonder how many washes it is going to take to get all the grains out. I think she'll still be finding them for weeks. We have watched the sun come out of hiding, lighting up the sea and starting a new day.

Last night's summer ball was just what we needed after the stress and hard work of final exams. I drank copious amounts of alcohol, I danced with Grace (actually, I danced gracelessly – it's the capital letter that makes the difference there.) I danced with Shelly too, before she went off with her latest acquisition for the night. It was a great night that felt like it would last forever. We couldn't bear to go home, so came here instead. I smoke my last cigarette and look at my beer splashed trousers and sandy jacket. I guess I've lost my deposit on that, but who cares right now? I felt like James Bond for the evening, with the most beautiful woman in the world on my arm.

I wasn't so dapper when I turned up at Grace's parents' house last Easter. I was a mess. I'd spent the journey running the conversation with Julia over in my head. At the time it had seemed to make sense, it felt like I was finally getting some of the answers I wanted so badly. Looking back, it raised more questions than it resolved.

Grace answered the door as the taxi drove off – fuck it, I had a whole envelope full of cash! Her face registered first surprise, then dismay as she realised why I was there. She grabbed me fiercely and pulled me tight without saying a word, then led me inside and started making mugs of tea and asking a hundred and one questions.

I was glad of the tea, I had spent most of the night stranded on the platform of some god-awful station in the back of beyond, huddling inside my leather jacket to try and keep warm until the first train of the day arrived.

I told Grace as much of my story as I could, which made it a bit sparse on detail. I told her about Julia waiting for me, how they knew everything and how she had promised to explain more but wouldn't let me go through with my plan.

I have worried for a while now that Grace may be humouring me, or think I'm going mad. Mysterious people that only I ever see, past events that I can't tell her any details of. I can't even tell her about my disappeared friends. I know I am short on evidence for any of this, and that I'm asking a lot of Grace to believe it.

I ask if it's okay to stay, just for a day or two.

"It's fine, I told mum and dad you might be coming, they're looking forward to meeting you. They're both at work right now, you can surprise them when they get back. Probably not as much as you surprised me, it's great to see you."

I get another hug.

"You look knackered, do you need to sleep?"

"Yes, I didn't sleep much last night. I can contribute towards food."

I take out the envelope and pass it to Grace. She looks puzzled as she reads the inscription on the front and can't stop that look from changing to surprise when she looks inside. She pulls out the wad of twenty-pound notes.

"There must be a thousand pounds here, is this your savings?"

"No."

I show her another, smaller and crumpled envelope with my own cash in.

"Julia gave it to me before she went."

"Why would she do that?"

I shrug.

"Travelling money, she said. These people are weird, they gave me money before, when I changed college."

There have been other times too. Times when I have gone to check my balance at the cash point and found I had more than I thought in my account. Not huge amounts, but enough to keep me solvent. It never showed up on my monthly bank statements. At first I put it down to me being either much better or much worse at budgeting than I thought I was, but it was too regular an occurrence to be a coincidence. I also got a cheque for interest on my savings that was completely out of context with the amount I had in the building society. They insisted it was correct and showed me some complicated calculations to prove it. I didn't argue too much.

Grace looks at me. I know she wanted to believe me before, now she had a real tangible piece of proof in her hand. Now she knows I am not completely delusional. Either that or she thinks I'm a bank robber. She takes me upstairs and puts me in her childhood bed. The room smells of girl. It is pink and fluffy with ornaments and trinkets on the shelves and ledges. There is a teddy bear on the bed and a poster of Duran Duran on the wall, I will rib her about that later. In the interest of balance, there is also a fair collection of empty mugs, glasses and dirty underwear left on the floor. Grace kicks the discarded underwear under the bed and helps me pull off my boots, before I collapse into the bed and fall straight asleep.

Later Grace brings me a sandwich. She puts it on the bedside table and slides in next to me for a hug which turns into something more passionate, resulting in more underwear on the floor.

I meet Grace's parents, who are great. They seem to quite like me, and her younger brother doesn't seem to be able to leave us unattended for more than 10 minutes at a time, he is the ideal chaperone. I insist on seeing baby photos, and Grace's parents are more than happy to oblige, to her indignation. It is comforting to be surrounded by the warm hubbub of family life, laughter, teasing, tantrums, all the elements of normality.

Grace in her natural environment is different from Grace at college. She is more confident, more….whole. She takes me to the places she knows and gives me a commentary on her childhood, where she used to go swimming, where her best friend from primary school used to live, where she fell off her bike and took the skin off both her knees.

We were passing the youth club, where she had her first kiss (Darren Fields, if you're interested.)

"Am I going to meet any of your friends while I'm here?"

There is a short awkward silence.

"Probably not."

"Okay, embarrassed of me?"

"No, embarrassed of them."

I look at her and wait for further explanation.

"I didn't enjoy school by the end, there was this group of girls that had it in for me."

I think I can guess the rest of this story. I went to a big school, and was lucky not to have been the victim of bullying. In fact, I may have managed to join in with some low-level tormenting of my own early on in my school career. I had been mortified when I was called into the headteachers office, expecting the cane – or worse. Instead, he sat me down and explained how the boy we had been picking on was feeling, how he had asked to change schools, how he had stopped eating and was too afraid to come to school.

I won't say it made me a better person, but it made me less of a bully.

I held Grace in my arms and told her it was okay, I didn't want to meet anyone who would treat her badly. She holds me back and looks at me earnestly.

"It's okay, things are different now. Life is better. You've made it better."

I find it hard to believe this, given the help and support I have wheedled out of her, the needy me that wants people to feel sorry for him. Not to mention the precarious situation with my history and being a 'person of interest.' Nevertheless, I take the compliment and vow to myself to try, really hard, to be better.

While I am there, I help Grace's Dad tidy the shed, hold the ladder while he clears the guttering and remember to offer to wash up after meals. In this cocoon of normality, I lick my wounds and regain my equilibrium.

Eventually I return home and spend the rest of my time buried in my books with my music isolating me from the world outside.

Since then, the intervening time has seen lots more study, followed by lots of exams and end of course submissions, all leading up to the Summer Ball.

Grace stirs on the sand.

"Shall we go to bed now?"

"Good idea, I think we should. Come on."

I help her up, transferring my tux to her bare shoulders. She shakes some sand from her hair.

"Yuk, this'll take forever to wash out."

"I'll help'"

"You won't, but nice of you to offer."

We go back to her room and sleep.

*

I help Grace's dad pack her things in the car as she prepares to leave for home. The halls are surrounded by many similar cars being loaded to capacity while people swap phone numbers and addresses and promise to write. Grace comes back from a tearful hug with Shelly to say goodbye to me. There's not much to say, we said our farewells last night.

"See you in two weeks then?"

"Yep, and you're coming back here after?"

"Sure thing, I'm missing you already."

"Me too, I'll write every day."

"Bloody liar."

"Well, every week then."

"It better be more than that."

"I'll see what I can do."

Grace's dad clears his throat. We take the hint, we kiss and Grace leaves.

I do write more than once a week, and we both visit one another. But now it feels different, as if we are treading water somehow. We are in limbo between now and the cusp of adulthood. I have a job lined up at the school where I did my placement. They rang the college and asked for me specifically. I will be starting in September and am simultaneously frightened to death and excited. Grace could not get a job locally, they are quite scarce. She managed to get one closer to her home, which means we will have a long-distance relationship. I am sure we can manage it.

The promises of regular visits and phone calls, along with the letter writing are kept up. After the turmoil of the last year our separation is a wrench, I do not like to be apart from Grace and I'm disappointed that we are not closer. On dark nights, when the only thing that makes things right is the touch of another person, I miss her.

Chapter 19
Untitled

September is hard. The approach of Autumn has always been a time of excitement and anticipation, with the prospect of a new year ahead. There is the promise of fresh starts and new adventures. This year is different. This year it brings nothing but bad dreams and painful memories.

I have been doing long days, working into the evening and trying to get things done before the weekends. Grace is the same. Our plan of meeting every other weekend has already gone out of the window, with both of us having a mass of work to do and being tired. We met up at graduation and spent a night at an hotel with our new found wealth. It was so good to catch up and spend time together, which made it that much harder when she had to leave. As the autumn progresses the leaving becomes harder each time we meet.

I am not living at home any more, although I still visit regularly, mostly when my laundry gets too much or I need a hot meal. I have a flat in town, it was a real bargain, an advert went up on the staffroom notice board and I snapped it up. I can still hardly believe that nobody else wanted the flat for the price. It's quite small and I had to buy a lot of things to get it set up, Mum and Dad helped, but it's a place of my own and will be great when Grace comes down to visit.

I rang the number on the card when I moved, as I had been instructed. A voice on the other end listened to me tell them who I was. Before I told them why I was calling they interrupted me and read out my new address for me to confirm – before I had told them what it was. They then thanked me and hung up.

The first week in my new flat an envelope was put through the door early one morning. It had no stamp, only my name written in vaguely familiar neat blue handwriting. Inside was a front page of a newspaper, it was the following days paper, with a headline about a story I had been dimly aware of, an Australian court had ruled that ex MI5 agent Peter Wright was not in breach of the Official Secret Act with his book Spycatcher. In the space at the top of the page the word 'SOON' had been written in that familiar handwriting. I mulled it over, clearly something to do with the Official Secrets Act, but why soon? What will be soon? What's going to happen?

Still more questions than answers.

Next week is the last week before my first half-term holiday. I admit I am looking forward to it, Grace is coming to stay and it will be good to have a week to unwind. I am enjoying work, but need to recharge my batteries a bit. I have taken myself for a walk on the beach. It is very windy, and not the same walking by myself. I make the return journey along the beach and decide to stop in the pub to warm up before I complete my journey home. By the time I come out of the pub the wind has picked up even more, and it has started to rain. I hurry home and drape my clothes around the place to dry, before sheltering in my bedroom.

I lie in bed listening to the wind hammering rain against the window, it is getting fiercer by the minute. I doze and then wake suddenly to the sound of a large crack, followed by a wrenching, tearing sound. I look out of my window and see that a branch has broken off an old Oak in the small park across the road. I am mesmerized by the swirling wind and rain, in a daze I go out the front door and walk over to the park. Before I get there, my pyjamas are soaked through and clinging to me for dear life as the wind tries to whip them away. I walk over to the broken branch and stand there being buffeted and pushed so that it is difficult to stay upright, wet leaves whipping past me like bullets. My mind is in a different place, a different time. I look up, the rain stings my open eyes and the wind howls and screams and the rain washes away my pain as it flows over me. I don't know how long I stand here with my arms outstretched, there is nobody else about and the darkness protects me as I weep.

*

Grace comes to stay for a few days at half-term. She likes my new flat and we have a good time. She makes my Mum's week by going over for tea one evening, and we revisit all our old haunts. It is like meeting again, we become reacquainted and have lazy mornings and early nights. On her last night we argue.

"Are you still going to apply for jobs here?" I ask.

"There are no jobs to apply for, when there are, they're already taken."

"There are though, you just have to keep looking."

"Yeah right, what about you looking near me? I like my school, it's going well."

She's right, I could move. But a part of me freezes at the idea when she suggests it. I feel safe here. I say nothing.

"I just think it would be better if you got away from here, spread your wings and get a fresh start."

"Yeah, that worked out well last time I tried it."

"Come on, that's over. Anyway, you'd have me to keep you out of trouble."

"It'll never be over though."

"Now you're being melodramatic."

"Sorry, that's how I feel. I need to be here for now."

"You're not even considering it are you? I want to be near you, don't you want that?"

"I do, I just don't know if I'm up to it."

"I'll help, you'll have me to hold on to. We can do it if we do it together, look how much you've changed since I first met you. You're stronger now, more resilient. I just want to be with you, this travelling back and forth is killing me."

"I don't feel strong, and I'm sorry the travelling isn't worth the effort. I'm travelling too."

"I didn't say that, you can be so obtuse. At least think about it, have a look at some of the jobs that are coming up, there are some really good ones."

"You've been looking for me?"

"No, just looking. Say you'll look too."

"I'll look."

But I won't, I know it and Grace knows it too. It leaves an awkward silence that I fill by making a cup of tea and suggesting we walk on the beach in the dark.

I wish we hadn't argued, we made up before she left, but it felt bad. We'd never argued before and it left a lingering unpleasant feeling. I don't know what to do about it except keep doing what we are doing and hope things work out. Because sometimes hope is all we have.

I busy myself with the next term and get lost in my work once again. It has a rhythm and pulse that is easy to set your life by – start times, end times, lesson times, holidays. It is all set out and you follow the path. The lessons themselves have no such structure, I decide what happens and whether to direct it or just go with the flow, it is absorbing, exhilarating and exhausting in equal measure and the weeks fly by.

Alice

Alice's new role has continued to take her away for periods of time. When it is only for a day or two, she asks for updates from her newly acquired PA. Sid is never far from her thoughts and is always the first thing she checks up on when she gets back. Dan is no longer asked to supervise, especially since it emerged that the undercover operative he put in place to watch Sid was a friend of his from University. It was Jones who had bought this to O'Brien's attention, O'Brien had not been impressed. When Alice is away for longer than a day or two, O'Brien supervises Sid personally.

Not that there has been much to supervise. After returning from his Easter trip he seemed to settle, working towards his finals for his degree and then enjoying a leisurely summer. She was notified every time he took a train, which becomes quite predictable in the autumn when he is visiting his girlfriend regularly.

On the day of Sid's graduation Alice travelled to the college and found a seat at the back of the auditorium. The room was crowded with proud students and prouder parents, each round of applause as enthusiastic as the one preceding it. She watched as Sid crossed the stage and collected his handshake and certificate, then left as unobtrusively as she had entered.

At around this time Alice and her colleagues had been carefully watching the progress of Peter Wright's Spycatcher book, a set of memoirs from his time in MI5. Typical showboating MI5, hardly covert when they're always shouting to the world about what they're doing.

However, it seemed that some secrets are, ultimately, not as secret as people thought they were, and that some stories could be told without violating the Official Secrets Act. Not only that, but her information network was keeping her updated with the prospective changes to the Act itself, which would come in the next year or two.

She didn't want to encourage Sid to spill all his beans, but wanted to reassure him that he was less likely to be locked up indefinitely just because of what he knows. She sent him the report to give him some hope and encouragement as he embarked on his journey into adulthood.

Alice spent an increasing amount of time working on the Intermediate-Range Nuclear Forces Treaty. Although the UK was not directly involved, they were very much a part of the process. She worked on mostly low-level observation and working party tasks, helping ensure that the wheels turned smoothly at the top. This final leg was crucial to the agreement, any minor discrepancy or anomaly could trip the whole process up, or at least stall it for a time. What Sid knew could potentially derail the whole process if it all came out. Questions would need to be answered and everything would need to be renegotiated from a different starting point.

The relief when the agreement was finally signed was huge. It was double for Alice, as it meant Sid was no longer a direct threat to national security. She personally delivered the envelope with the following days paper in it to his flat and then checked into a hotel, where she passed the day reading briefing papers and writing reports.

Chapter 19 (continued)

Early in December another envelope comes through my letter box, appearing in the morning, same familiar neat blue handwriting as before. This time it contains the front page of tomorrows New York Times. The headline reads 'Reagan and Gorbachev Sign Missile Treaty', at the top of the page the name of a pub in town and the time 8pm is written in the blank space. I think I understand, but I want to be sure. Part of me is desperate to know, to find out, to understand and get some release. I read every word of the article, then read it again. I think of little else for the rest of the day, I am distracted at work and the kids get free rein on the day's activities as I sit at my desk with the article spread out in front of me.

I arrive at the pub just after seven, I can hardly keep myself away that long. It is practically empty on a weeknight, I buy a pint that I sit and nurse while I watch the clock slowly count down the seconds. I am facing the door and don't see anybody come in, Julia clears her throat as she sits down next to me. I would ask her where she came from, but know that I won't get an answer. Instead, I offer to get a drink, which she accepts.

"So, here we are again," Julia sips her gin and tonic and looks at me smiling.

"I'll get to the point, you've waited long enough for this."

"Please do," I sip my beer.

"You've read tomorrows paper I guess."

"Cover to cover, what does it mean?"

"It means that years' worth of hard work has finally paid off, we are actually getting rid of some missiles. It also means that the sort of moving, hiding and disguising things that my company was involved in can finally stop."

I take that in and let my brain process it.

"So that was a nuke? The thing we found was a bomb?"

"Not exactly, it was something else. Something we didn't want anyone else to see when they came to inspect our bases. And technically you didn't find it, you stole it."

I shrug, "Why was it there?"

"It was being moved, someone thought it would be fine, it turns out they were wrong. When it went missing it risked causing an incident, an international incident. It could have disrupted the whole process, years' worth of talks and negotiations all balanced on a knife edge. Do you see why it was so important that we kept it quiet?"

"I do, but what about Lisa? How could you ever explain that?"

"I can't, I have to live with the decisions we made every day, just like you do. One of the things that keeps me going is knowing that this treaty is something that Lisa would have wanted, something that she would have thought it was worth making sacrifices for. I never knew her, but I knew about her."

"What about the others, are they all okay?"

"All fine, all moved on, like you. I'm not sure they all have your resilience, but they're getting there with some help."

"Are you helping them?"

"They all have different handlers, I never actually met any of them."

"What about Sue?"

"She's fine. She didn't know anything, we got to you just in time by the sounds of it. There were other people involved, not all of your friends kept secrets so well."

I think how close I was to dragging Paul and Sue deep into this whole sorry mess. I exhale slowly and ask, "So, I can see her now then?"

"If you want, it might be best if you think of a story first though, it has to be watertight. We still don't really want this getting out. The less people that know the whole truth, the better."

I think about this for a moment.

"I can't see her, can I?"

"Probably best not, we won't stop you. But we will still be watching for some time to come. If I was you, I'd stay where you are and enjoy the life you've got, it could be a whole lot worse."

"Maybe I will, I don't know what I'll do."

There doesn't seem to be much else to say. Julia has got to the end of her drink, she puts her empty glass on the table and looks at me.

"You kids were so lucky you know, some people said we should just keep you in the centres to be safe. It took the boss a long time to convince the committee we could do what we did. I'm glad you didn't let us down."

"How did you know so much? Was my room bugged?"

Julia laughs. She asks me to pass her my leather jacket from the back of my chair. She then produces a small pair of scissors from her bag and makes a cut in the lining. There is a small disc stitched to the inside of the jacket, she cuts it free and drops it into her bag with the scissors.

"We didn't know everything, but we did know a lot, you don't go to many places without this."

She hands my jacket back to me and I stare at her.

"Were there people watching me?"

"We asked people to drop by every so often, we could never manage to watch you all the time, but it was important that you thought we could."

"You bastard."

It is half-hearted, almost joking. I actually feel relief that it wasn't just my paranoia running riot. I feel relief that it is all over at last. There is a lot to take in.

"I'm going now, I've got a long journey ahead of me. Do you want to watch me go?"

She winks at me and points at her legs. I see she is wearing her tight trousers and I blush. But I watch her bottom as she leaves anyway, she turns at the door and says goodbye then she is gone.

Chapter 20
1990

I am counting. I am counting continuously and meticulously. I started the day with 29 children in tow, and am determined to end the day with the same number. As I shepherd them across the busy street on our route to the museum they chatter excitedly to each other, confident that I will hold up the traffic for as long as is necessary for them to cross over. The cars wait patiently and I thank them.

It is the summer, and I finally feel like I am finding my feet as a teacher. I've made some mistakes along the way, and learnt from them. Some days it's almost like I know what I'm doing. In April I ventured on another class topic about space travel, the first time since I was a student. No cataclysmic explosions this time, the space shuttle Discovery safely delivered the Hubble telescope into orbit. We made an entire solar system out of various sized papier mâché balloons to honour the occasion.

We also did a topic on countries of the world, which necessitated watching the World Cup, which took place in Italy. We made the semi-finals this time, before going out on penalties. I was able to watch the matches guilt free this time, having no-one to 'spend more time with.'

I had been to visit Grace that Easter.

"Have you looked in the Times Ed? There's a ton of jobs coming up here."

I hadn't.

"Yes, there's a couple I'm thinking of applying for."

"Liar."

I say nothing.

"I don't think I can keep doing all the travelling. It's like I never have any time for myself."

I know what she means, it's pretty exhausting.

"Shall we give it a break for a while, have some weekends to ourselves?"

"But I'll miss you."

"You won't, you're always busy when I come down, and I'm always having to juggle things about to fit around the weekends."

She's right of course, but that doesn't make it easier to hear.

"I thought you would look for other jobs now it's over."

I had told her about that last meeting with Julia, most of it anyway. She held my hand and said she was glad it was done, and I think she was.

"It's just so hard, I want to be with you, but I'm scared of changing things. It's like it would break the spell or something. You're the best thing that happened to me, you saved my life."

"Melodramatic again." Grace shakes her head and rolls her eyes making me laugh. "I think you saved me too though, we were right for each other. It's changed now, we've moved on. We're not at college anymore, time to start being grown-ups."

"It sucks," I whinge.

And it does, but Grace is right. We have moved on, it is time to start making adult decisions, even though I don't want to. That is how it ended, not with a big bust-up, but kind of fizzling out as it reached its natural conclusion. I still wonder if I could have made it right, probably. I know I wouldn't have got through that time without her, and I still love her for her kindness and understanding.

We both cried of course, and promised that we'd stay in touch. So far, we have.

*

As the end of the school year approached I had arranged this class trip, as a treat. It seemed like a good idea at the time, right now it seems quite stressful, as number 29 finishes crossing and we head up the grimy pavement towards the museums, the children taking in everything and everyone around them as they gaze in awe and wonder. We are not short of spectators ourselves as we weave along the pavement, past cafes and shops, alongside the clamour of the traffic and through the dance of the pedestrians. We are on the last leg of our journey and I am sweating in the hot summer sun. I follow number 29, or Charlotte as she is properly known, as she follows the other children, who follow Mrs Johnson towards the museum.

At a table outside a café something takes my attention, I'm not sure what it is – a glimpse, a movement, the sound of a voice. I am still moving forward with the tail-enders and slow down to look back over my shoulder. I scan the people sitting at the tables, trying to put my finger on what had called to me. I don't see it at first, then I do. There is a girl, no not a girl, a woman. She has a careful plait of long brown hair and is sitting with her back to me. She is sharing her table with a man in a suit who looks about my age. I cannot see her face, but there is something about her posture, about her presence, that makes me sure I know what that face would look like if she did turn my way. There is something in the Sue-ness of her.

I have now stopped completely and have turned to face the café. My mouth is dry and I am feeling slightly dizzy. I am sure as I can be that it is her, but I need to know, need a better look, to speak to her, to see her again. The sound of her laughter carries to me over the sound of the busy street and then I know for sure. I take one step in her direction when a small hand slips into my own.

"Sir, it's this way. Come on or we'll miss the dinosaurs."

I look down at Charlotte's face, concern at the edges of her expression. I look ahead to the disappearing line of children and then glance back once towards the woman in the café.

"It's okay Charlotte, we won't miss the dinosaurs, come on."

I smile down at her, and we walk hand in hand to the museum, where I start counting again.

Chapter 21
Postscript

That was all years ago now. My leather jacket with its ripped lining and blood-stained sleeve lives at the back of the coat cupboard, possibly it doesn't even fit me anymore, I daren't try. Those days, weeks, months and years all looked big from the front but small from behind. Life has been good to me, I have had lovers, had fights, had triumphs and disasters. I never did leave town, preferring to stay where I was, too scared to move.

I am still in touch with Grace, her husband is okay – not as nice as me of course. No, who am I kidding? He's a great bloke, we get on well. They had a lovely baby girl. I used to send her presents at Christmas and a few days after her birthday. Grace is a fantastic mum, we met up a few years ago (they came on holiday here at the seaside). I often feel a pang of regret that it didn't work out for us. I sometimes wish things had been different, or that I had been braver. But as they say, if wishes were horses, there'd be shit somewhere.

I have not settled down with anybody else. Grace wasn't right for me, but neither was anyone else in the end. I have come to the conclusion that love is something that can only be ignited with the flaming passion of youth. I have no ties, I even keep my family at a respectable distance. If people are not close to me, I can't hurt them, can I?

In 1994 I finally got round to taking driving lessons, after years of prevarication. I passed my test first time in spite of my nerves and some silly mistakes. I got a steal of a deal on a used car, it's always worth keeping an eye on your staff message board. A month or so later someone crashed into my new car. I say crashed, it was a small shunt at some traffic lights. The man got out of his blue Ford Escort and we swapped details. Later I organised for my car to go to the garage and have the taillight on one side replaced and a bit of minor bodywork, which was all the damage was. They did it in an afternoon.

A few weeks later I got a sizable cheque in the post from the other mans insurance company. The letter with it said it was for 'injuries sustained'. I rang up to query it as I had not sustained any injuries, and I am basically an honest person - when I'm not stealing nuclear missiles. The lady on the other end of the phone was adamant that this was correct, that it was for me and that it was normal practise after an accident of that nature. Nobody else I knew had heard of this before. I kept the cheque in its envelope for two weeks before I cashed it and paid off the car loan I had taken out.

I often suspected that Julia's guiding hand may have been behind some of the events that had helped me along the way, or just plain good luck. It irked me that I could never be completely certain if it was my own hard work and effort, or the pulling of hidden strings that got the results.

Life wasn't all plain sailing either. I've only ever been abroad twice. Both times I rang the number on the card to let them know I was going. Both times my passport was taken into a backroom by officials, who then reappeared with more senior looking officials, who took me away for a more detailed breakdown of where I was going? Where had I been? Why was I going? Why did I go? Who did I see? How long did I stay? What with that and the strip searches it was enough to put me off flying.

In 1996 I got ill. I had a cold that turned into a cough that turned into a chest infection. I ended up sitting in the doctors' surgery coughing my guts up and hoping for some antibiotics. What happened next was the doctor made a brief phone call. I didn't hear what she said because I was so busy coughing. She then took me to the front of the building, where an ambulance turned up with its full lights and sirens going and put me in the back.

In hospital I was taken on a trolley to a large room with no other patients. A nurse fussed around me under the direction of a doctor, who stood making notes and asking me various questions that I was coughing too much to answer. While this was going on a seemingly endless stream of people began wheeling machines and equipment into the room. Then Doc arrived. He looked the same as he had ten years ago, just more wrinkled. He shooed everybody else out of the room and turned to me.

"Hello again."

I wave.

"How's things?"

I cough.

He then proceeded to run all manner of tests and checks, humming to himself and making notes while he worked.

"Am I going to die?"

"Yes."

I look at him in horror. Did he just say what I thought he said? That wasn't the answer I wanted.

"We're all going to die, entropy is real."

Great, it turns out Doc is a bloody comedian. Who knew after all this time? He finishes what he is doing and then turns and gives me a smile.

"You're fine, a nasty chest infection but you'll get over it. Although you really should give up smoking you know?"

I did know, and I did give up after that.

I never did get in touch with the others, although I often thought of it. Something held me back. I also came to realise something that I'm sure Julia knew, once college finished people spread to the four winds like seeds tossed into the sky. The promises to keep in touch and always be friends are superseded. Life comes along with other plans for you, and you grow older and wiser. Or just older, it's down to you.

The recent rise and rise of Facebook has led me to start looking for people's profiles. I find the ones I can, and see that they are well, purely stalking of course, though maybe I'll click that friend request button one day. Sarah started a pottery business, she makes some of the finest jugs in Northumberland apparently. Jo is busy raising a family and Stewart is still teaching, like me. Paul died a few years ago, I was sorry that we had never got back in touch, it just never happened. I didn't try hard enough. Truth be told I didn't try at all in the end.

Sue disappeared. I looked, but couldn't find any trace of her. I guess her parents moved or something. I still look for her occasionally, but haven't found her yet. I don't even know if I want to anymore, I have my life and I expect she has hers. We all do, except Lisa.

I could find no information about where Lisa was laid to rest. One cold day in October, under a slate grey sky and with the late afternoon temperature dropping, I visited Greenham Common. It's a common again now. No protests, no peace camps and, most importantly, no missiles. Now it's a place to walk, let your dog run and enjoy the beauty of the countryside, although there are few people venturing here today. I took the photo of Lisa and the gang that I had kept for all these years. I skewered it to a low branch on a small tree and said goodbye.

Steve Beed was born in 1964, since then he has seen men walking on the moon, been chased by a wild elephant and been on the TV – which makes it sound all much more exciting than it actually was.
He has a beautiful wife and three grown up children and has been a teacher since finishing college in 1987.

You can write and tell me how much you liked this book at:
stevebeed64@gmail.com
In return I will let you know about new books that are in the offing.

You can follow my blog at:
https://steevbeed.wordpress.com

Printed in Great Britain
by Amazon

46386034R00116